GOLDEN FLAME

A Charlotte Lavender Adventure

Terry Ann Taylor

DEDICATION

To my mother-in-law Ann for her wisdom and to her son for his love.
Journeys are spiritual adventures that occasionally bring kindred souls
together with inexplicable force.

ACKNOWLEDGEMENTS

Researching the historic timeline for Charlotte Lavender has been an absolute pleasure.

Special acknowledgement must go to the Gum San Chinese Heritage Centre in Ararat, the Golden Dragon Museum in Bendigo, the informative Castlemaine Art and Historical Museum, and the Kyneton Museum.

Thanks are due to the friendly and knowledgeable volunteers at the Bendigo Joss House Temple, a significant and spiritual building of the Chinese community and to the small town of Chewton, the original Forest Creek settlement.

In Melbourne, I extend special thanks to the Chinese Museum in the heart of Chinatown with its period displays and gold mining scenes.

In print, my wonderful visual bible was *The Victorian Gold Fields 1852-53* by Michael Cannon with notable, gifted and historic illustrations by S.T. Gill with his perceptive plates depicting life in the goldfields.

Significant books that allowed a peek at life in nineteenth century Melbourne and on the gold fields Included Jean Gittins' *The Diggers from China*; Geoffrey Serle's *Golden Age*'; the infamous French courtesan, Celeste de Chabrillan's *Memoirs of Life in Early Melbourne 1852-58;* the Marquess of Salisbury's youthful account in Lord Robert Cecil's *Gold Fields Diary* about a journey in 1852; and finally, the English translation of Antoine Fauchery's *Letters from a Miner in Australia.*

I am also grateful for the extensive library of NSW and its obliging staff at the Governor Marie Bashir Reading Room, and the breathtaking State Library of Victoria with its classical domed reading room where I spent many an enjoyable day viewing their gold related archives.

Finally, thank you to my editor Kim Farnell for her careful eyes in catching everything from typos to continuity errors. Any mistakes are my own.

CONTENTS

1

THE CAPTAIN

John Robinson: South Atlantic Sea, 3 September 1853

The deck lurched violently under my sodden leather boots as my hands slithered along the dank cedar railing. Unrelenting waves pounded bow and starboard, as sailors scurried to secure flapping sails and tighten deck ropes. I had ignored the crew's demands to retire to my cabin, my drenched clothes now a testimonial to my defiance. The ship had been lucky to pass St Paul with little interference, but upon waking this morning the winds off the South American coast had whipped up, and with them a squall of hammering rain and restless dark green seas. The sailors called it *pitch-pot* – five degrees of latitude on either side of the equator where storms gathered and burst into torrents of rain. Glancing south, I saw another layer of cimmerian clouds rumbling towards the ship. The sea, dispirited and murmuring in a foul temper, spewed a torrent of spray upon the deck.

Captain Gabriel Sterling was stoically stationed at the *John Robinson*'s wheelhouse, his hands firm on the wheel as he duelled with the turbulent seas. The ship was sturdy, but it required all his expertise to control the crew and temper the sails.

Moving cautiously to the bridge, I fought against the unrelenting rain and wind to position myself close to the wheel. A sea mist enveloped the vessel from starboard to port in one seamless grey shroud.

"Captain Sterling, how long do you think this storm will prevail?" I yelled, my words barely audible above the grinding sound of the sea. The Captain's head jerked in surprise at my voice, his eyes slits in the driving rain.

"Miss Lavender! What are you doing on deck? Go back to your cabin immediately! My task is to get you safely to Port Phillip and not lose you overboard!" Sterling roared, gesturing fiercely towards the first class cabins. His features were barely visible above the collar of his great oilskin coat.

"Captain Sterling," I heaved, waiting for an infinitesimal break in the wind. "You may be in charge of running the ship," I gripped the railing as the ship pitched aft, "but I have obligations to the passengers and their morale." I was screeching in a most unladylike manner in order to be heard above the blustery and ear-piercing conditions.

The Captain cursed under his breath and fired off an order to his burly second mate who braced his legs and took hold of the wheel. A further string of expletives rained down upon the head of Mr Sanders who was stationed precariously on the stairs. A steady tirade of words rippled harshly in a chain of command along the deck.

I was aware that the Captain had regarded me as a thorn in his side ever since we had departed Kingston. Fortunately, his crew had been far more amenable to my requests, especially Mr Sanders. Regrettably, the Captain was not cut from the same cloth and ignored my simple demands, treating me with tight-lipped contempt. His tall and rugged form was impervious to my womanly charms.

Alexander had been poorly since we'd commenced our journey and had insisted that morning that I confront the commanding officer regarding his discomfort and welfare. Normally, I would have ignored the Captain, but some perverse part of me enjoyed his vexation. Also, I required definitive information to allay the fears of my fellow passengers and my sulking brother. It had been my father's doing, inspiring and organising this band of merchants to sail for the gold colony. But my parents, sadly, had missed the ship, due to my father's estate manager and long-time friend succumbing to consumption only days before our departure. Now, with my brother indisposed I felt obligated to enquire, not only for his welfare but also for that of the other passengers. While Alexander was sick, I was my father's representative on board. Clasping the handrail with renewed determination, I raised my chin determinedly.

Captain Sterling ignored my unrelenting stare, his face impassive and grave as he watched the sky above. I grappled for my balance as the ship was buffeted by another gust, my limbs aching with the effort. From the corner of my eye I could see the commotion on deck as the crew struggled to tie the sails into place.

Mr Adams, a fellow merchant and passenger, had informed us that Captain Gabriel Ethan Sterling was extremely capable. He had a wealth of knowledge that had ensured his quick rise through the ranks. At an age when many a sailor was still a master's mate, Sterling had – through determination and skill – acquired a respected name within the international shipping world, hence his being granted the opportunity to master the *John Robinson*.

Wiping rain from his dark brow, he adjusted the collar of his coat more firmly and turned to face me once again. The ship rolled and suddenly lurched, sweeping my feet from under me. Swiftly, a large firm hand seized my floundering body and steered me aft.

"Captain Sterling, unhand me! You're hurting my arm, you... you brute!" I exclaimed, thrashing out at his solid but rigid form as he manoeuvred me indelicately along the passageway towards the nearest cabin.

"Miss Lavender, I apologise for any violation of your sensibilities, but remain in your goddamned cabin! Your presence on the deck is foolhardy, as well as a distraction to my men," he growled, grappling furiously with the handle. As he pushed me through the doorway I gazed up – his face was stern and unrelenting, A steady stream of water dripped from his fringe to his eyelashes then down his nose to pool on his collar. His stormy green eyes flashed in ill temper.

I nearly stumbled over the threshold and turned to protest, only to be greeted with the slamming of the cabin door in my face as the Captain retreated.

"Infernal man!" I stamped one saturated boot on the floorboard. "Was it so difficult for him to be civil? All I requested was a little consideration of passenger comfort."

The ship pitched forward and I quickly gripped the edge of the bunk for safety. A shiver coursed through my body, one of anger rather than cold. Glancing towards the dull light, I was astounded to see a slim young boy, barely twelve, stoking the remnants of ash in an iron brazier. His hazel eyes were large and bewildered as he assessed my behaviour. Clearly, I had been placed in the Captain's cabin. I had observed this sleek dark haired boy scooting around the deck, running orders from his commanding officer.

"Young man. May I share the warmth?" I composed my features and moved closer to the fire.

"Yes, miss. The name's Jesse. Captain's cabin boy at ya service." He saluted cheekily, plainly thinking this a great joke.

"Well, Master Jesse, it is lovely to meet you. I am Miss Charlotte Lavender." I curtsied and stumbled briefly with the weight of my soaked skirt and the movement of the ship.

"Yes, miss. I seen you on deck. Master Sanders says you are pretty but Captain says you are a confounded nuisance."

"And you?" I thought it best to ignore the Captain's comment.

"A fairy, sparkling and blue." His eyes were lit with a burnish glow and a charming smile transformed his young lean face into that of a glorious Rubens cherub. "Mr Burnes says you move like a fairy too, popping up everywhere!"

"Thank you, Master Jesse. I am certainly not a fairy but I thank you for the handsome description."

"Miss, would you like some whisky? The Captain swears by it for emergencies!"

"That sounds heavenly, Master Jesse," I replied, giving him an encouraging smile.

No sooner had Jesse moved towards the Captain's whisky decanter than the cabin door swung open once again and my poor abigail Mary was unceremoniously deposited on the doorstep by a rangy sailor. Her petite but rounded frame was buried in a disarray of fabric. With a squeal she eradicated herself from his arms before bustling to my side. The sailor, laughing at her distress, gave me a lewd wink before disappearing.

"Thank goodness you are here, miss. The rogue grabbed me from behind and muttered something about the Captain. He bundled me along the corridor with his hands in places, miss, that well… Master Sanders should be informed about the wandering hands of his crewmen! Most indelicate it was, miss. Most disrespectful. I don't know how we weren't swept overboard. The water was sloshing around my feet." Pausing for breath, she suddenly noticed my dishevelled state. "My goodness, you are soaked, miss. Let's get you out of those sodden clothes before you catch your death of cold!"

"Mary, for goodness sake calm yourself," I snapped before turning to the young cabin boy with a smile. "Now thank you, Jesse. A small swig would be appropriate before I change."

Mary watched the young boy suspiciously as he passed the whisky tumbler into my shaking fingers. Hand on broad hips, she swayed like a roosting hen as the ship lurched to stern. Her lips pursed in indignation as Jesse retreated towards the door.

"Miss, if I might be so bold, I would reckon you change from that wet clobber like your Mary says. Captain's woollen dress coat hangs at the end of the bunk." With an impish smirk he skipped out of the cabin into the turmoil.

"Little villain!" Mary grumbled at my side.

I was aware that propriety dictated that I should refuse use of the cabin and the Captain's coat, but another pitch of the ship warned me that it would be useless to protest – the storm was intensifying. Thank goodness the Captain had organised Mary to attend to me. I was shivering uncontrollably by now, and I feared succumbing to some dreadful consumption that would confine me to my cabin. I untied the ribbons of my sodden straw bonnet and threw it aside. Mary removed my pelisse, full skirt and crinoline. My shaking hands struggled with the intricate buttons of my blouse, forcing me to relinquish to Mary's ministrations. She expertly stripped me of my stiff corset before hanging my assortment of garments over chairs and brass hooks. I breathed a sigh of contentment as, encased in the warmth of the Captain's wool cloak, I settled into an elaborate heavyset armchair. My body jerked up and down as the ship crested the cacophonous swell.

I let my gaze move over the meticulous order of the cabin as

Mary pottered about. Maps and charts were rolled up protectively in a pigeon-hole dresser. A large mahogany table, plainly used for charting, stood stoically near the south paned window, its patina glowing in the soft light of the dying ashes. Several leather strapped chests were placed below, no doubt containing the Captain's treasured instruments. Chinese silk banners in vibrant colours hung majestically from the rough timber mouldings. The embroidered scenes and delicate brushwork offered an enticing splash of the Orient, creating an exotic and grand backdrop to such a humble abode. A tallboy positioned near the bunk appeared the only personal effect, with its accompanying mirror and brushes securely restrained.

"It's a bit gaudy." Mary sniffed as she inspected some of the banners. "A bit inappropriate for an Englishman's cabin. Some of the figurines are questionable, miss. Why would the Captain force you into his cabin? I think you should have a word with Master Alexander when he is less poorly. Seems to me that the Captain is a surly chap and not at all gentlemanly. Oh, my goodness! Look at the carvings on this box, miss!"

"Mary! This conflict and drama has given me a frightful headache. Please put down that box and help me to the bunk."

Dropping it with a loud thud she waddled to my side. Her round obstinate face showed her displeasure. Clasping the edges of the bed, I wrinkled my noise at the musky aroma, the undeniable odour of an active man. Wrapping and tucking the coat snugly around my dishevelled form, Mary retreated to the commodious armchair in a huff.

My foggy thoughts were with Alexander and poor Gibbs, his valet. My brother's indisposition was making him a loathsome travelling partner. I prayed that the inclement weather would improve; Alexander needed his sea legs. He was acting so childishly at present and it grieved me that the other passengers had so little patience with his behaviour. I wondered whether this trip to the antipodes had been well thought out; our adventure was steadily becoming a nightmare.

Numbly, I drifted into sleep wondering whether it was due to the soothing effect of the whisky or Mary's prattling. I forgot about the storm and sailed away on the wings of Hypnos.

Sunlight streamed in through the panes of glass as I woke, playing on the timber ceiling and the brightly coloured banners. The ship gently pitched with only the distant chatter of crew penetrating the cabin. Thank goodness that was over. I stretched and rose, gingerly swinging my legs over the edge and adjusting my twisted chemise as I discarded the heavy coat in the lovely comfort of the warm bunk.

"I presume you slept well, Miss Lavender?" a deep rumbling voice enquired.

Startled, I squeaked, glancing futilely into the dim corners of the cabin and rapidly pulling the cloak to my chest. Captain Sterling reposed nonchalantly in the armchair, his cat-eyes twinkling wickedly at my discomfort.

"Captain Sterling, this is highly improper. Where is your cabin boy, Jesse? Where is Mary?" My eyes whipped around in a frenzy trying to penetrate the darker confines of the cabin.

"All is well, Miss Lavender. Jesse has only this moment roused your abigail and they will be back shortly with dry clothes."

Looking at his unruly hair and clothes, it was plainly obvious that he had not slept or rested during the night. I wondered how long he had been staring at my unseemly clad figure in his warm bunk. As if reading the thoughts swarming furiously in my head, the Captain gestured towards the window.

"It is only daybreak, Miss Lavender. I apologise for the intrusion. However, it has been a long night. I sought to find peace and refuge in *my* cabin. Clearly, I was mistaken."

"This is highly improper, Captain Sterling. May I suggest you vacate the cabin until I leave? Like a true gentleman?" I pointed defiantly at the cabin door. My head was still groggy and my voice rang harsher than I expected.

"Miss Lavender, may I remind you that your insistence in venturing to the deck during the storm occasioned the entry into my cabin. Only a lunatic or a knucklehead would venture on deck during a storm."

Astounded at the Captain's effrontery, I dropped to my feet, flushed with indignation. I was suddenly conscious of my tumbling hair and stray strands sticking unattractively to my flushed cheeks. As I attempted to adjust the coat to cover my exposed ankles, I realised

I was giving the Captain an eyeful of my décolletage. Blushing, I wrapped myself protectively into the folds of the fabric, endeavouring to remain composed. Unperturbed green eyes watched my attempts at modesty with amusement. The effrontery of the man!

"What type of captain are you? I was merely concerned for my brothers welfare. Surely someone as pig-headed as yourself understands the need to communicate with the passengers during trying conditions. After today I can only imagine what the whole ship will be gossiping about! May I remind you that I was forced into this cabin – by you. You are a bully, Captain Sterling. An abominable tyrant!"

"A bully, a tyrant, they are stern words for a scantily clad woman," he chuckled.

I raised my chin a notch and gave the ridiculous man my most scathing look – the one I reserved explicitly for put-downs.

"Miss Lavender, I accept your apologies and bid you good morning. I suggest you wait for your abigail before parading yourself before the whole crew. May I suggest that next time there is a storm, you remain within the confines of your own cabin. I would hate my morality to fall prey to examination!" His lips curled in an unpleasant smirk.

"Your morality! Huh! Captain Bligh! You wouldn't know what good manners were if you tripped over them!"

Untangling his long legs from the comfort of the chair, Captain Sterling rose and approached me, his look demonic. I remained rooted to the gently rocking floor, one hand clutching the bedpost as I squared my shoulders ready for his assault.

He strode past me, and wrenched the cabin door open, growling into the corridor. "Jesse! Goddamn it, boy!" Within moments Jesse had appeared at the door, an amused twinkle in his eye which suddenly disappeared upon seeing his Captain's displeasure. "Jesse, assist Miss Lavender and ensure she is escorted to her cabin by two bells." He lowered his head to avoid the beam and stepped past the lad, striding purposely towards the quarterdeck.

"Sorry, miss. Mary started gossiping with a long stringy man and I got distracted," Jesse stated sullenly, closing the door behind him.

"All is forgiven. Please fold my damp clothes and I will be gone as soon as Mary can dress me." No doubt Mary had found the easy ear of

Gibbs, my brother's sullen valet, and was sharing a colourful picture of the evening's events. Cursing under my breath, I busied myself with pulling the bunk covers back into place.

Thankfully, Mary soon arrived with dry clothes in hand, and with young Jesses's back turned, I was swiftly dressed. I dared not stay long in the Captain's cabin with the other passengers rising for the day. I would complete my ablutions in my own cabin.

"He burst into the cabin without regard for your modesty or privacy. I was tempted to give him a tongue lashing," said Mary. "But you know what he is like, miss, and you were a lamb, fast asleep and oblivious to the world. He stood peering down at me like I was a bug and pointed to the door. It was that confounded cabin boy. He insisted on talking to every sailor we encountered."

Jesse muttered beside me, jostling Mary and me along the corridor.

Out on deck, the early morning light revealed the damage to the *John Robinson*. Sails and ropes were strewn upon the main deck as the scurrying crew attempted to set order to the clutter. Luckily, no passengers were on deck, I glanced up to see the rigid figure of Captain Sterling, his feet apart as he stared out to sea which was now a dark greenish blue under a perfect cloudless sky. His normally broad unrelenting shoulders rounded with fatigue as he rose with the swell.

I suddenly remembered his penetrating eyes as he had appraised my dishevelled state. *Well, Captain Sterling. Two can play at such a game!*

2

VIRAGO

For the next few days I solicited an onslaught of passenger grievances that I referred to the second mate. I also encouraged the passengers to share their concerns with Mr Sanders. A stylish young man, with an endearing mop of flaxen hair who'd appeared to pander to my needs, Mr Sanders was the epitome of an Englishman with his lithe figure, pleasant manners and attentiveness. His ease of conversation and obliging attitude endeared him to the lady passengers, although at times I felt he was too obsequious.

"Definitely, Mr MacGuigan. The Captain would be most interested in that observation. I truly believe our inconveniences distress him as much as you," I said as I strolled the poop and weather decks before luncheon.

"Mrs Adams, I heartily agree the crew should be more observant of the children. It's a matter I am sure is close to the Captain's heart," I shamelessly acceded, fanning myself briskly.

"Certainly, Mrs Hargreaves. Decorum is essential even on a ship and young men and woman should seek healthy restorative practices on different sides of the vessel. Truly shocking accounts. The crew should be alerted. The Captain must be fully aware of the consequences."

By the third day I was aware that a degree of unrest rippled through the crew. Several of the older seamen had scoffed at the passengers as they assisted them on deck that morning. While I had previously enjoyed a pleasant word or two with the younger members of the crew, they now appeared to avoid the passengers, especially the ladies.

Mr Sanders will hear of this. Sailors offending paying passengers – never!

I felt uplifted, dressed in a buttercup-hued walking dress with lovely princess seams that accentuated my shapely lines. Mother had acquired this dress and several others from the catalogue of the House of Manning in Dublin. Mr Alfred Manning was all the rage at present, dressing Her Royal Highness and the Duchess of York. Its delicate fabric rustled deliciously as I took a turn of the deck, carrying my matching parasol that sported an indulgent silk ruffle. The weather had settled to a balmy seventy-three with a moderate humidity, so Mr MacGuigan had shared with me. It was a lovely day and I was in excellent spirits.

"Miss Lavender, if I may. A quiet word seems in order." I glanced up to see Captain Sterling at my side, his lowered voice full of malice. Before I had time to comment, his hand firmly grasped my elbow and propelled me towards the saloon.

"Captain Sterling, unhand me you, you, barbarian," My impassioned plea fell on deaf ears.

As we entered the saloon, he gestured beyond the polished mahogany dining table with its matching carvers to the padded slipper seats. I glided over and gracefully sank onto the soft leather, my countenance I hoped appearing indifferent as I met his eyes in defiance. His face flushed, for once appearing at odds with his impregnable exterior. Hostile green eyes appraised me with displeasure. Turning to the bar he signalled for the steward to leave. The young man dropped his cloth and took flight.

"Well, Captain Sterling. What has provoked this disgraceful violation? Is this another indication of your overbearing temperament? I demand an explanation." I sat upright, my back stiff and resilient as I stared him down.

"I apologise, Miss Lavender, if I ruffled your elegant clothes or violated your sensibilities. However, I have far more pressing matters that require my attention."

"Yes, I can imagine you do – doubtless to the detriment of the paying passengers. I will be informing my father of the intolerable conditions and your unyielding manner." I snapped my parasol shut, enjoying the effects of my words on my companion. His expression changed from one of vexation to fury before my eyes.

"If you must know, Miss Lavender, I have a mutiny erupting on my ship."

"What?" I was unable to stop my eyes widening in surprise.

"You heard me. A mutiny!" He extended his arms in exasperation and began pacing the cabin.

"Well, sir, that has nothing to do with me. Surely you can control your men? I imagine you are well armed. May I suggest you have this conversation with my brother or Mr Adams?" Lowering my gaze under his dark scrutiny, I fussed with the wrists of my taffeta gown, the diversion sufficient to settle my nerves.

"My first officer has been busy buffering complaints from the passengers and attempting to ensure the crew are mindful of their ridiculous requests."

"How noble of Mr Sanders! At least one member of the crew is sensitive to the plight of the passengers." I shifted uncomfortably in my seat.

"Sensitive or not, the nodcock has agitated my crew, who as you can imagine are a surly lot after being away from home for six months. If I may remind you, Miss Lavender, the only thing between your chastity and them is a strong allegiance to my command." He smirked.

I leapt to my feet with indignation, striking him with my gloved hand. A flash of suppressed emotion flickered in those bright verdant eyes. "How dare you take ungentlemanly liberties on such a sensitive matter! This meeting is concluded!" Gathering my skirts I attempted to glide past him. Captain Sterling stood his ground, rigid and uncompromising, hands defiantly behind his back.

"May I remind you, Miss Lavender, that if any unrest erupts I am ill equipped to take on the majority of my crew. I trust you will review your interference and act appropriately. Good day!" Turning on his heel, he stepped over the threshold and into the corridor.

What an insufferable man! Dismissing me as if I were some insolent servant or petulant child. *How dare he treat me in such a manner?* I was tempted to rouse my bedridden brother and drag him up to the abominable man. Weaving through the corridors I found Mary busily rearranging my gowns within the travelling trunk. "Mary, leave me in peace. Your fussing gives me a headache," I exclaimed as Mary tilted her head to one side.

"Miss, I'll bring you a nice cup of tea! That will do the trick for your headache. It would be the sun. You should be mindful that too much sun is bad for your skin and your health. I promised your mother you would be well covered on deck, and look what happens. Here you are barely covered and —"

"Mary, enough! Please, leave me in peace. Go and talk to Gibbs and see how he is faring."

With a pout Mary closed the trunk with a firm snap and bustled out the door.

I threw myself onto the bunk, distraught and embarrassed, my eyes welling up with tears of shame. My obstinacy and stupid pride had created a perilous situation on the ship. *Foolish, foolish woman!* This constant sailing and monotonous activity had frayed my nerves; the food was excessively bland and the living conditions cramped and unhealthy. It was, however, my mindless and thoughtless disregard for the Captain's authority on board, that unnerved my spirit. I had acted poorly, with little thought of the consequences. I was above such pettiness, and Alexander for one would be disappointed by my spiteful manner. I felt ashamed. After wiping my tears and adjusting my fair hair before a small but elegant toilette mirror, I ventured next door to my brother's cabin.

Knock! A feeble voice beckoned me in. Alexander lay motionless on the cabin berth. His normally adorable locks now framed his lean face in lank clumps. The room was stifling; the smell offensive. I jammed open the door, making a note to have a word with Gibbs, but for the present allowing the breeze from the corridor to lessen the odour.

"Alexander, I have allowed this pitiful behaviour to linger far too long. This afternoon you will accompany me up on deck. I insist – and please, none of that disagreeable language. I will summon Gibbs to dress you appropriately." Ignoring his muttered profanities, I called a steward to locate his valet.

Steeling myself, I made a firm decision. *I will be the model of politeness, the model passenger. And when I reach Port Phillip, I will no longer have to endure Captain Sterling and his caustic tongue!*

During a lunch of salted pork and vegetables I mentioned surreptitiously to my fellow first class passengers my concern for the welfare of the crew and their constant trials.

"You must admit, Mr MacGuigan, their welfare has a tremendous impact on our ease of travel. If we can alleviate any problems or misunderstandings, it will allow us to sail smoothly. I apologise for the pun, however it has come to my knowledge that the crew feel low." I emphasised my comments by touching Mr MacGuigan's arm. His face lit up with delight at my flirtatious touch.

"That is ridiculous, Miss Lavender, ridiculous. How can the crew feel low when they are hard at their – exquisite! – I mean, duties." He fumbled in embarrassment, raising his napkin to his luxuriously engineered moustache, its red tinge at one with his plump scarlet lips.

"Exactly, Mr MacGuigan. But it is in our best interests to wave a white flag of peace and ensure a courteous and pleasant journey. We must, at all times, demonstrate the meaning of good breeding and gentlemanly indulgence."

Turning to Mrs Adams I said, "And my dear Mrs Adams, was not it only yesterday that Able Seaman Withers rescued young Oliver from the mast?" Placing one dainty hand on my heart I smiled benevolently at my companions.

"I see your compelling argument, Miss Lavender, and I for one are humbled by your concern," remarked Mrs Adams. "I will ask Mr Adams if he may be prevailed upon to release a barrel of rum. He could certainly spare one from his stock. I would imagine the crew would enjoy a night of merriment. What say you, Mr MacGuigan?"

"A truly noble gesture, Mrs Adams," he said, his moustache twitching.

I simply smiled.

3

CIRCE

"Ah, Miss Lavender. I find you once again involved in passenger needs."

I had been preoccupied, listening intently to Nellie Brownlea recite the alphabet, when I glanced up to see Captain Sterling casting his leonine shadow over the seat. Luckily, my wide-brimmed bonnet partially obscured my face so he was unable to see my irritation at his intrusion. I wished I had worn my 'ugly' with its half silk hoops to totally block his appearance. Goodness gracious, the man had no limits! He had pestered me at least twice today, earlier approaching me during my morning constitution.

"Captain," I bowed my head slightly in acknowledgement, and then turned obstinately to young Nellie, as her youthful voice droned through the letters. Mrs Adams, a staunch advocate of strong Christian values, had impressed upon the Captain the necessity of creating a school. It had the two-fold effect of curtailing the flighty activity of the children during the morning and creating peace for the crew at work.

"Good Christian guidance to ensure that the minds of the young were forever attuned to their fortuitous destiny," Mrs Adams pronounced to the passengers, her massive bosom heaving in satisfaction as she glanced skywards.

Willis the sailmaker had erected an awning over the mizzen bow, allowing a protected area for the lessons. Mrs Adams had enrolled the services of passengers who declared their interest in assisting with various tasks of reading and writing. I regarded it as a means by which to reduce the boredom of the long journey rather than any Christian calling. However, I must admit that the few hours a day with the younger children were satisfying. And a little Latin with the older boys in the afternoon brought back fond memories of Alexander and myself in younger days.

Glancing at the shadows on the deck I noticed the Captain's feet were still riveted to the one spot. The infernal man had not taken the hint that I was occupied. Shifting young Nellie's reclining body from my side, I stood, brushing the creases from my elegantly styled lavender morning gown before raising my eyes impatiently to meet the Captain's gaze.

"Yes, Captain Sterling. Is there something you wish to discuss with me?" I asked, suddenly conscious of his commanding form. A light southerly breeze tousled his unfashionably long dark auburn hair, revealing an intelligent well-tanned face, and his startlingly green eyes fringed by dark lashes watched me unwaveringly. His normally hostile demeanour was replaced by a surprisingly courteous pose, one eyebrow raised in what appeared to be amusement at my scrutiny.

"Miss Lavender, I wished to thank you for your sensitivity to the issues we discussed last week. I believe your guiding hand instigated a pleasing outcome for the crew."

"Well, Captain Sterling, I am sure you are mistaken." My hands surprisingly nervous, reached up to adjust my bonnet ribbons.

"I am in your debt, Miss Lavender. I shall certainly be mindful of your generosity for the remainder of the trip," he declared before turning abruptly to discuss the educational progress of the children with Mrs Adams. I attempted to hide my surprise although my mouth stood agape as I watched his receding broad back.

Whatever did he mean by 'mindful of your generosity'? The man was a conundrum. Confused, I lowered myself to Nellie's side to continue our lessons. That was the problem with Captain Sterling; it was immensely difficult to judge his character. With the other passengers he was charming, his expression sincere and his voice pleasant. However, when it was a question of exerting his authority, his whole being was immediately transformed. His voice became stern and uncompromising and his physique unyielding and rigid. I surreptitiously observed him strolling from group to group conversing with my fellow travellers. His banter was agreeable and welcoming. From this angle his profile was exceptionally appealing. Shaking my head in wonderment I willed my senses back to the task at hand and started to read one of Nellie's favourite stories.

That evening in the saloon I observed Captain Sterling I hoped with a certain amount of equilibrium, as I bantered with my dinner partner Mr MacGuigan, an agreeable and affable pastoralist from Kingston who was clearly enraptured by my company. He was of Scottish descent, a stout man of an undefinable age who had sadly lost his wife to consumption last year. He was travelling to the New World intent on forging a new life for himself, hoping he could encourage his children to follow him. For all his idiosyncrasies, his company was surprisingly soothing to my inner restlessness. I suspected his cordiality and attention was not solely for companionship on the journey. I certainly did not intend being the next Mrs MacGuigan! Needless to say, he was well read – a little too pre-occupied by his livestock, but generally a pleasant companion.

During the past few weeks, the Captain had refrained from joining his first class passengers in the saloon for the evening meal, instead claiming to have duties on deck. This evening I was transfixed by the sight of a witty gentleman who casually lounged in a fine Flemish style chair at the head of the table. A glass of claret in hand, he chatted knowledgeably with Colonel Williamson concerning India whilst keeping the wallflower Miss Hamilton amused with tales of China. I was amazed to overhear that he spoke four languages, his most fluent being Cantonese.

I must have been a poor companion to Mr MacGuigan with my lacklustre replies. My ears were alert to everything being said further up the table as I nodded and smiled at my partner's words. What was the Captain up to? It certainly did not help that the candlelight highlighted his tanned facial features against his crisp white evening shirt. His usual hostile countenance was now relaxed and congenial; his smile mellow and carefree.

No, I must be hallucinating. I quickly stole another glimpse between courses.

"Miss Lavender, I do not think you are with us tonight," commented Mr MacGuigan. Blushing, I glanced furtively towards Captain Sterling. Confound the man! His amused face watched my discomfort.

"My apologies, Mr MacGuigan. A slight headache plagues me this evening, but I was finding your account of the new botanical strain of wheat for the colonies intriguing."

Gabriel coughed, raising his napkin to his mouth to hide his mirth. I could hardly contain my scowl. *Insolent and odious man.*

"Ah! Then, Miss Lavender, I will attempt to speak softly to avoid any undue distress," Mr MacGuigan replied, gently patting my hand before continuing his monologue on the agricultural benefits of English wheat. For the remainder of the meal I ignored the Captain and continued to banter pleasantly with Mr MacGuigan and Mr Sanders.

After dinner I strolled out onto the poop deck in the company of Alexander. The evening was calm and the sails fluttered in the light breeze; there was but a light swell in the ocean as it cradled the sky singing with stars. A banquet from the gods!

"Magnificent evening, Mr O'Toole!" I commented to the burly sailor as he kept his eye on the sails above.

"Best time of the day, Mistress Lavender." He grinned, his smile wrapping around a large toothless gap. "Quiet and peaceful on deck. No young uns fighting and squabbling!"

I nodded in agreement. Even the best constitution and patience was tried by the children slipping between legs and skirting around the ladies with their grubby hands. Their mothers' bold indifference was at times trying, especially in the face of possible danger to their offspring.

After a few laps of the upper deck, I noticed that Alexander was becoming green. It confounded me that a gentle swell of the ship could turn a strapping man into such a blithering mess.

"Charlotte, stop smirking. You are beastly. This was your idea. Trust you to convince Father that we travel ahead. I am retiring to the sanctity of my cabin. Good evening, my pet!" With a quick peck to my cheek he lurched to one side and raced for the stairs.

"Alexander, I will look in to see how you fare. I am positive some fresh air will relieve my headache. I will be in shortly," I said to his retreating back.

Alexander had kindly agreed to accompany me when it was apparent that my parents would be delayed. My parents had not been happy with the arrangement, but knowing they would only be a few months behind swayed their decision. Thank goodness! The stifling society of Jamaica had jarred my nerves. Contrary to popular belief, fashion and flippancy were not the extent of my skills. That my life consisted of only frivolity and mindless pursuits rattled me. It was difficult to convince any gentleman that beneath my exterior lurked deeper emotions and intelligence.

But I was to blame in many ways. I had a tendency to play the frivolity card when it suited me, and I had learnt early that men were creatures of habit. A pleasant smile or a kind word opened doors that harsher words or skills could not. Could this be regarded as manipulative? Maybe, but it begged the question that if you were true at heart and believed you were doing right, surely the means justified the end? A line from Voltaire popped into my mind: *To succeed in the world it is not enough to be stupid; you must also be well-mannered.* It was all folly! I had been the personification of womanliness and still my restlessness persisted.

I blamed it on Papa – his tenacity and vision were intoxicating. From a young age I had insisted that whatever Alexander pursued I would have the same opportunity, even to school! Alexander had been my valiant warrior. Maybe it was the remoteness of the West Indies, but I had from an early age formed a close bond with my brother. It was therefore natural that as he progressed through the classics, I followed. My mother had been despondent at my obstinate behaviour. Ladies should concentrate on womanly pursuits, mindful of their transition into marriage. Transition into marriage! It reeked of boredom and suffocation. Luckily, my father, immersed in the running of the plantation, turned a blind eye to my unyielding independence. Now I had reached the age of twenty-one, my mother had become totally disheartened by my forthright views and what she perceived as unladylike behaviour. There was nothing like a poignant piece of Latin or Shakespeare to drive suitors away. The saving grace for my mother was my appearance. Cornflower blue eyes, sultry blonde ringlets and an alluring face – one she believed would eventually capture a heart or hand! Maybe Port Phillip would offer an opportunity for a new beginning, a new resolve.

With a sigh I glanced over the stern. The silver wake shimmered as the moon painted the tips a pearly lustre.

꙰❦꙰

I had wished the affable Mr O'Toole a fond goodnight before taking my last round on the poop deck. The soft breeze was invigorating; the pungent salty tang energising to my senses. The boredom and monotony of sea life fell from my memory. The gentle movement of the humming vessel beneath my feet was calming and soothing to my soul.

Looking towards the bow, I was surprised to see Captain Sterling on the main deck. I had imagined him enjoying the continued flattery of my fellow passengers. However, here he was! What started out as an innocent observation from a distance had escalated into an uncomfortable moment of voyeurism! His usual stern features had moved progressively from delight to distress – or was that agony I perceived? His hands clenched and unclenched the railing as he gazed longingly at the clear night sky and its luminous points. I wondered what tortuous memories or thoughts were plaguing him. It was the curse of ship-board life that privacy was such a scarce indulgence.

Disconcerted and awkward at what I had witnessed, I attempted to walk casually towards the first class cabins, hoping to discourage his imminent approach.

"Are we not kindred souls tonight, Miss Lavender? The southern skies are truly magnificent this evening."

I spun around. Gabriel Sterling had bent his head to whisper. His mouth was so close that his warm breath tickled the side of my exposed neck. Soft hairs quivered before a shiver rippled from neck to knee as I inhaled his distinctive manly odour. I looked up to see his eyebrow raised in query. His provocative gaze wandered down my body in a most disturbing way. I was aware that my silk dress was disconcertingly tight around my legs, the skirt pulled by the gently breeze, no doubt exposing my womanly outline. I felt vulnerable as our eyes locked and I stood riveted to the deck, my body tingling with anticipation. Without a further word he bent down, his warm breath caressing my right earlobe.

"Goodnight, Miss Lavender. Sleep well. I look forward to your company in the morrow," he murmured before strolling confidently into the darkness.

I was so furious that all I could do was stare as he sauntered away. *How dare the man?*

A little kissing and flirtation did not hurt anyone but this was highly inappropriate. I scolded my disloyal body. *Had I actually leant into the Captain's body expecting a kiss?*

My chest heaved as I threw curses quietly to the wind. Pulling my Indian shawl tightly over my shoulders, I retreated to my cabin.

4

RETRIBUTION

Mary bustled into my cabin with a restorative morning tea, a look of consternation on her face as she approached the bunk.

"Miss, Are you ill? I told Gibbs the pork appeared too pink! I will complain to the cook. God forbid, he could poison us all! And you with such a delicate stomach. Your mother will be horrified!" she declared, touching my throbbing forehead.

"Mary, please stop your fussing. It was just a uneasy night. Breakfast would be fine. Are there any eggs left? I could not face any more salted pork this morning – or biscuits! Also, mention to Alexander that I am indisposed today and give my apologies to Mrs Adams."

"Everyone is out of sorts this morning, miss! Gibbs is running around flapping his wings in protest at the laundering. Master Alexander even had a few curt words with the Captain, which is highly irregular for him." Distractedly, Mary pushed a lank strand of dark hair, back under her once white cap.

"The Captain…" I said in a subdued voice.

"The man has been cursing and pacing the deck since early morning. Setting the crew on edge. Even poor Mr O'Toole received a tongue lashing over the mainsail. Don't know what has got up his nose, miss. The good news is the we are passing the Cape of Good – something – and swallows, pigeons and even an albatross are hopping about!"

Had last night's intimacy left him as furious with his own indiscretion? I doubted it!

"Now Mary, off you go. No more gossiping, I am a little weary."

"Certainly, miss, but I suggest that a dose of cod liver oil will get your spirits back!"

My glare prompted her to make a swift exit.

Curse the man. The first class passengers would be horrified if they heard of the Captain's inappropriate behaviour, more so my brother! But making allegations towards the Captain would be counterproductive to a congenial time on the ship. I was aware that several of the ladies were already watching me, showing their disapproval with speculative glances, especially after the cabin incident. Any hint of impropriety would significantly damage my respectability. What an abominable situation to occur on such a confined craft! We had only been at sea for forty-five days, and depending on the westerlies, we could be in close proximity for another forty-five. At home, I would have scoffed at the smallness of society, but sea life was a totally different state of affairs. The close proximity of passengers ensured that any uncivility was scrutinised.

The best plan was to approach Captain Sterling and discuss his unbecoming behaviour with him personally. Surely this would be advantageous to both of us? He would apologise and continue his bull-headed attitude on the ship and I would retain some vestige of dignity. He was certainly an intelligent man and conversant with social obligations. It would be in my best interest to forgo my time on deck today – perhaps my absence would evoke contrition on his part. Resolved, I rolled over and fell into a peaceful sleep.

꧁꧂

Fortuitously, I had borrowed a novel from the Captain's library and the diversion was soothing. The ship had been rocking gently all day; obviously the crew were working hard at capturing every ounce of wind. Thankfully, my cabin was located conveniently within the passage and received a pleasant breeze. I had ensured that my bunk was lined with a number of pillows, the lace comfortable and luxurious to the touch. Darwin's Voyage of the Beagle rested on my knees as the sunlight streamed pleasantly through the porthole.

Mary had mentioned that below deck the poor second class souls sweltered with not enough air circulating through their corridors. Today they would be on deck creating havoc with the equilibrium of the ship. That suited me!

Dozing off during my reading I was jolted by the sudden surge of the ship. Bracing myself against the bunk, I heard pans and utensils clang to the floor as several ladies screamed from adjoining cabins. Children cried out as the ship lifted from the sea as if bewitched before plummeting with an almighty crash.

"Secure your possessions, brace yourself and stay in your cabins," yelled Mr Sanders, his loud voice reverberating down the first class passengers corridor.

Peeking around my cabin door, I raised my voice above the clatter, attempting to remain poised. "Mr Sanders what is the meaning of this intrusion?"

"Aargh, Miss Lavender," he said as he took in my dishevelled appearance. "A storm is brewing in the distance. We expect unsettling weather. The Captain has requested all passengers be bunkered in their cabins, miss."

"Thank you, Mr Sanders."

Well, if the Captain insisted I be confined to my cabin, I would languish in my nightgown and forego any attempts to dress for dinner. Pulling on my dressing gown for warmth, I was suddenly thrown onto my bunk with such force that it knocked the wind from my lungs. I grasped the edge, attempting to regain my breath. The side of my head ached from its impact with the wall. Bracing, I waited for the next roll as the ship lurched and slid down the side of the wave, a daredevil ride into oblivion.

The day seemed endless with the storm raging incessantly outside. I remained huddled in the corner of my bunk as seawater ebbed and flowed through boards in my cabin, and my trunk played tag with the scurrying rats that hastily squeezed through the planks. I looked on in shock as darkness enveloped my haven. The uproar overwhelmed my senses. The vibrating strain of the ship's hull, the relentless pounding of the waves above, the hysterical crying and screaming, the thud of the cargo. Even the pitiful cries of the livestock from the bowels of the ship. My head nearly exploded with the grim sounds. Battered and bruised, I pulled my pillows and blankets closer to buffer my body against further bumps as the ship lurched, thrust and creaked into the chilly southern seas.

❧

I couldn't remember falling asleep, but now I eased into a sitting position, stretching my sore limbs and tentatively rubbing my aching shoulders. My head still ached from the knock sustained during the storm, whilst my arms and legs throbbed with bruising. I steadied my wobbly legs on the damp floor, feeling weak as I attempted to open the cabin door. Unexpectedly, the door was flung open with Alexander disarrayed and dishevelled in its frame. I glanced in aghast at my brother before letting out a peal of delight. "Oh Alexander, darling," I exclaimed, throwing my arms around his waist and burying my head in his crumpled shirt.

"Charlotte, you are a minx. How will you ever repay me for this hardship? It does however appeal to my sensibilities that you will be forever indebted to me." He growled but placed his arms tenderly around my shoulders. "Gibbs has twisted his ankle and several passengers have sustained injuries. Mrs Adams has unfortunately – or maybe fortunately – broken her leg."

"My goodness, how are you aware of this?" I asked, staring up at his feverish eyes. "Are you unwell?" I reached up to touch his forehead.

"Couldn't feel better. Strange as it may seem, I have been energised by the crisis. I have been assisting Dr Edmunds in his ministrations."

"You! Assisting the surgeon? No!" I exclaimed in bewilderment, stepping back to observe my brother in this new light.

"That Captain Hook upstairs became aware of my agility and seconded me to medical duty."

"Is he mad?"

"My sentiments exactly. On a brighter note I was able to assist the good doctor capably but the sight of blood was particularly unsettling." He winced. "However, my organisational skills in classifying the urgency of the cases was undeniably well received. And Mrs Saltram has been delegated to nursing duties."

"Alexander, you are a puzzle."

28

Adjusting his collar nonchalantly he rested a soft blue gaze upon me. "Gads, woman, you are a mess. Society would have a field day with your appearance. I will send whimpering Mary along to assist in your dress, but ensure it is modest. I need your presence immediately in the surgeon's cabin." He retreated into the hallway.

I stood in the doorway shaking my head in disbelief. If Mother could see her children at present, she would have hysterics! Hearing movement, I glanced up, expecting Mary. However, Captain Sterling's towering figure stood rooted to the boards, appraising me through bloodshot eyes. His dark auburn locks were plastered to his pallid face.

"Miss Lavender, I regret the intrusion. I saw your brother leaving and thought you would be suitably attired." He bowed his head in deference. "I see you are fine. I suggest that the doctor inspects your bruises. He may have a soothing salve."

With a curt bow he melted into the night. His whole demeanour appeared fatigued; his shoulders surprisingly slumped for such a robust man. Turning on my heel and nearly slipping on the floor, I cautiously moved to my bunk to await Mary. How did the Captain know I had bruises? Cautiously, I rummaged in my trunk for my hand mirror. *What a fright!* I appeared demented, with my hair ruffled into a birds nest and a colourful bruise swelling on my hairline. I gasped in horror. And I had not said a word during the Captain's discourse, standing meekly in my dressing gown. I, Charlotte Eliza Lavender, had been lost for words.

5

THE CONFRONTATION

I had expected Captain Sterling to grace the infirmary with his presence but he remained elusive throughout the day. I enjoyed Dr Edmunds' company; he was an old friend of my father's and had landed a place on the ship due to his affable temperament and competent medical skills. Long widowed, he was travelling to Port Phillip for adventure. His fascination was not gold but people, and his amusing stories kept me distracted all day. He administered tonics and bandaged several passengers' sprains and burns but the seamen had borne the brunt of the storm. Captain Sterling had allowed a special disbursement of rum for those injured. Many had abused the kindness, arriving with all manner of mysterious illnesses. The doctor had sent them off with a sharp word.

"Their life would not appeal to me," declared Dr Edmunds, catching my eye. "Their country is their floating ship, their house a hammock and their two most important pleasures are smoking and drinking!"

"Some people have simple pleasures, Dr Edmunds. They are well-travelled." I replied as I unwrapped another packet of damp bandages.

"Yes, I suppose you are correct. However, our companions have a far more practical opinion of the world. The charms of travelling are equated to which country has superior tobacco or cheap drink."

He smiled conspiratorially and then called in another seaman. "Perkins, sit there and put your foot on the stool. Excellent. I was telling Miss Lavender about the beauty of Polynesia."

"Bloody Polynesia. Sorry, miss, for the language! Stupid country, nothing to smoke, nothing to drink. The American States, now that is the place, miss, marvellous. Excellent tobacco and good brandy, but mind you, miss, weak beer!" he said confidently through a toothless grin.

Dr Edmunds winked at me before turning to his patient's lacerated toes. Stifling a smile, I passed a cup of rum to Perkins.

"Very good of the Captain, miss! But he is always fair, Sterling. Must be his age or him being an orphan. My fourth time on the *John Robinson*." Perkins winced as Dr Edmunds pulled a stitch through his big toe.

"How do you know he is an orphan, Seaman Perkins?" I asked dabbing at his bloodied cut.

"O'Toole! Said Captain Sterling worked his way up from a nipper with the chink's junks to the *John Robinson*. Fought all the way."

"I can imagine!" I muttered under my breath.

"Yes, miss. I could see him fighting those chinks single-handedly. Mountain of a man and those chinks would have been trying to crawl all over him." Perkins swore, excusing himself with a cheeky smile. "Fair tobacco in Hong Kong and good brandy but bloody expensive. Those chinks know how to sting you."

Dr Edmunds chuckled as he finished his last stitch.

Thankfully, after we had finished with Perkins Mrs Lamont arrived to relieve me. However, I was disappointed to retire to the confines of my cabin, away from the activity and sailors' tales. They were a strange group of men, although the majority had grand and glowing stories about the headstrong Captain. From spice adventures in Indo-China to sailing the African coast, to the seas of India. It sounded exotic, mysterious and compelling.

Too fatigued to summon Mary, I dozed fitfully within my loosened stays, awakening at daybreak with a kink in my neck and throbbing shoulders. Mary had been distressed at my independence but greeted me cheerfully with a breakfast tray, plus the gossip that was circulating the ship. There were strange bed partners discovered during the turbulent weather! Feuds over cargo damaged or misplaced! Tempers raised by stolen items. It was simultaneously surreal and tedious. Captain Sterling would no doubt require an immense amount of patience to pacify the injured parties.

My breakfast tray was almost bare and I groaned in despair. "Biscuits again, Mary?"

"Sorry, miss, but the cookhouse was a mess, nearly swept overboard, and the cook refused to provide any food until the carpenters repaired the galley. He promised dinner, thank goodness, but I believe it will be salted beef with dried potatoes. The stores are low now and the fresh food that was left was ruined by the salt water sloshing through the hull. I have a good mind to complain to the Captain. But I took pity on the man – he looked exhausted and everyone wanted a piece of him!"

"Thank you, Mary! At least the tea is hot!"

"Captain was kind enough to allow a portion of his own supplies and Jesse supplied the hot water."

"Damnation!"

"Pardon, miss?"

"Nothing, Mary. The blue morning dress will do nicely, thank you, and stop fussing." I rubbed my temples in exasperation.

"Sorry, miss. One more moment as I fix the curls at the back. There! All finished. I'll come back and mop the cabin when you're on deck. You would not believe the things I have discovered floating through the corridors. It would make your face pale," she declared, disappearing in a flurry of skirts.

Once on deck I surveyed the commotion with trepidation; several of my fellow passengers were still confined to their cabins. Mrs Adams was resting under doctor's orders under the mizzen awning, whilst beside her Mr Adams was schooling a few boys in mathematics. Mrs Adams smiled stoically as I enquired about her health before moving along with a pleasant greeting to all and sundry whilst keeping my eyes on the quarterdeck. I noted that Mr O'Toole was currently at the wheel whilst Mr Sanders was discussing the finer points of the foremast repairs with Mr MacGuigan. I continued my stroll around the poop deck, discussing the harrowing events and injuries with Mrs Lamont, a sugar merchant's wife originally from Chiswick, who viewed my company with scepticism. I cringed at the lady's conversation; she was a pious bore. However, she did make the day pass more quickly.

My tolerance was ebbing and still I had not seen the brooding Captain Sterling. After another turn of the deck with Mrs Lamont, I excused herself – there was only so much I could take of her incessant tittle tattle. The sun was already beating down on the deck. Shortly, it would be too exhausting to be outside without shade and my delicate bonnet would give little protection.

I had come to enjoy the early mornings, the sails fluttering overhead, the exhilarating rush as the ship skimmed and shimmied across the iridescent waves. My gloved hand steadied me at the railing. I contemplated my life before this arduous journey – how naive I had been! This was not an adventure but a trial, one of the magnitude of Ulysses'. Closing my eyes briefly, I revelled in the salty mist clinging to my lashes, lips and exposed skin. Mornings such as these were uplifting; I felt energised, even magnanimous.

"Miss Lavender! I find you rested? I apologise for interrupting your thoughts and reflection."

Slowly, I opened my eyes, focusing on a distant point out to sea, my face slightly shielded by my stylish blue-ribboned bonnet. "Good morning, Captain Sterling!" I replied sharply, turning to confront him.

He looked dreadful. Dark smudges lay below his normally vibrant eyes whilst deep wrinkles creeped upon his temple. His face was drawn and serious except for a whimsical curl of auburn hair on his forehead. I wondered whether to play the affronted lady and tear strips off him for his behaviour or to be a passive gentlewoman. He had every right to be apprehensive. Although he commanded this rat infested ship, my father held the strings. Captain Sterling would be sailing Chinese junks off Hong Kong if I told Papa what had happened. Manhandling a lady, compromising her character, taking undue advantage of a lady's sensibilities – the list would be endless and, oh, so satisfying.

Lost in thought, I was suddenly aware of the Captain clearing his throat. "Miss Lavender, it is my sincere…" He paused as I raised my gloved hand to silence any further words.

"Captain Sterling, past events have not endeared us to each other. I am of the opinion that the remainder of the journey would be best served by burying the hatchet and ensuring a level of professional distance. Our paths would not normally cross and this is obvious from our discord."

I did not miss his grimace as his startled green eyes travelled over my face in disbelief – or was that resentment? I coolly opened my laced parasol with a flourish and, noticing Mr MacGuigan approaching, promptly excused myself and glided away.

✿❀❁✿

For the next week I avoided the Captain as far as I could, which was difficult on the *John Robinson*. Dinner was a tiresome affair. Captain Sterling had continued to grace the first class passengers with his presence during the evening meal, bewitching them with his affable manners and stories. Delighted, the company had integrated him into their reading and card groups. I was furious. Surely the man had far more important things to attend to? I decided to raise this issue with Alexander, who had succumbed to playing whist, partnering Miss Hamilton, a quiet and intense young lady who was originally from Cornwall. Adele Hamilton was joining her father in the Colonies and had acquired Mrs Adam as her chaperone for the duration of the journey. I was not disposed to her company with her severe grey clothes, unassuming character and mouse like disposition. Why was it disturbing that my brother and Captain Sterling enjoyed her company?

"Well done, Miss Hamilton. Capital move," beamed Alexander. "We have outplayed you tonight, Captain and Mrs Lamont."

"You have played a great hand this evening, Mr Lavender, with your gifted companion Miss Hamilton. You are both to be congratulated." The Captain's warm smile rested on his female adversary, her blush evident even from my reading corner in the saloon. Alexander flashed a good natured smile at Adele as he collected the cards. I was disconcerted to see Miss Hamilton's face transform, a delighted smile escaping her lips as she basked in the warmth of the gentlemen's approval.

"Miss Lavender, excuse me, Miss Lavender. It is your turn to read the next chapter." Mr MacGuigan roused me from my reverie, holding out the book for my consideration. I smiled and raised my hand to my mouth, feigning a yawn.

35

"Oh, Mr MacGuigan. I am sorry to disappoint you. However, I am weary and if I may be excused, I will join you once again tomorrow." I stood and bowed to the remainder of the circle. Monstrously slow nights, unbelievably monotonous company – when would this journey end? According to Alexander's estimation and his conversations with the Captain and crew, it would be another twenty days or so, depending on the wind and seas, before we reached Port Phillip.

6

SOUTHERN OCEAN

At noon every day Mr Sanders communicated to the passengers the exact latitude and longitude of the ship. On the Captain's instructions, he gathered whether the wind was good or bad and this inspired the adventurous to calculate the distance still to be covered. Mr Adams enjoyed this part of the day, instilling into his young students the benefits of arithmetic and calculus. Occasionally, as a treat, the Captain Sterling attended with some of his astronomical instruments and explained to interested parties the bearings and positions.

The temperature in the Southern Ocean had plummeted, so today only a few passengers had attended Mr Sanders daily communication. We were apparently sailing at twelve knots an hour and the roaring forties had us in her clutches.

"Ahoy, starboard." Perkins exclaimed. "Whales."

Removing my gloved hands from a fur muff, I clutched onto the balustrade. About a mile from port, two jets of water rose above the waves to a height of fifteen feet. A massive fin dipped in the air and disappeared, then a tail. It was breathtaking. Alexander exclaimed in excitement, his arm warm around my shoulders.

"It is magnificent!" I declared, beaming.

"You have a red nose!"

"Prig!"

"Let me escort you to your cabin, Charlotte. The wind is becoming icy. Look at the grey in the sky."

"One more moment, Alexander! It's been so dull confined to my cabin for days. The hail has at least disappeared from the deck."

In the distance, menacing spikes bobbed up and down. Icebergs from the south! A sailor's nightmare; the mainmast was manned constantly with a lookout. I hoped the poor seaman got double rations of numbing alcohol at night for his sufferance.

"Come on, Charlotte. I hope your constitution is up to salted pork and dried potatoes tonight!"

"Alexander, surely not!"

"All our stores are depleted. We are down to salted pork unless Mr MacGuigan can be persuaded to part with a lamb!"

"Heaven forbid! Maybe I can charm him into it tonight. Oh, for fresh meat!"

As we approached Terra Australis talk became more feverish about spotting land. The wind consumed our days. Were we going fast or very fast? Were we on the right track? If the wind jumped up three points, my fellow passengers pondered whether we were gaining or losing time. The days rolled into each other and still no land. At dinner, we made bets and discussed latitudes and longitudes! The Captain was quiet at these times, clearly enjoying our ridiculous speculations. He knew exactly where we were!

"Miss Hamilton, I hope I find you well this evening." Captain Sterling extended his hand to assist Adele Hamilton to the table, ignoring me. Alexander had shifted me to one side, greeting Adele and the Captain. The effrontery of him! The evening passed in much the same vein as always. There was polite talk regarding the activities and misadventures of the day, an uninspiring meal, coffee or tea with the ladies, then an evening of cards, reading or games with the other first class passengers. I could feel my ill humour simmering beneath the surface.

I had been particularly attentive to my dress this evening and Mr MacGuigan complimented my choice of gown. The exquisite material shimmered from blue to green in the lamplight and his eyes glanced suggestively over my décolletage. Elderly Mrs Lamont pursed her lips in displeasure as she sauntered past.

Feeling a need for fresh air after dinner, I excused herself and escaped to the deck. The evening was glorious, relatively quiet except for the flapping of the sails and rigging above. The temperature was milder than it had been and the breeze tantalising. The glow of lamps and soft chatter alerted me to the crew working at the bow, whilst the steerage creaked with the pulsating set of waves. I glided along the poop deck, at rest with the universe. Tonight the stars were the heroes of the night sky, spread as finely as an intricate beaded wedding veil, glimmering and sparkling from overhead to the distant horizon. It was breathtaking to be part of Erato's ethereal wonderland. The muse of love, with her lyre summoning Jason to a voyage of passion across a lovelorn sky. I smiled at the thought.

"It would be remiss of me to not remind you, Miss Lavender, that there is danger in wandering the ship without an escort or lamp," declared a rumbling and familiar voice. I spun around in confusion, lost within my thoughts of the Argonauts. Captain Sterling leant leisurely against the mizzen mast, watching me with interest.

"I am always mindful of my steps, sir! Do I need to remind you that I pace this deck daily?"

The Captain levelled his gaze, the corners of his mouth twitching. "I was referring to unscrupulous advances that may occur in the dark."

"You, sir, are no gentleman," I replied, my heart racing as his lithe and masculine body unravelled and moved towards me, panther in movement, unusually soundless for his formidable size.

"But, madam, you have already reminded me once before that I am no gentleman," he leant down and whispered. Even in the darkness I could see his mocking eyes sparkle with amusement. I had no choice! I tilted my head upwards, grasped his evening lapels, rose on the tips of my slippers and kissed him full on the mouth. I savoured the startled then sensual touch of his soft warm lips. He tasted and smelt exquisitely of claret with a mix of cheroot and – surprisingly –cherries. My ungloved hands slid down his evening coat as our kiss deepened and a dizzy rush of yearning swirled through my body, making it soft, pliable and unsteady. Skilful lips, soft and supple, traced my own, eagerly forcing mine into blissful obedience. What had started as a pure reflex now descended into lust. My aroused compliant body leant provocatively into his embrace. A muted moan escaped his mouth as he stiffened at my touch. Suddenly, in one swift movement, the Captain lifted me firmly off the deck and placed me several feet into the darkness.

"I suggest you retire for the evening, Miss Lavender," he said sharply, as his eyes avoided my gaze. His voice was laboured and strained.

"As you wish, sir," I replied coquettishly, attempting to regain my composure as my legs quivered with anticipation. It had been desire – pure desire – nothing more, nothing less. It must have been those fanciful thoughts of Erato! In that sweeping moment I had craved him, passionately and intensely. Surely woman should be able to express their desire? Whether they acted on it was a point of propriety. Well, my propriety and lack of restraint had flown overboard. No doubt it would come back to haunt me!

7

Mr Lavender Intervenes

"Charlotte, I do hope you are not dallying with the Captain," said Alexander whilst leisurely strolling the deck mid-morning. He had overcome the worst of his sea sickness, and since the raging storm he now ventured more often onto the deck. In fact, he had enjoyed the company of the timid Miss Hamilton earlier for a brisk morning constitution. His day suit of light grey set off his cerulean eyes beautifully. No wonder Miss Hamilton was besotted!

I stiffened at his comment. "What makes you say that, Alexander? It is an inappropriate question," I replied, unconsciously adjusting my bonnet strings with nervous hands.

"Come, Charlotte. Do not play innocent with me. I have noticed your surreptitious glances follow the Captain." Alexander watched my face intently. "Not to mention his gazes. It will be only days before the whole ship is aware of your behaviour. May I remind you that we are not in Bath or London, but on open sea, confined to a vessel, captained by a seaman employed by your father. If you wish to embarrass him and me you are on the right road to do so!" He growled between his clenched jaw. "Charlotte, I am aware the voyage has been tiring, and your character – well, your character lends itself to flirtation – but the man is an employee! I had expected more decorum and composure from you." He shook his head in disappointment.

I snorted indelicately, releasing his arm to grasp the newly polished timber railing. "Embarrass you? How quaint. I suppose your relationship with Miss Hamilton is totally above board. I've seen you fawning over her in the evenings. Whatever do you see in that mousey tedious woman? La, the woman is beneath you, Alexander!"

"So this is your form, move the gossip to me. May I suggest, dearest, that you carefully consider the implications of this inappropriate dalliance. I would be reluctant to call the man to task if you are discovered in a compromising situation. I certainly cannot visualise you as a captain's wife keeping the home fires burning as he travels the world. The adage 'a woman in every port' comes to mind." Alexander smiled and touched his hat instinctively as several passengers drifted by before returning his hard gaze upon my pale face.

"You are disgusting, Alexander!"

"Does the truth hurt so! Come, come, Charlotte. I know enough of your character to realise a submissive and humble life is beyond your sensibilities. We will be arriving in the colonies shortly and the scandal would certainly weave its way home, as bad news inevitably does! Think of your father if not of yourself."

I contemplated Alexander's words as I gazed in thought out to sea. Yes, I had to admit my impetuous nature had run wild of late. Although he was devilishly handsome and worldly, Captain Sterling was certainly not of my social sphere and unlikely to be on my mother's list of suitable suitors. In the light of day, I felt foolish as I reached to take my brother's arm again.

"It will finish, Alexander. It was only sport, something to amuse me on board. Do not worry about my virtue!" I remarked flippantly, feeling my chest clench with deceit.

"I am glad to hear that but it was not your virtue I was concerned but your heart," he said softly before propelling me towards the steadfast Miss Hamilton.

Yes! It must finish! It would never do! What lunacy had overtaken my body? My father would be outraged, my mother mortified at my indiscretion. As Alexander chatted to the sheepish Miss Hamilton, I dared a glance to the upper deck. Captain Sterling's stood proud and undaunted gazing towards the horizon as he consulted the chronometer with O'Toole.

I decided that the only way to broach the subject was to approach it head on. I had observed the Captain dismissing his second mate from the quarterdeck and, bracing myself, I slowly made a path towards his command centre as other women passengers milled around the deck.

To ensure the other ladies would not fault my presence, I queried the Captain politely regarding the weather and the ship's longitude. We exchanged pleasantries, but I was constantly aware of the underlining tension between us. His body moved with a natural fluidity and vigour as he pointed out to sea. His head was bare with strands of hair whipping at his intense and strikingly sun-baked face. A slight white scar was noticeable on his hairline. I wondered what adventure had brought upon that particular injury.

Fortunately, the other ladies continued to their exercise, Mrs Lamont watched me intently with crossed brows as she moved towards the poop with Mrs Adams.

"Miss Lavender?" questioned the Captain, his sharp iridescent eyes watching me intently.

Turning I ensured the ladies were sufficiently out of range before lowering my voice. "Captain Sterling, it is necessary to explain my behaviour. I propose we meet in the saloon at a mutually acceptable hour."

"May I suggest at six bells? I will relinquish my command to Mr Sanders and await your company." His voice was controlled and firm. A quiver rippled down my spine. Adjusting my hat, I breezed past, furious at my disloyal body. Shivering, I sought out Mr MacGuigan to quell my flurry of emotions and musings. There was nothing like a lecture on agriculture to dampen the tumultuous feelings within my chest. I had been a fool and must seek to right the wrong. I was aware of the Captain's eyes burrowing into my back, No doubt he scowled as I charmed my fellow passenger into accompanying me in a stroll.

After a taxing morning of irksome socialising with the older ladies of the ship, I arrived at the saloon with Mary, at the designated time. "Mary, please ensure we are not disturbed. The Captain wishes to discuss a delicate matter with me."

"But, miss, wouldn't it be more appropriate for me to sit in the corner of the room?"

"That is totally out of the question, Mary. I shall ensure the Captain leaves the door ajar."

"Yes, miss. But may I suggest —"

"No, you may not, Mary," I declared, brushing past her indignantly.

Captain Sterling's tall, muscular form was draped nonchalantly on the leather bench, his green eyes penetrating and guarded as he appraised my arrival. I had purposely chosen a modest teal day dress that buttoned demurely to my neck, the unassuming cloth giving me strength in my actions.

"Captain Sterling. Prompt as ever," I said for Mary's ears. Tentatively, I lowered myself demurely into an armchair opposite him, disconcerted that he appeared aloof and cool, refusing to stand as courtesy dictates at my entry.

"Now, sir, about last evening…" I started in a soft conspiratorial manner.

"Miss Lavender, if you have come to beg for your virtue, I can only imagine it is entirely too late! Have you shared your favours with Mr MacGuigan as well?"

My eyes flew open in shock. "How dare you!" I declared, leaping to my feet. I could feel a deep burning flush scold my cheeks and my eyes narrowed in contempt as with one swift movement he grabbed my hand and dragged me onto his lap, delivering a jaw crushing kiss upon my furious lips. I should have put up some vestige of a struggle; it was unladylike! But instead, I melted against his broad chest. My body hummed within his embrace as his lips gently relaxed to enjoy my compliancy. Soft puffs of air trailed from the edge of my mouth to the curve of my ear, warm lips gliding delicately over my tingling skin.

"You may fight this now, Charlotte, but one day you will plead for such a touch." The Captain whispered in my surprised ear before releasing his hold. Unceremoniously, he deposited me on the leather seat and rose. "You may be assured of my discretion, Miss Lavender. I take my leave. I trust you will enjoy the remainder of the journey." With a slight bow and his face impassive, the Captain left the room.

Dazed, I stumbled out of the room flying for my cabin, Mary in hot pursuit. "Miss, miss. Are you all right? Should I send for Master Lavender?"

"Mary, please leave me be. Busy yourself elsewhere. I wish to rest for a short moment. My megrim has returned." Dismissing my worried abigail, I curled up in my bunk pulling the blanket over my head, shuddering with resentment.

8

Melbourne

Port Phillip Heads, Colony of Victoria

Land. Oh, blessed land! The Port Phillip promontory jutted out towards Bass Strait, its shores carpeted in luscious moss as the lighthouse stood majestically, upon the headland. Its enormous light was chiselled from meticulous planes of luminous glass and shimmered in the early bright. A lonely sentinel guarding the gifts of the bay!

Directly across the channel, in contrast to this peaceful scene, was its nemesis, a scary jumble of grey angular rocks, jagged and threateningly large, plummeting menacingly into the swirling sea. High on the pyres of stone were the skeletal remains of wrecked ships. It was a graveyard of mistakes and ill-fated decisions. Skilfully, Captain Sterling manoeuvred us through the channel before the pilot boarded us for the forty mile journey through the bay.

It was the vibrancy of the birds that first stole my breath away! I stood riveted to the spot, crammed with the other passengers against the rail, watching with fascination the craggy bays and opalescent beaches in the distance. Birds coated in striking green, yellow and blue enraptured us, screeching and squawking at our intrusion. Seagulls latched to the masts, whilst below black birds scrutinised the deck for morsels left by our enthusiastic minions. Clumps of rocks rose majestically from the tranquil waters, bemused seals slipping unruffled by our presence into the calm waters. Playfully they rode within our wake, their funny moustached faces grinning with mischievous delight.

The day was perfect!

I clung to Alexander and breathed in the warm spring air. So bizarre that it was October and yet it was spring already in this southern land. Our journey was thankfully at an end. We intended to stay in Melbourne for a few weeks to visit acquaintances, and then Alexander had proposed to visit the goldfields in an explorative venture. This would give us an opportunity to regain our 'land legs' and enjoy the luxuries of town.

I had sensed the Captains presence on the quarterdeck since early morning, and had sneaked a glance whilst he was busy commanding the men to the sails. His firm booted leg was braced against the wheel, and his town coat hugged his broad shoulders while his white shirt highlighted his tanned features. The man was outrageously handsome this morning, his eyes flashing with excitement as he confidently directed his men to their duties, his dark auburn hair whipped and tousled in the gentle breeze.

The hardened O'Toole was smiling with pleasure, his mood reflecting that of his Captain's as he barked off instructions with a jaunty tease to the seamen below. Sanders had retreated to the foremast, no doubt to enjoy the spectacle.

As we approached the wharf, at least seven ships heaved at their mooring cables beside us, a forest of masts wavering in the breeze. Flags flying, from American to Dutch. To the right, was another mass of black vessels from England, their numerous sterns reading "London" or "Liverpool". Goodness! It was bedlam with the endless shouting of disgruntled crew as cables and anchor ropes rubbed and pulled in all directions.

From the lapping waters below, small boats rocked with hawkers bellowing out trade names and soliciting labour. In their mad hurry to be the first to our ship, they jostled for position, cursing and swearing at each other as their bows and sterns collided.

"Ahoy, the *John Robinson*. Any carpenters or bricklayers on board? I promise excellent pay, full board, good lodging," yelled a dubious character clinging to the edge of his small rocking skiff as his companion deftly manoeuvred alongside us.

"Cook, male or female, for prime hotel. Generous profit share!" bellowed a chubby man as he shoved his foot out to stop the collision with an approaching rowboat.

Clearly, the colony was desperate for workers, so desperate that they needed to intercept passengers before they landed in Melbourne! Gold fever!

Several of the crew rained items upon them for amusement which was received with catcalls. O'Toole ordered the men back to work, and before long we were settled upon Queen's Wharf.

After waiting for an excruciating two hours, a column of smoke moved eerily from the mouth of the Yarra Yarra towards the shore. Unfortunately, we must now endure three hours aboard a steamer to travel eight miles to the centre of Melbourne. Thankfully, Alexander had engaged Mr Sanders to assist with negotiating our fare, although it was still an exorbitant five shillings per passenger – and that was to sit on our luggage.

We farewelled fellow passengers and gave our thanks to the Captain. Well, Alexander gave his regards and I stared past Gabriel's looming figure towards the commotion. I threw a quick glance his way and my cheeks flared as a wry smile crossed his face, his eyebrow raised in amusement at my evident discomfort. Infernal man! Exasperated, I turned on my heel, mumbling my thanks before seeking out Mr MacGuigan for assistance. It was disconcerting that his mere presence unnerved my sensibilities. Well, goodbye, Captain Sterling. *May you rot in hell!*

The steamer was an atrocious welcome to our new home. It felt unstable and was poorly fitted out. The deck was overloaded with parcels, luggage and passengers. We huddled against each other as we travelled up the narrow but deep Yarra Yarra. The traffic was horrendous; at one stage we were nearly crushed between two larger boats that passed by regardless. On either side of the river the land was uncultivated – a few scraggly livestock rummaged within misshapen trees. Finally, we reached our destination. The steamer sailors hurried us off quickly, depositing our luggage with little care onto the dock as they headed back for their next inflated fee.

"Absolutely outrageous!" Alexander said as he swayed in indignation. "Three pounds for our luggage. This is highway robbery."

"It's a fair price, gov. You ask the carriers," stated the surly man.

"Well, I will report this to higher authorities. This is thievery."

"You do that, gov, but your luggage will stay here," the carrier sneered.

Alexander grumbled and eventually conceded, handing over a small advance fee, the remainder on consignment. Gibbs had been left with the bulk of our trunks with express instructions to guard the luggage with his life! This was an unfortunate predicament considering that Gibbs' build did not allude to pugilistic endeavours. His slight gaunt figure was exactly what Jesse had described as *stringy*.

"For goodness sake, Alexander. Let's stop haggling and find a suitable hotel." My shoes were already dirty from the filth on the dock. "I desperately need to change my dress. It's already ruined and I crave a meal not laced with salt or brine!"

"Very well, Charlotte. This way. Father had it on good authority that the Criterion was suitable. He wrote in advance for lodging. Devilishly bad luck if they have not honoured his letter. It is apparently well-favoured and is grand by colony standards."

The carrier followed us, his face set in a most unattractive grin as he pointed out landmarks. All around was a hive of activity, people shoving and bumping into each other. Poor Mary was lost for words and tottered beside me in bewilderment. I clung to Alexander as he attempted to protect me from the full brunt of the chaos. The beautiful sky of early morning had been replaced with rolling clouds and fine mist as we trudged despondently towards our hotel. My skirt was ruined as I dragged it along the street through mud holes, debris and indescribable filth.

The Criterion was an attractive renaissance-style building, sitting royally beside an ad hoc array of timber stores and shanties on Collins Street. The carrier proudly called the area the 'Paris' of the colony. I had laughed at this. Inside, the obsequious hotel manager graciously shared that the hotel had been the proud creation of American entrepreneurs Weder and Moss. Its imposing three-storey facade and vaudeville theatre was a testament to the boom of the gold rush. I was thankful the room didn't move and it was bigger than a hatbox! After the confines of a cabin, this was a palace. The bed was covered in satin sheets, a most disturbing reminder of the frivolity of the diggers.

After a bath, my hair washed, dried and braided by Mary, I reclined blissfully on the garish chaise longue. A tray was ceremoniously delivered with a vast quantity of fresh produce from heavenly fresh bread to blood oranges. I soon discovered that this opulence came at an inordinately high price. With the influx of miners, the colony farmers struggled to meet the demands for fresh produce.

Alexander had promised to meet me for dinner later in the dining room; he had a few errands to run and introductions to attend to. While he was energised, I was exhausted!

It was heaven! It was magical! After the months on board the *John Robinson* and its hardships, the world had returned to its correct axis!

Languishing on the chaise, I drifted into a peaceful slumber. No children, no crew yelling orders, no clashing of pans, crashing of plates, gales of wind or thunderous rain, just silence.

Roused from my restful nap, I succumbed to Mary's skilful hands and prepared for dinner. I had chosen a cyan laced gown inspired by my favourite designer Mr Alfred Manning. The fashionable House of Manning! Its scandalous cut lacked the normal hoops so resplendent in England at present, but fitted my trim waist perfectly. Its pretty petticoat was covered with an additional overskirt, accentuating my attractive curves. One last glance at the full mirror assured me of its graceful fall. With gloves and reticule in hand, I glided confidently out of the room.

"What a pleasure to see you once again, Miss Lavender. As always, a picture of perfection," stated a familiar masculine voice as I descended the staircase. Nearly losing my footing, I turned to see Captain Sterling leaning nonchalantly on the railing above, his dress a touch casual for evening but undeniably emphasising his virility and imposing size. A lock of auburn hair defiantly fell over one twinkling green eye.

"Have you no pride! What is the meaning of this imposition?" I declared, hotly wielding my fan.

"Imposition? I beg to differ. I am merely staying at an exceedingly convenient Melbourne hotel. It was not my intention to burden you with my unwelcome presence." His eyes flashed with mischief as he observed my bristling temper. "But since we are both guests, may I have the honour of escorting you to dinner?"

"Honour! What do you know of honour? Pooh!" Steadying my nerves, I descended the remainder of the staircase, attempting to ignore the chuckle that rang in my ears. Incorrigible scoundrel! I would ask for another room. How could I possibly sleep knowing he was on the same floor?

Alexander was already seated, having given up on my length of toilette, but as I approached he smiled and rose, warmly extending his hand in welcome to the Captain who had followed me. "So glad to see you again, Captain. Will you dine with us?" he enquired, raising a surprised brow towards my flushed face.

Before I could reply, the Captain motioned towards another table. "Thank you Mr Lavender, but I have another party to join. Enjoy your time in Melbourne, Miss Lavender. Always a pleasure."

As Alexander pulled out my chair, Gabriel bowed politely but as he moved his fine shoulders back he winked conspiratorially over my brother's bent head. Shocked, I tumbled onto the chair like a sack of potatoes. My nemesis strode confidently to a corner table occupied by several fashionable couples.

"Charlotte, for one moment I thought you had overstepped the boundaries," Alexander said, easing into his chair. "Are you ill? Your face is exceedingly flushed?"

"Alexander, don't be ridiculous. I am fine! Maybe a little flushed by exertion."

My brothers eyebrows shot up in query.

"Oh, for goodness sake, Alexander! It was a surprise to me that our esteemed Captain was staying at the Criterion! He is an abominable man, sadly lacking in manners, I am bewildered at my initial partiality." I fidgeted with my starched napkin. Behind Alexander, I observed Gabriel's genuine warmth and affection on greeting his dinner companions. He kissed several cheeks and pumped the men's arms enthusiastically. His distinct deep voice chuckled at their remarks.

Dinner was ruined; the excellent piece of lamb barely palatable. How dare he laugh and flirt with the ladies, his elegant companions enjoying his wit and humorous tales. I listened half-heartedly to my brother's conversation regarding his advantageous business and banking introductions during the afternoon. One of my ears was constantly attuned to the corner table conversation.

The odious man was doing it on purpose, attempting to inflame my agitation. It didn't help that one of the ladies was monopolising him, patting his arm constantly in jest, her raven hair framing luminous brown eyes longingly resting on his suntanned face. *How dare he enjoy himself!* His normally sturdy body appeared relaxed and pliant, his verdant eyes playfully enjoying the distraction.

"Charlotte, my dear. What do you say?" repeated my brother, vexed at my lack of attention. "Charlotte, for goodness sake!"

"No need to yell at me, Alexander. I am weary this evening, that is all. The journey has been taxing for my nerves."

"I merely suggested that we delay our journey to Ballarat for a few weeks. It will give you time to recover and me time to access business possibilities. I have an introduction to the Melbourne Club which I intend to make full use of, plus several civic contacts. I am confident you will enjoy some pampering before we attack the frontier!" Alexander proceeded to describe the new and ornate civic buildings of the city. "Charlotte, wealth literally oozes through the pavements. Everyone is moving at a frantic pace; the energy is decidedly invigorating."

I smiled. The past months at sea had taken a toll on Alexander. It was wonderful to see this transformation, this vibrancy. Well, if Alexander was enthused, I would be too! This town would make a pleasing change.

"I am so glad that you are revived by our surroundings. A few weeks in Melbourne would be delightful after our strenuous journey. I will pen a letter to Father and Mother tonight to inform them of our safe arrival."

"Very well, my dear. May I escort you upstairs?"

"No, Alexander. I will leave you to your cigar and port. I promise to be far better company tomorrow." On tiptoes, I kissed his cheek before gliding to the staircase.

9

FRAGRANT WATERS

"Alexander, are you acquainted with a Mr Xavier Willoughby of East Melbourne?" I enquired. "We have been invited to a dinner party at his home this Sunday" I waved a beautifully inscribed card that had been delivered earlier. The name was not familiar and certainly not of one of our acquaintances from the *John Robinson*.

"No, but the name sounds familiar. I did share a port with a man called Sutton after you left last night, one of the Captain's cronies, but I was tired and a bit foxed. I have a meeting at the Club this morning and will discreetly enquire as to their standing. It is highly irregular to have received an invitation without an introduction or visit!"

"The card is tasteful," I replied, nibbling delicately on my toast as I contemplated the golden Chinese dragon emblazoned on the reverse.

My constitution was still fragile, and I favoured a light breakfast. I wasn't sure whether it was the agitation of having Captain Gabriel Sterling so close to my quarters or the rigours of the sea journey that had unsettled my constitution.

"Well, it is unorthodox – however, this is the colonies! I will leave you now, my dear, and join you for dinner this evening." Alexander proclaimed, rising as he adjusted his gloves and stylish French silk top hat.

I beckoned for another pot of tea while I contemplated my day's activities. Mr Wren at the front desk had suggested a walk to the recently planted Fitzroy Gardens and a stroll along Collins Street that harboured a plethora of stores. I decided to summon Mary and enjoy a little exercise; my legs were still uneasy on dry land. Rising, I headed for the foyer. A solemn spindly man hunched over the desk. His glasses were perched precariously on the edge of his Gallic nose.

"Excuse my intrusion, Mr Wren, but have you perchance seen my abigail, Mary? The other staff have been indifferent to my requests." I asked, my exasperation made obvious by my fingers tapping on the desk.

"Miss Lavender! A delight! I must admit the desk has been extremely busy this morning but I will discover her whereabouts and send her up immediately. I apologise for the inconvenience and will certainly speak severely to my staff for their lack of sensitivity." An obsequious bow dismissed any further questions.

"Thank you, Mr Wren. This is most vexing. I had planned a turn in the park and a walk down Collins Street." I indignantly spun on my heel right into the arms of Captain Sterling. I stumbled and his strong arms gathered me into a brief embrace as he deposited me firmly to one side.

"Miss Lavender, I fear your land legs elude you!" he beamed, his splayed left hand still encircling my trim waist as his catlike eyes gazed down at my upturned face. I could feel the heat of his touch through my fine fabric, his hand lingering possessively as my breath rose and fell erratically. The Captain's full lips parted in a winning smile. "You are not well, Miss Lavender?"

"Captain Sterling, unhand me this instant," I gasped, my voice cracking as I defiantly drew my carriage taller.

"I am at your service, Miss Lavender." He bowed, still smiling.

Mr Wren, coughed briefly to seek my attention. "Miss Lavender, my apologies. A note was left by your abigail with our young Kitty. From what I have gathered the news is not favourable."

I snatched the note from his hand and opened it with exasperation.

Miss, I beg your forgiveness but I have run away to be with Gibbs.
Yours truly, Mary

"Silly, silly girl!" I choked, my hand flying to my mouth in distress. Captain Sterling's arm reached out to steady me.

"Kitty has informed me, Miss Lavender, that they have absconded to the fields." Mr Wren commented, peering over his reading glasses with concern.

"The fields?" I declared in alarm, I felt the blood run from my face.

"The goldfields, I fear. The purge of every employer in this fair land." Mr Wren's balding head shook from side to side. He suddenly reminded me of an ancient and absurd egret, resplendent in brown and green stripes.

"Thank you, Mr Wren. Miss Lavender may need a restorative beverage. Would you please send something to the lounge?" the Captain suggested.

"Immediately, Captain. Most disturbing news," Mr Wren clucked as he turned to his assistant, still shaking his head.

Captain Sterling grasped my elbow and propelled me to a comfortable turquoise sofa in the morning lounge. Thankfully, it was empty. After the refreshments had been delivered, Captain Sterling poured a restorative brandy. I was still staring at the note in disbelief!

"Miss Lavender, if you wish I will make enquiries for you at the Cobb and Company office. We may be able to ascertain whether they headed by coach towards Ballarat, Castlemaine or Maldon. However, it is a lost cause. I am already missing half my crew due to the fever – the other half are now on a warning. Heaven forbid them making another strike!"

Captain Sterling handed me a glass of brandy, I acknowledged his kindness with a tight smile. I had mixed emotions. On one hand, I should refuse the Captain's assistance, but on the other I relished his natural capability and comforting presence.

"Thank you, Captain, but I shall ensure Alexander is aware of the situation and makes the necessary enquiries. How could they! Alexander's valet and my abigail," I groaned and downed the brandy. A delightful warm sensation coursed through my body as I accepted another glass without hesitation and swiftly emptied that.

"Stranger things have happened," he declared, a sly smile playing on his lips.

The brandy had brought warmth to my cheeks and my shock had been replaced by a soothing melodious ambience. The restorative drink was certainly invigorating!

"Captain, please do not let me interrupt your day. After this glass my legs will be sufficiently recovered to carry me to my room." I stifled a giggle. My legs, I could hardly feel my legs – why was I mentioning them to Captain Sterling?

A delightful mellowness moved through my body as I breathed in deeply the subtle fragrance that was him. Did he realise how sinfully handsome he was at present? His unfashionable long auburn hair, streaked by the sun with a chestnut hue, fell carelessly over one eye. His large hand was constantly pushing back rebellious strands from his forehead whilst those mesmerising sea green eyes burrowed into my soul with an unnerving intensity. I was melting under those eyes, my whole body tingled, as I leant in closer. Breathe, Charlotte, breathe! My stomach quivered and in one involuntary movement I indelicately unloaded my meagre breakfast onto Gabriel's lap.

"Oh, my goodness. Oh, my goodness!" I cried, rummaging in my purse for a handkerchief as I realised the extent of my disgrace.

"Do not be distressed, Miss Lavender. I should have been prudent. Alcohol in the morning is probably not the most appropriate choice for a lady with a poor constitution." Gabriel rose, frowning as the remains of my breakfast dripped down into his boots. "It is probably in our best interests if I escort you to your room." He extended his hand with a concerned gaze. Hurt by his words, I retaliated.

"How dare you accuse me of poor constitution! This is your doing, Captain! Plying me with alcohol at such an hour. This is low, even for you! What will people think? This is mortifying." I held my throbbing head in distress as I wiped the spittle from my mouth.

"Miss Lavender, if we don't make haste to your room, the morning tea crowd will view your indelicate situation." Ignoring my discomfort, he grasped my elbow once again and steered me forcibly towards the main staircase before I could protest, barking off orders to a surprised Mr Wren for water and a maid.

Stumbling at the stairs, I could barely contain my humiliation as Gabriel swept me into his arms and climbed the timber staircase. His powerful arms effortlessly carried my slim figure several levels.

"Captain Sterling, put me down at once. This is unseemly!" I stated, wriggling in his arms, attempting to modestly control my billowing skirt.

The Captain paid no heed to my protest. To avoid a scene, I buried my face into his firm muscular chest, hoping to avoid recognition by other hotel guests. The young chambermaid, Kitty fell in behind. He strode into the room and deposited me gently on the silken bed, commanding Kitty to fetch cold cloths for my forehead and ample water for my toilette.

"I will leave you to recover, Miss Lavender. I am sure Kitty will be a capable attendant." He smiled fleetingly at Kitty as she fidgeted and blushed near the bed, then turned abruptly and left me to an atrocious headache.

I muffled a feeble protest before closing my eyes in submission as Kitty undressed me. The man was a nuisance to any sane woman. Drifting into a fitful sleep, I suddenly remembered his ruined trousers. I must ensure that Alexander offered to pay for a new pair. A vision of his well-built body striding from my room had surely increased the pulse in my forehead as I recalled his gentle arms and compassionate disposition.

☙❦❧

After a nap in which I cursed the Captain who invaded my dreams, I joined Alexander for afternoon tea. He had come bounding into the dining room in great excitement, his wheaten hair tousled from the cool September winds howling from the south.

"Well, Charlotte. I have no idea how we have come to receive such an sterling invitation from the Willoughby's, but I have been assured that the family is extremely respectable. Mind you, some fellows were at little in awe that we had received an invitation. The Governor dines with them regularly. Xavier Willoughby is a dynamite, a ship magnate, originally from Hong Kong. They have only recently moved to Melbourne."

"Wonderful, a social outing is just what I need. Being cooped up in this hotel is taxing. Are they fashionable?" I enquired, dabbing at my mouth. The mutton was unusually satisfying this evening.

"Rather! I hear the two daughters are extremely attractive, their company highly sought."

"Well, I shall ensure an acceptance of their invitation is delivered promptly this evening!"

We dined quietly in our suite. It was a pleasure to listen to Alexander's excitement, concerning the colony's potential business opportunities and areas for investment. He was pleased by the promise of an introduction to several government officials regarding the planned extensions to the new Victorian railway network. Gold was bustling the town into a fervour, and money was being thrown at services, rail, roads and public buildings. Melbourne was becoming a hub of the world, and its founding fathers wanted its buildings to reflect its position. On a brief walk down Collins Street, I had observed all manner of classical revival buildings under construction, the largest being at the top of the hill – the Gold Treasury with its elaborate columns and Greek inspired frieze. Clearly, in this new colony and new city, it was important to show permanency, wealth and consistency. Turning to the classics for inspiration was a path that was currently in vogue within Western Europe. Even in Jamaica, public buildings were impressive copies of classic revivals in London. Apparently, the artisans were here, some already disillusioned by the goldfields. Money was burning a hole in the pocket of the men who had cleverly taken advantage of the boom. Importers, exporters, grog suppliers, ironmongers, shipping magnates, transport companies, all manner of enterprises. I could see why Alexander was so excited and inspired.

Retiring early, I had commandeered the services of a young girl named Linny on Mr Wren's recommendation. Young Linny worked in housekeeping but craved to be a lady's maid and travel the world – this was her opportunity to test the waters.

Alexander had promised to look into the flight of my ungenerous abigail and his wayward valet. I had a sneaky feeling that after the disastrous experience on the *John Robinson* with my brother, Gibbs had felt that digging holes on the goldfields would be an easier task. What persuaded Mary to join him, I could hardly comprehend.

The absence of Captain Sterling was a relief. His only contact comprised an unusual medley of local flowers to apologise for the previous morning's indiscretion and enquire about my health. I penned a simple 'thank you'. A socially acceptable note. He had been elusive the last few days; Mr Wren advising that he had been leaving early each morning for his ship. I left the note in Mr Wren's capable hands!

By Sunday evening, I was on tenterhooks, distracted by the absence of trusty Mary. Young Linny assisted me with my stylish ensemble. Her eyes lit up at my finery and accessories. She had carefully pressed my evening dress, a daring French inspired gown that complimented my eyes. Its moiré duck-blue silk was embroidered with stylised flowers. Matching braid and Brussels lace edged the neckline that scooped elegantly across my bosom. I had decided to wear my hair high with a simple braid, and with Linny's assistance twist curls to my shoulders. I hoped this would accentuate my colouring and fine neckline. Finally, my young trainee placed a blue and white ivory comb at my crown. She had done exceptionally well; I was exhausted!

"Incomparable as always, my sister, You do me justice!" Alexander bowed as he placed my hand on his arm. His attire was the height of English style – a tight-waisted coat creating a pleasing masculine line to his lithe figure. The exceedingly expensive carriage ride was brief but uncomfortable on the uneven dirt road. Alexander had haggled with the driver for fifteen minutes over the price. A month's pay for some men!

The elegant East Melbourne home was hidden behind beautifully landscaped grounds. The sweeping carriageway passed intricate cast iron gates before continuing down a line of exotic bushes of ginger, hibiscus and even splashes of my favourite, heliconia. Tantalising tropical fragrances wafted in the air as the lamps flickered their welcome on the columned portico. Surprisingly, the home was not Eastern inspired but of Greek revival with elaborate finials. An elderly Chinese butler, resplendent in a scarlet red cheongsam, greeted us at the entrance, escorting us through an imposing foyer lined with large Asian urns to the drawing room. Its gold embossed wallpapers and frescoes were exquisite and tasteful. Briskly announcing our arrival, the butler bowed and withdrew, his long queue swishing from side to side. The exotic mixture of East and West; a dramatic effect.

"Miss Lavender, Mr Lavender, welcome. Marianne Sutton. We are so glad you could join us this evening. May I take the liberty of introducing my husband, Charles, my sister, Adele and my brother, Trent. Mr Lavender I gather is already acquainted with my husband." She smiled briefly before turning to an imposing gentleman with greying whiskers. "May I further introduce our distinguished guests Mr William Wright and Dr David Jones and his lovely wife Cecilia, recently down from the goldfields. They have kindly joined our dinner party."

Dr Jones gave me a bold wink.

I curtsied but froze on the spot – these were the elegant people who had enjoyed dinner with Captain Sterling a few nights ago at the Criterion, I felt ambushed – was this Captain Sterling's doing? Marianne must have noticed my fleeting look of apprehension as she stepped forward and claimed my gloved hand in affection.

"Miss Lavender, we were made aware that you were newly arrived from Jamaica, and as we are both starved of company, we could not hesitate but make your acquaintance. Isn't that correct, Adele?" Marianne sent Adele a pleading look, clearly to solicit her good wishes. I was poised to bolt. Scanning the room, I felt that this may not have been a good idea after all, but I would have to make the best of the situation.

I knew there was mischief afoot, but it would be social suicide to insult my elegant and wealthy hosts. The two ladies were certainly not starved of style; they wore the height of fashion in exquisite silk ensembles, the lace undeniably Belgian. The older Miss Willoughby was willowy, with doe eyes and a winning smile, her dark ringlets wound in intricate fashioned pearl combs. It was, however, the younger sister, whom I had noticed draped over Captain Sterling at the Criterion, who was exquisite. Her almond shaped eyes fanned by ink black lashes were certainly alluring and seductive. And her golden gown with its organza panels accentuated her pleasing figure and décolletage, while her shining dark hair was simply gathered, its length cascading down her back entwined with silk florets. Miss Adele Willoughby was an exotic and delicate flower.

Alexander had immediately moved from my side to converse with her. I summoned my social graces as armour and smiled at Marianne. "Thank you for the lovely invitation. I must admit it was unexpected but we have looked forward to this evening with pleasure." I retrieved my fan from my fringed purse at my wrist, my cheeks flushed by the turn of events.

"Miss Lavender, please let me introduce my father." Marianne escorted me to a rosewood sofa, conveniently placed near the fire, where a distinguished gentleman reposed. His hearty square face lit up at my appearance, clearly enjoying my handsome form. His attire was stylish, a tailored black evening coat with a velvet collar and an embossed grey waistcoat that snugly fitted his robust form. He would have cut a dashing figure in his youth, although his curling dark hair was now peppered with grey above matching eyes. His ruddy face was wind burnt and lined, undoubtedly from years in the sun.

"Miss Lavender, the girlies have darn well fussed over me all day. It's the bloo.. infernal gout, blast…foul inconvenience. I apologise for not rising but please be seated. Not every day am I introduced to an English rose!"

I smiled at the old term.

"Father, behave yourself. Poor Miss Lavender has barely arrived and you are already being incorrigible." Marianne protested, her elegant gloved arms crossed in mock dismay.

"Marianne, leave me to entertain Miss Lavender. You will have your hands full with Wright and Jones. Keep Charles close by. I want no bloodshed!"

At my look of horror Mr Willoughby chuckled, a deep roll of thunder. It reminded me of another rumbling voice. Marianne shook her head at her father before gliding back to Cecilia Jones.

"I apologise for my language, Miss Lavender. I enjoy teasing my overprotective daughters! The arrival of Dr Jones has set the fox among the hounds, so to speak. It should be an entertaining evening."

"Is the fox a friend or foe?" I asked.

"A perceptive woman you are, Miss Lavender, not just beautiful! I will not bore you with colony gossip!"

"I am intrigued. Please?"

Old man Willoughby eyed me before slapping his good leg with amusement and leaning confidentially towards me. He raised one bushy eyebrow in devilish mirth. "Wright is the Chief Gold Commissioner for the goldfields and our Dr Jones is a bit of a revolutionary. Poor bast– fellow has taken it upon his head to represent the miners' rights. Trent invited him unbeknown to Marianne. Blood… good surgeon and dedicated to his motley group of diggers." He signalled the butler for drinks.

"What the blood…. hell is that? Hock?" Mr Willoughby growled at the water placed in front of him.

"Missy Marianne orders!" The aged servant grinned, his teeth surprisingly even, as he handed me a sherry.

"Who is the master in this house?" ranted old man Willoughby.

Hock retreated with a smirk.

After a pause, which I thought was due to pain, Mr Willoughby gestured towards Mr Wright who was plainly a military man, his physique rigid and commanding. He was deep in conversation with Alexander.

"Wright's a fair man. Well liked in the service but the miners' fee and the way it's enforced has roused sleeping beasts. It's a prickly subject at the moment. Our Colonial Secretary is a spineless old bastar… Mmm, well, I am sure you will hear enough in the coming weeks; the darn journalists revel in chicanery! If it's not the persecution of the Celestials it's the woebegone miners. Now, Miss Lavender, enough about politics! What brings you to marvellous Melbourne? Certainly not its society!"

I explained our plans and my Father's interests in Jamaica. Mr Willoughby listened with great interest, his deep authoritative voice soothing as he interjected occasionally with some informed advice. Funnily, he reminded me of an older version of Captain Sterling.

"Has Father led you completely astray, Miss Lavender? I apologise but he has a deep appreciation of beautiful woman." interrupted Mr Trent Willoughby with a winning smile.

"Go away, boy, with your fancy words. I am enjoying Miss Lavender's company!" A flicker of displeasure crossed Trent's face at his father's comment.

"I am sorry to interrupt your tete-a-tete, Father, but dinner is served. May I lead you into dinner, Miss Lavender?" He bowed, his handsome face, open and inviting. The older Mr Willoughby attempted to stand, grimacing he gestured towards a servant for assistance. Rising, I placed my gloved hand upon the young Mr Willoughby's firm arm.

"Thank you, Mr Willoughby. It was a most entertaining conversation," I curtsied before being led to the dining room.

"Miss Lavender, I thank you for your courtesy to my father. He enjoys a lively chat, especially with a charming lady."

"I can assure you sir, the conversation was enlightening," I rested my gaze upon his classic features.

Surprisingly, I was enjoying myself. Trent Willoughby was undeniably a handsome man. His raven hair tapered to rest on firm shoulders, his eyes an exotic deep brown that complimented his fine chiselled features and pleasing disposition, all wrapped within an athletic body. He moved beautifully and I wondered whether he danced as well.

"You must allow me to show you the sights, Miss Lavender? We have some fine parks, only recently planted."

"That would be lovely, Mr Willoughby. I have been looking forward to strolling through the gardens."

"I am your humble servant," Trent proclaimed, with a brief bow, before assisting me with the balloon back chair. His warm breath upon my neck sent an involuntary shiver down my back.

The table was resplendent in the finest silver. A handsome epergne in the form of a palm tree created an imposing centrepiece, cascading with fruit from the East. Mangos, pineapples, bananas, lychees and dragon fruit adorned the dish. The china was beautifully crafted and decorated in Chinese temple scenes, the silver tableware unquestionably French, maybe from Thiers. I was accustomed to fine dining, but was impressed with the display before me – the Willoughby's had exotic but exquisite taste.

Alexander had been assigned to a seat next to Miss Adele Willoughby and I could see the glowing satisfaction on his face as he entertained the young lady with tales of exploits from his recent journey. Old Mr Willoughby sat at the head of the table, his face flushed from exertion – or was it due to the claret he had insisted on? Mr Trent Willoughby chattered good-naturedly beside me, answering questions regarding the exotic Chinese murals that lined the room.

"The Hong Kong landscape you admired on our entry was painted by Jian Jinglun, a famous Hong Kong artist. It celebrates the change of seasons and depicts the Chinese zodiac of the family."

"The Chinese zodiac?"

"The Chinese animal zodiac depicts traditional animals for the year of birth. Unlike the western astrological chart that is governed by the month, the Chinese zodiac is determined by the year. A repeating cycle every twelve years." He smiled indulgently at my confusion. "So you will notice on the mural that Adele is depicted as a rooster and Marianne as a horse."

"And you, Mr Willoughby?" I asked good naturedly.

"I am a snake or shé in Chinese." He grinned, his brown eyes sparkling.

"And does each animal have defining traits?"

"Of course! The rooster is courageous and honest, whilst the horse is kind and straightforward. Traits that describe my sisters." He smiled pleasantly.

"And yours?" I continued in a teasing manner. "The snake?"

"The snake is intelligent, wise and lively," he said with obvious pleasure.

"A paragon amongst men?"

"You tease me, Miss Lavender. My zodiac downfall is that I am a private person and more determined when I have a goal." Trent leant back in his chair, observing my reaction.

"Well, determination is not a bad thing, Mr Willoughby. I would imagine in your line of work that it is important for good business acumen."

"You have won my heart, Miss Lavender! And I insist you call me Trent, as I shall call you Charlotte. If it were not an indelicate question, I would be happy to disclose your zodiac animal. Suffice to say, I am going to be bold and declare you a monkey. Witty, clever and a bit naughty." He gave a cheeky grin.

Our laughter was interrupted by an exclamation of delight from Marianne. "Gabriel! We thought you had forgotten our evening. Please take the chair beside Mrs Jones. Luckily, we have just this minute been seated," she clucked enthusiastically.

"Gabriel, dear boy, I hope this tardiness is no reflection of your onboard mismanagement. How goes the *John Robinson?*" asked old Mr Willoughby, his face alight with eagerness.

"Please accept my apologies, sir, for the lateness of my arrival. We have had a unsettling day, but I will not elaborate now with ladies present. Maybe over port later." Gabriel kissed the cheeks of Adele and Marianne with fondness, his usual confident demeanour laced with a touch of apprehension. I wondered whether that was due to my presence? After shaking the firm hand of his host, he proceeded to his seat.

"I trust you were not harmed, Gab?" Trent enquired, his eyebrows knitted together in concern. I had also observed a slight redness and swelling to the Captain's brow.

"Not at all, Trent. Let us not speak now but enjoy the company." Gabriel acknowledged his fellow diners, including my brother, before resting his gaze upon me and offering a curt bow of recognition. "Miss Lavender."

"Captain Sterling," I acknowledged with arched eyebrows. Infernal man. The evening had started out so pleasingly. I turned to Mr Trent Willoughby with a winning smile.

"A dragon," he grinned conspiratorially, looking across at Gabriel with shining eyes.

"My apologies, Mr Willoughby – Trent?" I queried, my head bent to one side in confusion.

"Gabriel, his zodiac sign is a dragon. Capable, courageous and confident!"

"And its shortcomings are?"

"Hot-headed, controlling and arrogant."

"Trent, I truly believe the Chinese zodiac is most enlightening!" I chuckled, raising my glass for another refill.

Although I was enjoying the lively banter with the gorgeous Mr Willoughby, I was unfortunately conscious of my other dinner partner opposite. His usually powerful body relaxed in mellowness as he conversed with Cecilia Jones, a claret glass casually held in his firm capable hand. A warm and stirring sensation coursed through my body – that glance at his hand had set me off. Visions of his hands plying me with alcohol at the hotel and gently carrying me to my suite popped ridiculously into my head. Disturbingly, I was conscious that even with the personable and eloquent Mr Willoughby beside me, my treacherous eyes still wandered regularly towards the Captain.

After dinner, the men retired to the billiard room whilst the ladies enjoyed tea in the gold drawing room. I found myself sandwiched between the two Willoughby sisters as they discussed the fashions currently in vogue and listened intently to my comments regarding society in London.

"Miss Lavender, sometimes it is refreshing to be an expatriate. I do not think my constitution would cope with the criticism and disparaging comments that form polite society in England. I hear it can be brutal," said Marianne, her eyes wide with concern.

"Yes, I have close friends in London and after the camaraderie in Jamaica they have found society in England tiresome."

After further discourse on English *soirées*, Marianne stated, "Miss Lavender, please. You must call us Marianne and Adele. Any friend of Gabriel's is a welcome addition to our circle."

"Well, Captain Sterling is but an employee of my father's but I would happily ask you to call me Charlotte," I replied, disconcerted by Marianne's warmth towards the Captain.

"He has always been a dear boy, even as a child. My father adores him, I think he sees so many of his own qualities in Gabriel. His tenacity and strength of character hide a generous and sincere soul. Do you not agree, Miss Lavender – Charlotte?"

I flinched, stammering in confusion, then I quickly composed my features, lowering my eyes. *What had that confounded man said to these ladies?* "I – I am sure his qualities are commendable," I said eventually.

"He was but a lanky young boy of ten when my father rescued him from the clutches of a despicable trader in Hong Kong harbour. Gabriel was undernourished, abused and dirty. His amiable character and loyalty was infectious – he seemed to fit perfectly in our home. Even as a young boy he was profoundly protective of us, especially of Trent. Imagine, both parents dying at such a young age! Both distinguished missionaries. Gabriel soon became another dear brother." Marianne, dabbed her eyes, with her exquisite Belgian lace handkerchief. "Do forgive me for my sentimentality."

Adele leant across and patted her sister lovingly upon her knee.

I smiled and gave a perfunctory reply of empathy. I was mystified by their conversation regarding Captain Sterling childhood. My conclusion was that Captain Sterling had implied some *tendre* on my part. Marianne supplied a few more childhood stories before the gentlemen returned from their port.

Dr Jones was flushed, and I wondered whether it was maybe due to a heated conversation with Mr Wright – who was also high coloured – or their consumption of whisky. Old man Willoughby appeared smug and amused as he chatted comfortably with the Commissioner. Cecelia Jones patted the sofa beside her, obviously concerned by her husband's appearance. Trent and Gabriel were the last to materialise, their easy banter bringing a smile to Adele's face. I gave Gabriel a withering look as he approached the sofa. Fortunately, he changed tack and turned to Adele.

"Adele, may I accompany you on the piano?" he suggested, avoiding my penetrating gaze.

With Adele's sweet soprano voice and the rich, warm baritone of Gabriel, the duet performed was entertaining and delightful. Captain Sterling had a surprisingly number of endearing strings to his well-defined bow.

For the remainder of the evening I conversed with the enchanting Mr Trent Willoughby, taking our leave at eleven. I, with a promise that he would call at the hotel for a stroll in the newly formed Fitzroy gardens the following day.

10

THE JOURNEY

I had dressed carefully that cool morning, selecting my most fashionable blue bonnet, one trimmed with an unusual shade of green lace, with a matching blue pelisse in a pleasant contrasting superfine wool. Sitting demurely and ensuring my skirt folded beautifully around my seated form, I fastened my purse with a firm snap. Mr Willoughby certainly would be rewarded with a graceful and refined picture of elegance in the Criterion foyer. My lace-gloved hands rested serenely on my lap.

"Good morning, Miss Lavender." A rumbling voice interrupted my ministrations. My eyes flew up to greet the dancing green ones of Captain Sterling.

"Well, Captain Sterling. Don't tell me you have arrived to create havoc with my constitution this morning! Is it to be whisky or will you throw me over your shoulder for amusement?"

He raised his hands in surrender. "Am I not yet forgiven, Miss Lavender? What is my punishment?" He beamed, his smile crinkling the edges of his eyes in mock deference as he bowed.

"Punishment?" A slight smile tempted my mouth. "Well, my punishment will be to ignore you, Captain." I raised my eyebrows in defiance, suddenly straightening my back to stop any desire to laugh. "I am presently awaiting your friend Mr Willoughby. We have organised a lovely stroll. I am sure you have important business to attend to, sir?" I rose as if to take my leave but the Captain stopped my departure by placing his steady hand gently upon my elbow.

"That is the crux of the problem, Miss Lavender. My dear friend Willoughby has been called away urgently on business and begs your forgiveness. He has instructed me to escort you to the tea rooms until his meeting is over." The Captain's brow furrowed in obvious apprehension.

I was not happy. Should I entrust herself to the vexatious Captain for a walk before I met with Mr Willoughby, or scorn him, remaining in the hotel until Alexander arrived? Boredom won over!

"Linny, you may stay at the hotel, Captain Sterling will be escorting me to Mr Willoughby," I said to my young charge.

꒰⭑꒱

The day was magnificent; the beryl sky made a wonderful backdrop to the delicate clouds easing their way through the sunshine. The air was still chilly as a slight breeze wove through the buildings. I was pleased I had had the fortitude to wear my pelisse, and reluctantly admitted the imposing presence of the Captain protected me from the full force of the wind that swirled on the street. He fell into easy step with me, ensuring his stride was tempered.

We walked in silence until Swanston Street, the Captain checking his bearings as we proceeded towards the construction site of the new treasury building. It was certainly pleasant to be out in the fresh air watching the activity on the street, despite the dust. Swallowing my pride, and disconcerted by the lack of conversation between us, I attempted to make small talk. I had been harsh in my assessment of his character – had he not been concerned and attentive the other morning for my health? He had also been instrumental, no doubt, in the dinner invitation to the Willoughbys' and that alone should endear him to me.

"The Willoughby ladies hold you in high regard, Captain Sterling?" I said, watching his reaction from hooded eyes.

"Yes, Marianne and Adele were attentive when I was growing up in Hong Kong. No doubt they shared my story with you. They are proud of their father's philanthropy and my unfortunate childhood beginnings. It makes for an interesting and tragic story!" he commented with a pleasant chuckle.

72

"They were sensitive to your plight and appeared genuinely proud of your achievements."

"Marianne has always been protective of me, almost a second mother, Adele, however, set me on a pedestal and is particularly partial to tales of my adventures – an exaggeration of the truth at times. When she was younger I was her hero." He turned and smiled sheepishly. My stomach lurched in response. I was convinced that Adele still thought of him as her knight in shining armour.

"Trent keeps me level headed. They are the closest I have had to family; I owe them my life."

I contemplated his face for a moment. His normally commanding and rigid features softened as he turned his gaze abruptly skywards. "You now know my dark secrets, Miss Lavender."

"I doubt that, Captain Sterling." I smiled apprehensively, as he laughed beside me, his hand running distractedly through his tousled hair.

"Mr Trent Willoughby seems a sophisticated gentleman," I stammered self-consciously, turning to view the passing trade.

"Yes!" he declared curtly. His arm stiffened under my light touch.

I regretted the comment, and plunged into an inane conversation about foliage. From the bustle and filth of Collins Street, we entered an English paradise within the city, an expansive area dotted with young elms and floral beds. As we crossed the small street of Landsdowne, which was barely a track through the park, I noticed a black carriage travelling at a gruelling pace, the horses frothing at the mouth as it sped up the mucky thoroughfare. As it approached, Gabriel protectively pulled me away from the kerbside. The driver skilfully pulled his motley team to a halt beside us, his battered cabbage hat pulled low over his dark eyes.

"Get in, gov. That also means your fine lady," he declared, glancing around before withdrawing a battered pistol from his greatcoat. Gabriel instinctively stepped closer, crushing my arm to his side. "No ideas, gov, or the lady gets a bullet." The man spat out his words with a chilling intensity as he watched Gabriel's furtive glances.

"How much, man? I will match any amount that has been outlaid!" Gabriel declared reaching for his purse.

"Keep those hands at your sides, gov. We don't want your money. Not now, anyway!" He grinned and then his sinister laugh echoed in the cool of the morning.

I was petrified, pulling my body closer to the Captain's powerful form. My initial shock had now given way to terror. Killed on the streets of Melbourne, thousands of miles from my home. My parents would be inconsolable. Swallowing, I braced myself and stepped out from behind Captain Sterling, confronting the villain.

"Sir, my brother will be pleased to compensate you if you release us. I am certain we can come to some arrangement."

My voice quivering slightly with fear as Gabriel clutched at my arm.

"Listen to this, Harry. They are throwing gold at us. Get in!" The man spat with contempt, pointing the pistol to the carriage door. A solid built and ugly rogue descended from the carriage. Although his collar was pulled high, it was clear that his face was a painter's nightmare. He'd clearly been ravished by the pox and had one eye slightly closed as well as a severe scar travelling across his chin. A villain from a penny fiction! His gun levelled at our chests.

"Don't underestimate Harry, gov. He is a fine shot even if one of his eyes ain't working properly," chuckled the surly fellow upfront.

I could feel Gabriel tense beside me, his expression changing as he summed up our situation. He obviously had anticipated a social morning and with that in mind had most likely left his pistol at the hotel.

"Surely you are not going to allow them to kidnap us, Captain Sterling." I squealed, attempting to disengage myself from his large hand. He cursed under his breath, holding me firm.

"Careful there, gov. I don't want any trouble but I am sure Harry would love to give your missus something she would remember." The man laughed, his beady eyes sizing me up.

I shivered, but stood firm, opening my mouth to remonstrate once again. Gabriel gathered me by the waist and unceremoniously dumped me inside the carriage.

"That's it, gov. Show them who's in charge! Now, no funny business or your missus loses a fine set of ears," He shifted back to the centre of the board, placing his pistol under his coat. The man called Harry leapt in opposite us, the blackened windows creating an eerie and menacing light that matched the mood within.

"I will hold onto the lovely, You stay there, gov." Reaching across, he grabbed me with one grubby massive arm, Gabriel attempting at that precise moment to wrestle the gun from our assailant's hand. Unfortunately, with agility unusual for such a big oaf, he hit Gabriel squarely on the brow, knocking him out. I let out a high-pitched cry as the Captain slumped to one side against the tattered squab.

"You have killed him, you brute," I cried out, squirming in my seat attempting to avoid the man's groping hands. Blood streamed down the side of Captain Sterling's tanned face.

"He'll be fine, just sore in the head. Now, my lovely, let's see what charms you have under these layers," said Harry as he pawed at my bodice.

Keep calm, Charlotte. The man was going to assault me and there was no-one who could come to my rescue. The Captain lay unconscious as the carriage rocketed down the road.

"Unhand me you, you brute." I brandished my flimsy purse at his head, my stupid stiff crinoline and petticoats a frustrating burden as I tried to kick his legs.

"I likes them feisty. Give me a kiss, you puss." One hand held my arms together in a vice-like grip while the other stroked my chin. "Lovely soft skin you have, missus." He lowered his mouth to mine as I spat and bared my teeth.

"You will purr like a cat after I have finished with you, my pretty kitten," he whispered, his foul mouth pushing my head back against the padding, his tongue pushing brutally between my soft lips. Disgustingly, he moaned with desire. I could hardly move. *Was this how woman were molested, overpowered and raped?* I tried to summon my strength – to no avail. Once again, he moaned but this time his body started to fall. Releasing my arms, his hefty form dropped heavily to the floor, Gabriel's fine ivory knife was wedged to its hilt within his ribs.

"Oh my Lord, oh my Lord!" I whimpered, throwing herself onto the other bench. My gloved hands frantically wiped saliva from my lips as I attempted to pull my pelisse over my exposed shoulders. Captain Sterling bent past me to retrieve his knife, wiping the blade clean on the man's shabby dark vest. Whimpering, I started to shake violently and tears streamed down my face as I attempted to overcome the hysteria which was consuming my body.

"Charlotte!" There it was again, my name through the tenuous fog. "Charlotte!" the Captain bellowed. His voice became more insistent as I felt his arms clasp me to his broad chest. The scent of him propelled me into consciousness.

"Charlotte, are you hurt?" The Captain removed my bonnet, stroking the back of my neck and shoulders as my sobs subsided into uncontrollable hiccups. Forcing myself back from the frenzy, I became aware of soothing hands and soft endearments. Dazed by the events, I sat cradled in his arms, feeling safe and nurtured, enjoying the nearness of his mouth as his words created puffs of warm air to tickle my exposed neck.

The deafening rattle of the harnesses and the scrapping sound of the wheels abruptly severed the moment and returned my battered body to the present. I stiffened in embarrassment. "Thank you, Captain, but I am restored now." With a slight shove, I moved discreetly from his embrace, firing a belligerent look in his direction. I fussed with my retrieved purse and bonnet, aware of his eyes scrutinising my flushed face.

"Miss Lavender." Troubled iridescent eyes searched mine as he handed me a freshly starched handkerchief. I eased back against the squabs while the carriage still lurched forward in a mad rush.

"You require this more than me, Captain. You are bleeding from your right temple."

He tentatively touched his forehead. "Only a small graze. I will survive."

"Honestly! Men! Lean this way please, Captain, and I will swab it as best I can considering this rollicking."

The Captain closed his eyes, I experimentally touched the wound and noticed his lips grimace. "Martyr," I mumbled under my breath as I attempted to clean his skin. The movement of the carriage made it almost impossible to continue the task. "I am sorry, Captain, but that is the best I can do at present."

Luckily, it was only a surface wound but it was accompanied by a nasty bruise that ran down his prominent cheekbone.

"Does your head ache, Captain?" I enquired as I was buffered against him.

"Like the dickens." Retrieving the handkerchief and tucking it into his pocket, he braced his body against the wall, closing his eyes.

The carriage continued its frenetic pace. Jumping would be foolhardy, I realised, especially with two passengers. If Captain Sterling had been by himself, he would probably have taken his chances. But with my bountiful assortment of clothing it would take me half the day to negotiate the doorway. Maybe if I stripped to my undergarments… I looked sidewards. Gabriel appeared to be resting, his chest moving in a quiet rhythm at total odds with the carriage.

As I considered various scenarios, the carriage started to slow to a trot. The Captain jerked forward, his head cocked sideways as he listened to the sounds on the road. "Miss Lavender, you must take this knife and place it securely, say, in one of your undergarments. I have the man's pistol, but we cannot rely on overpowering our kidnappers." He handed me a beautifully carved ivory handle with Chinese inscriptions. My raised eyebrow elicited a further comment. "A gift from Hock on my coming of age. It has been my firm companion for many years." He grinned lopsidedly, his bruise intensifying to a bright red.

The carriage rumbled to a halt, the horses breathing heavily in the background. Captain Sterling turned towards the door and pushed me firmly behind his broad back. I could feel the tension rippling through his muscles. My own were taut with anticipation.

As the door of the carriage swung open he cocked the pistol – our kidnappers were not that naïve. They were hidden from view!

"Captain Sterling, we suggest you relinquish the pistol and come out peacefully. We would hate to see you both killed for such a minor inconvenience." The icy voice was well cultured and familiar. The Captain glanced at me with a worried frown before tossing the pistol out the carriage door.

"You are a resilient man, Captain. Now please exit the carriage, and please do not be mistaken, we are well-armed and willing to shoot."

Gabriel eased his large shoulders through the door before turning to assist me. Cautiously stepping out, I glanced up briefly only to stare dumbfounded at our antagonist. The shock sent me tumbling unceremoniously into Gabriel's outstretched arms. Composing myself, I turned and confronted the miscreant.

"Mr Sanders!" I declared, my mouth gaping open in disbelief. I scanned his punch of mismatched companions. Several I recognised as crew from the *John Robinson*.

"Always at your pleasure! Miss Lavender, I apologise for the brutal handling. I can see that Harry was up to his old habits," remarked Mr Sanders, noting my dishevelled clothes and reddened lips.

"What is the meaning of this, Sanders?" Gabriel bellowed, his hands braced at his waist and his face rigid and uncompromising.

"The commanding Captain Sterling! Well, well. We are honoured! Not so commanding at present are we, sir? Now before we extend any further hospitality, I suspect you still have your lucky knife at hand."

Sanders gestured to Withers to search the Captain's boots and person. "I have no desire to kill you, Captain, but if you resist I will shoot."

Withers skirted over his boots, coat and trousers conspicuously aware of the smouldering anger permeating from Captain Sterling. "He ain't got any weapon, sir. Shall I check the missus?"

"No, Withers. The lovely Miss Lavender has already succumbed to rough hands. It will be my pleasure." Moving to my side, Mr Sanders attempted to touch my pelisse only to have a hand slapped fiercely across his jaw.

"How dare you, Mr Sanders! Lay a hand on me and I will have you hunted to the end of the earth. I am carrying no weapons and I am prepared to empty my pockets if you wish. But do not lay a hand on me!" Seething, I raised my head high and eye-balled the officer.

Before I could say another word, a hand snaked out to return the slap, stinging the side of my cheek. *God, why was it that some men had the audacity to hit ten times harder on reflex?* I cradled my cheek, glaring.

"I would not be so impulsive next time, Miss Lavender," Sanders jeered, grabbing my chin and wrenching it upwards.

"Good God, man. The woman has already been violated by your man. Give her some dignity." Captain bristled, his fists flexing as he attempted to quell his temper. Stepping forward he towered over Sanders.

"No further, Captain. Mr Sanders would be disappointed if I plugged you," the gun-waving Withers exclaimed.

Releasing me, Sanders stared at the Captain, a contemptuous glare distorting his usually affable and pleasant features. "I think we may have found your Achilles heel, Captain. Withers, escort Miss Lavender into the house. Let Hattie strip her – even though I was enjoying myself immensely." Sanders smirked, but his eyes locked onto Captain Sterling with distaste.

The Captain appeared now relaxed and focused. He had probably been in enough situations to realise the importance of a cool head. His attention was concentrated on Sanders, However, one finger tapped against his thigh, leisurely if not a little tensely. "Well, Sanders! What is it your require, money?"

"Not so simple, Captain! Let us adjourn to the house, to more civilised surroundings," Sanders pointed to the doorway of an imposing facade.

I mentally assessed our surroundings. We were at least two hours hard drive from the city. The property consisted of a single-storey elegant home that had a sweeping covered verandah, the handsome local brickwork pointed and highlighted by rendered columns in an English style. The numerous sash windows were closed, thick drapery covering the panes. Set back from the main road, it was hidden by a large natural garden, with an extensive planting of bushes, and a stable was visible from the driveway. Sanders prodded the Captain towards the tiled portico and through the front door which was surrounded by etched glass panels.

"Please turn to your left, Captain, and sit at the large desk. We have some papers to sign."

Gabriel hesitated until Sanders' pistol roughly shoved him forward.

"Remember, Captain, the delectable Miss Lavender is well guarded and on my word can be easily mishandled. If you wish, in front of you!" Sanders sniggered. I was propelled down the hallway towards a garish and plump woman, big busted with flaming red hair. Her gaudy dress accentuated her impressive cleavage – she no doubt believed it was also her best feature. I presumed this was Hattie!

"Get over here, raise your hands and no funny business." She jerked me to her side, ripped off my pelisse, tore at my sleeves and ran her plump hands roughly down my bodice, before removing my chemisette with a rip. I let out a squeal as she pushed up my skirt, forcing me to hold the crinoline, before efficiently inspecting my undergarments. Blushing with indignation rather than embarrassment, I pulled my petticoats and skirt into some form of order.

"Withers, you can have her back now," she yelled, her teeth black and uneven. Withers sauntered from the front room to retrieve me, but not before he gave Hattie a peck on the cheek and squeezed her rump. Slapping him upon the shoulder, Hattie gurgled with laughter and disappeared down the hallway. Setting my shoulders, I glided down the corridor towards the raised voices of Captain Sterling and Sanders.

11

KEILOR

Withers pushed me through the doorway. I was devoid of my pelisse, gloves and shoes. I must have looked a pretty sight with strands of my hair tumbling out of the tight braid woven on my crown by young Linny, barely hours ago. Cocking my head to one side, I stood erect and uncompromising, watching Sanders with disdain.

"Miss Lavender, your delightful company is required to ensure the acquiescence of the Captain. Please be seated." Sanders rose, pointing to a dainty embroidered chair.

"Now, where were we, Captain? The terms are clear. Due to unforeseen circumstances you have been forced to relinquish the captaincy and cargo of the *John Robinson* to your capable officer, Hayden Sanders. The papers are before you, already prepared by a most obliging solicitor in Melbourne. All I require is your signature and we will have a most satisfying outcome," Sanders turned to ensure that Withers had the Captain well covered.

"You will not get away with this, Sanders. The authorities and I will hunt you down. I will not sign." The Captain sat back in the large leather seat, locking his livid eyes upon Sanders.

In an instant, Sanders had grabbed me by the arm, forcing me to his side. The Captain's steely eyes followed Sanders' movements like a hawk. Producing a delicate knife from his pocket, Sanders held the tip under my chin.

"You see, Captain, I too have learnt from the master about concealing a useful weapon." He glided the sharp edge down my pale and exposed shoulder. "A most becoming décolletage, Miss Lavender! It is a pity I need to spoil it." I watched in fascination and horror as he swiftly made an incision into my creamy flesh.

The Captain leapt from his seat, his eyes wild, his face seething with fury as blood trickled down my exposed arm. Initially startled, I was unable to control the sob that escaped my mouth. I pulled at the detached sleeve in an attempt to stem the bleeding. Biting my lip, I refused to allow another sound to escape my lips.

"What is it to be, Captain? Another incision a little deeper would be unfashionable for your sweetheart's fair beauty and décolletage," sneered Sanders, his face distorted in malice.

"How dare you, Mr Sanders. My father will see you are hanged. You are playing with fire, sir!" I spat with distaste, hitting out at Sanders' face with such pent up force that he dropped the knife. Unfortunately, before the Captain could leap onto Withers, Sanders had his hands around my neck.

"Not so close, Captain Sterling. I will twist her pretty neck. Now! I am bored with this delay, sign the confounded form," Sanders yelled holding his sweaty fingers tightly around my neck. The blackguard! The Captain placed the nib in the inkwell and scratched his signature on the form before throwing the offending paper across the desk. Sanders released his hold and grabbed the document, perused the signature and nodded to Withers. "Withers, escort the Captain and Miss Lavender to the honeymoon suite, then summon the others."

"Yes, sir. This way, Captain, missus." He grinned, saluting Sanders.

Gabriel pulled me gently to his side, his face as rigid as stone.

"Keep on walking, Captain, a little further." At the rear of the house was located a small roughly bricked outhouse, I presumed used by the family as a cool room, probably for storing meats and other perishables. Withers opened a large iron grille door and gestured for us to enter. The Captain, turning to protest, received a solid push to his shoulders that sent him stumbling behind me before the iron door was secured and bolted.

It was cool and damp. The Captain attacked the room like a bull in a china store, pushing and shoving items aside.

"For goodness sake, Captain Sterling are you mad?" I asked as he continued to pull the room apart.

"Snakes, Miss Lavender! Snakes and other harmful pests that lurk in dark places."

Squeaking, I leapt back to the door.

"That is certainly a logical move, right in the path of any escaping predator!" He swore.

"I would appreciate less sarcasm and more informative instructions, Captain! It's hard to understand your mind when you choose to disregard my presence!" I cautiously watched his progress with trepidation.

"Be assured, Miss Lavender, I have never disregarded your presence!" he retorted, climbing agilely onto the bench to peer through the small and dirty window. Satisfied, he returned to the floor. "Magnanimously, our captors have left us a few candles and a flint. And there is a bag of potatoes, some type of hanging salami and a pitch of cider." Placing his morning coat gently upon my shoulders, he busied himself with the flint.

I wondered where the owners of this lovely home had vanished to. Maybe they had succumbed to the adventure of the goldfields or were visiting family in Melbourne. A convenient hideaway for Mr Sanders!

"I should, by all rights, return this to you, Captain Sterling." I remarked, adjusting the braids that tightly crowned my head. He watched in fascination as I removed his knife from an intricate golden braid. He leant forward to retrieve it, his thumb briefly caressing my swollen cheek.

"You are a conundrum, Miss Lavender!"

"I take that as a compliment, Captain." His touch was still warm on my face.

"It was intended as one," he replied, shooting me the lazy lopsided smile that transformed his features. "Forgive me!"

"For what?"

"Exposing you to this!" He gestured at the surrounding room.

"Well, Captain, I am certain I will regret it but yes, you are forgiven." I pulled the coat firmly around my shoulders. "It has been a most enlightening morning."

"Gabriel, call me Gabriel! I think we both can be excused for the intimacy." He crossed his arms and leant casually against the bench, his eyes boldly scanning my tattered dress.

"I will relent and let you address me as Charlotte, but only for the duration of our internment," I declared, blushing slightly at the intensity of his stare. "Can he really do it, take command of the ship?" I queried, attempting to hide my discomfort by changing the subject. Gabriel frowned as he attempted to weigh up the consequences. His eyes dropped to gaze on the knife, as he twisted it confidently within his palm.

"Yes, he can take command of the *John Robinson*. He is my second in command, therefore the port authorities will not question his directives if he shows the signed document. He will most probably avoid England but take a lucrative load to China. The Chinese miners up north and as far east as Walhalla will pay extraordinary money to seek passage to their homeland. Too many of their own craft have been destroyed recently by dissidents. But that is but an assumption. There are so many opportunities open to Sanders with a lovely ship like the *John Robinson*." Gabriel contemplated the fine inscriptions on the knife's handle. "Confound it, if I had discussed my concerns with Trent the previous evening about my difficulties on board the ship, he would have had the occasion to investigate after our disappearance. Now Sanders can sail on the next tide, my friends oblivious to our danger."

"Hindsight is a wonderful thing but in this case, Captain – Gabriel – I think you are too harsh on yourself. Sanders has clearly had this planned for some time. He even has seconded some of your crew. What happened on the *John Robinson*?"

"Remember last evening at the Willoughby's when I was delayed?" I nodded.

"Young Jesse had arrived bloodied and bruised at the hotel. Apparently, some of my crew – or should I say Sanders' miscreants – had manhandled him and locked him below deck. He fortunately escaped, but the ship was torn apart. Several of my men were eventually discovered in the hull strung up by their wrists. Needless to say, with all the ships in port the authorities were uninterested in our on-board misdemeanours. I left several sailors on board and well-armed. The others had absconded. Unfortunately, with the lure of gold, I cannot even trust my most loyal men."

"Well, when we return to Melbourne, you have my word as a witness! Mr Sanders will be locked up in no time." I waved my hand with a stately flourish.

"Thank you for your sentiments, Charlotte, but first we must break out!" Gabriel smiled pensively, striding over to the locked grill.

It seemed only moments as I rested against the sack of potatoes, but I must have dozed off, my thoughts strangely consumed by the *John Robinson*. My arms ached, my head ached and my stays dug uncomfortably into my ribs. A strip of petticoat I had used as a bandage had unravelled itself from my wound and somehow during my sleep adhered itself to my bosom. The dried blood attracted flies. I jumped to my feet swatting frantically whilst attempting to rearrange the dressing.

"Do you need assistance, Charlotte?" Gabriel enquired, stifling a smile.

"Thank you, no. I am fine."

"As you wish," he replied, the amused infliction annoying me further.

Gabriel had given up on the lock and was now attempting to ease the window open. Its size appeared impractical for an escape. "Is there something I can do?" I asked, shedding his coat and moving to the doorway.

"Pray or find another sharp instrument to pick at the lock!" he replied curtly, concentrating his efforts on the edge of the window pane.

I considered his request thoughtfully for a moment and then resolved, started to pull at my braid to free a few hair pins. "Something like this?" I held up a metal pin triumphantly.

"You never cease to surprise me, Charlotte Lavender. Were you this resourceful in Jamaica?"

"You forget, Gabriel, I grew up on a working plantation in Jamaica with a brother as my only companion. Resourceful is my middle name." I smiled and handed him a few pins for good measure.

"I can't imagine you playing rough with your brother."

"Unfortunately, I was notorious. Even my nurse gave up – dressing me in pants for good measure."

"And what happened to that child?" His veiled green eyes appraised me briefly before turning to the grille.

"Well, that child reached an age where upon her mother took an interest. If you knew my mother you would understand how complimentary the term 'interest' is." I watched in fascination as he jiggled the lock carefully. Stubbornly, it did not budge.

Returning to the bench we shared a swig of slightly fermented apple cider and listened as our kidnappers made their escape. Doors slammed, hoofs pounded and they catcalled as they rode past.

"Beasts!" I spat out as the sounds dimmed in the distance.

The warm afternoon light was now streaming through the small paned window and shone directly onto the padlock. Gabriel had given up on the lock and was now attacking the lower hinge with his knife.

A movement at the grille door aroused my attention, but before I could alert Gabriel a slight and withered Chinese gentleman, resplendent in what appeared to be silk pyjamas, came into view.

"Master Gab, stand back and I will remove the lock," said a soft accented voice.

Gabriel jerked his head upwards to stare into his rescuer's face. The old man held a distinctively aged Malacca pistol. Without a word Gabriel dragged me into the outer confines of the damp room, his sturdy but capable body shielding me from I gathered the noise. I relaxed against his broad chest, distinctly aware this was becoming a habit.

The sound from the shot reverberated throughout the room. I jerked in reflex but firm arms held me secure.

"God damn it, Charlotte, stay still. The bullet may ricochet! Hock may be forced to fire another." His voice was muffled within my dishevelled curls.

"Who may I ask is Hock and is it necessary to hold me so tightly?" I mumbled. His shoulders quivered with mirth. A shout in Chinese and Gabriel bustled me to the door and into the fading light of day. The Willoughby's Chinese butler stood serenely before us, bowing from his waist. "Oh!" I said, dumbfounded.

"May I present Hock, my *a sŭk* or adopted uncle," Gabriel stated, "Hock, you remember Miss Lavender from Fragrant Sea?"

Hock stood with deference to one side of the door, his long dark queue draped across his shoulder as his sharp brown eyes appraised my appearance.

"Yes, I remember Miss Charlotte! We must hurry, Master Gab, I have horses in garden."

Without another word he disappeared, his soft sandals shuffling on the stone pathway. I was disconcerted by his comment. Was that a voice of disapproval or indifference? But the man had released us from a chilly fate. I would forgive his behaviour, regardless!

12

THE BISHOP'S ENVOY

Hock was true to his word. Two plump horses were tethered to a gnarled and bent paperbark tree that afforded shade to the now neglected kitchen garden.

"How did Hock find us?" I enquired.

Gabriel had asked the same question whilst I had rushed off to the privy. Apparently, old man Willoughby had sent Hock on an early errand to intercept the Captain. Hock had been crossing the gardens when he had witnessed our abduction and had soon procured horses from the Bishop's house stable on Clarendon Street. The rector had been aghast at the request. It had taken all of Hock's resolve to convince the indignant minister of the danger. Eventually, Willoughby's name swayed the matter. The family were generous benefactors of the Bishop's cathedral fund and were meritorious patrons. The stable hands had rendered due assistance to Hock with the mounts and one of the stable boys was despatched to deliver an urgent missive to the *Fragrant Sea* household.

"Well, that is a relief," I stated approaching the closest beast. "We should be back at the hotel and in comfort in no time."

"There is, however, a slight problem," Gabriel stated irritably.

I turned and looked at him, the tone of his voice sent alarm bells ringing in my head. "What type of slight problem may I ask, Captain Sterling."

Gabriel's frame noticeably bristled as I once again reverted to his formal title. "Sanders has not returned to Melbourne but headed for the goldfields with his men."

"Well, we are in luck. You may return to Port Phillip, take control of your ship and the law may deal with the contemptible Sanders at its leisure. Now hand me those reins please."

"Charlotte."

"Miss Lavender, please." My chin higher than usual.

"Very well, Miss Lavender. The *John Robinson* has disappeared."

"What! Disappeared! How can a ship disappear?" I asked, hands on hips, staring at the silly man in disbelief.

"My thoughts exactly, but Sanders is obviously the only one at present who knows her whereabouts, so I must pursue that avenue."

"I suppose that would be the logical deduction. Well, then, your man... Uncle... Hock, may see me home and I will allow you to continue this unsettling adventure. I will inform Mr Willoughby of your whereabouts. Do you wish me to deliver a message?"

Gently stroking the horse's flank, Gabriel cleared his throat, his voice now dictatorial. "Unfortunately, Miss Lavender, you need to accompany me on the journey towards Sandhurst."

"What? Sandhurst! Certainly not, Captain Sterling! It is your ship and may I remind you that I have been kidnapped. Alexander will be inconsolable." With my head held high and my hair in disarray, I hoped I personified the goddess Bellona, staunch war goddess of Ancient Rome. Well, war it would be; I would not go easily! I strode towards the steed. Gabriel stood rigid blocking my progress.

"May I suggest, Miss Lavender, that you remove your petticoats? They will certainly impede your comfort."

"Impede? May I remind you Captain that for the second time today I will be forced to suffer the vile and contemptible mistreatment of the opposite sex." My voice almost failed me as my face flushed with indignation.

"I am a liberal man, Miss Lavender, but if I must take you by force, I will not hesitate."

Our eyes locked. An immovable force loomed in my path. I turned and pranced back to the house. In the background I could hear Hock's harmonious voice, solicitously reminding Gabriel about smoke, fire and offending dragons!

"I leave in five minutes," Gabriel's commanding voice hailed as I slammed the back door.

I stripped off my undergarments with one ear bent to the dialogue outside. The crinoline was a little tricky, but my decorative petticoat took no time.

Apparently, concealed nearby Hock had patiently observed our detention in the outhouse and waited cautiously until our captors had absconded before securing our release. As they lowered their voices, I heard snippets about the Chinese camp at a place called Forrest Creek and the tightly-knit Celestials community. At this point they changed to a language in soft singing tones, which I presumed was Cantonese. *Infuriating!*

I was irritated! Not just with the news that Captain Sterling refused to head for Melbourne, but that they had been secretive, not sharing their plans with me.

Resolved, I gripped my full skirt and dragged it unceremoniously from the kitchen. I had re-pinned my hair and covered it with my battered bonnet in an attempt to protect it from the dust. My pelisse was torn but serviceable.

On my return Captain Sterling was mounted and I suddenly realised the implications of riding pillion on the big bay. Out of sorts already, I voiced my dissatisfaction. "This is highly improper, Captain Sterling! But I have come to expect such treatment from your hands!"

He leant down to grasp my hand. "Then, Miss Lavender, I have not disappointed you!" he mockingly replied, the sunlight catching the cinnamon highlights in his hair.

Hock had kindly remained unseated, stooping slightly to allow me to place my left boot in his clasped hands. With one swift movement, I landed in a flurry upon the beast. Adjusting my folds, I was unable to modestly cover my extremities. Captain Sterling's inconvenience was amply rewarded by the sight of my stockinged calves, indecorously displayed to the world! The bay shimmied to the side.

"Hold tight, Miss Lavender. The mare must become accustomed to our weight!"

Pouting, I entwined my arms around his waist.

"Are you comfortable?" The deep vibrating sound of his voice reverberated down the length of his body. Disconcerted, I mumbled acquiescence.

Hock had nimbly mounted and moved to our side. His horse's tail swished in rhythm with his black braided queue. "We have long journey, Master Gab. The devils ride swiftly towards golden mountain."

"I thank you, Uncle! As always, your quickness of mind and spirit humbles me." Captain Sterling bowed his head in acknowledgement, his respectful words in discord with my treatment. I suppressed the burning desire to emit a rude comment.

⚜

For the first mile Gabriel grudgingly walked the young bay, mindful of my comfort, but as we approached several parties of miners he quickened the pace.

I suppose it should not have been a surprise to see miners, as this was the main track to the goldfields, but the number of men surprised me. Men from all walks of life, if their dress gave any indication. Most were on foot, their livelihood bundled upon their backs, with food dangling in sacks from their shoulders. Around their waists a myriad of items hung: pans, dishes, axes, kettles, and they always had a firearm in hand!

Even as the last glow of sunlight filtered through the giant ironbarks, they wove along the dusty track from water hole to creek to town. A flow of men walking a path they believed would lead them to the holy grail of gold! It was a glorious dream! No masters, no limits, a wild carefree life! Social standing, wealth, independence and security could be made possible with one booming discovery.

"Idiots," Gabriel Sterling commented as we hurried past a few startled men huddled around a fire enjoying a billy tea.

"You are being ungenerous! I think it is a wonderful adventure," I stated, my cheek rubbing against the Captain's coat. I could feel my face prickle with the heat.

"A wonderful adventure. Huh!" he boomed skirting around a drudging bullock dray.

"Surely you of all men can understand the desire for success?" I continued obstinately.

"Miss Lavender, even in normal life there is a fine line between success and failure. Unfortunately, in this case their odds are even greater. Half of them will be back in Melbourne within a month, destitute!" he thundered in agitation as he attempted to calm the mount.

The catcalling and whistles had started not long into our journey and were now spreading like wildfire down the track. Familiar with the vagaries of men, I had ignored the initial crude comments. But by the third mile, the discharging of firearms at random intervals had Hock's horse clinging to our side and my nails digging into Gabriel's ribs.

"Aye, gov. Let the little missus down for some real mounting," called out a staggering Irish miner as he reached for the reins at one creek crossing. Even from my height I could smell the stagnant whisky on his breath. Gabriel booted him aside with a stream of curses, and, weaving between his jeering comrades, we made for higher ground.

This was not an easy task. The road was littered with wrecked drays, bullock skeletons and other debris left by the migrating travellers. A stage coach approached from the distance and Gabriel attempted to wave it down. Obviously, this was a grave mistake because the driver's companion sent a charge whizzing past our heads.

By this stage, I was clinging on in desperation as the beast, agitated by the commotion, shied and bucked. Wrenching the reins and spurring the horse into a gallop, Gabriel used all his strength to regain some vestige of control. He leant forward and I followed suit, clasping him so hard my muscles ached. I closed my eyes, clenched my teeth and prayed for firm ground and a hot bath!

We rode like Sisyphus escaping Hades.

13

Diggers' Trail

My thighs throbbed as I half collapsed onto the courtyard of the Diggers Rest hotel. I knew this to be its name because a large German herr had greeted our arrival with an enthusiast introduction and announcement. "Velcome to de Diggers Rest, Frau!"

Heinrich Doff escorted us with much ceremony into the main lounge and left us under the care of his robust wife Mathilda. Waves of nausea threatened to unsettle my stomach. I swayed unsteadily, and seeing my distress, Mathilda bundled me along the passageway to the first available room.

"Rest here, Frau Sterling. I will send in some water and a special dumpling kasserolle."

The dust and grime of the road clung to my clothes and irritated my skin. It suddenly dawned on me what she had said. Presumably, Captain Sterling in his usual high-handed manner had allowed the misunderstanding. Fumbling with my bonnet, I realised I had little patience or energy to complete the task. I lay back on the cot feeling muscles in unthinkable areas stretch and ache. I had regarded myself as a competent horsewoman, but riding pillion on a large bay had its limits. I shut my eyes and gave in to exhaustion.

Warm and capable hands stripped the bonnet from my head, as I lay prone on the bed. A warm cloth lightly patted my face and cleansed my hands. My pelisse and boots were removed and I was tucked into the folds of the bed.

"Thank you, Mathilda," I murmured dreamily, turning on my side, oblivious to the constraints of my corset. An unsettling hint of a familiar odour in the air stirred my senses as I drifted into a bone-weary slumber.

❦

I woke with an incredible thirst. My mouth was parched and my belly groaned. It must be near dawn, the time when you reach for the extra layers to ward off the last of the night air. Lying on my back I stared groggily into the darkness. Slightly lightheaded, I stared at the ceiling, attempting to recall the events of the previous day. Images collided in my mind. A soft snore woke me instantly from my contemplations. As I rose on one arm the cot creaked. I winced as my whalebone corset dug into my right breast.

In the dark I could make out someone asleep on a bedroll. Captain Sterling to be exact. Even in the diffused light of morning I could see his dark auburn hair gleaming on his pillowed coat.

"Captain Sterling! Gabriel! What are you doing in my room?" I threw my boot at his broad back. No shortage of a target there! The impact had the desired effect and he snorted with indignation and turned over.

"I am trying to sleep, Miss Lavender," he declared drowsily, rubbing his lower back vigorously.

"Captain Sterling, this is highly irregular and ungentlemanly."

"I would think throwing a boot would rate as highly unladylike," he mumbled into his pillow, yawning as he turned once again to face the wall. It was too dark to see his expression but I fancied his auburn eyebrow was cocked in mockery.

My stomach groaned and rumbled traitorously as I grabbed my pelisse and stumbled around attempting to find my other boot. A snort of humour rose from the floor! Exasperated, I left my boots, pulled my copious skirt into order and snuck out the door. Needless to say the firmness of the corset would make it near impossible to refit my shoes without assistance.

It was still cool and dark in the corridor but I could hear the faint sound of pans at work and voices coming from the back of the hotel. I imagined that Frau Doff and her husband would be early risers. From the few moments that I had spent in the front lounge it appeared to be a popular location. What was it called again? Diggers Rest! How appropriate. I hoped there were no unpleasant miners floating around.

Heading towards the noise, I bumped into a young girl hurrying along the back corridor. Her flaxen hair was tightly bound into a crown plait, and a pile of sheets larger than herself was balanced precariously in her arms. A Doff child for sure!

"*Entschuldigung*, Frau." She curtsied, her intelligent blue eyes taking in my dishevelled appearance and matted hair. "The outhouse is outside the back door," she indicated with a tilt to her head.

I mumbled my thanks and proceeded in haste, tip toeing over the dewy ground. Sighing with relief and still in my stockings I made my way back towards the delightful smell of fresh bread wafting on the early morning breeze.

Frau Doff greeted me with enthusiasm and in no time had me seated next to her burly husband, who smiled and nodded in-between mouthfuls. A plate of toast, eggs and bacon was deposited promptly before me, slathered in a large dollop of salted butter. I ravenously attacked my first meal in almost twenty-four hours, washing it down with a jug of her husband's special brew he had pressed on me. Mathilda clucked pleasantly when she saw the empty plate on her return from the front room.

"*Gut*, Frau Sterling," she exclaimed, her rough and reddened hands placed in satisfaction upon her broad hips. "I send Greta to help with your –" She raised her hands and gestured towards her head. "*Coiffure*," she said eventually, broadly smiling as I started to pat at the matted mesh which yesterday had been so elegantly curled for my rendezvous with Mr Willoughby.

Suddenly I had the vision of a muscular Captain Sterling sleeping on a bedroll stripped to his shirt. Before I could protest, Mathilda had bundled me gently out of the kitchen and towards my room. Tapping gently, I turned the handle and peeked inside. The room, thank goodness, was empty. Young Greta was not far behind, and competently assisted in the relief of my corset and skirt. After the luxury of a warm wash and Greta's deft hair plaiting, I felt quite myself. Maybe the lack of a mirror was an advantage!

I had decided whilst dressing that the best course of action in this situation would be to take control of my destiny. Captain Sterling had a ship to find and I needed a coach passage back to Melbourne. I entered the main lounge hoping Herr Doff would assist me in obtaining a ticket on credit. With my purse lost within the confines of Sanders' carriage, I had only the crumpled clothes I stood in.

"Herr Doff, I am —"

A firm hand grabbed my elbow from behind. "My wife thanks you for your hospitality, Herr Doff," stated Captain Sterling graciously with a slight bow to his head before unceremoniously steering me out the front door. Too shocked to even squeak, I suddenly regained my voice and stamped down firmly on the Captain's toes.

"How dare you! I am capable of making my own decisions, sir! Unhand me." I attempted to move back towards the inn.

Captain Sterling spun around, arms folded, our bodies locked in an impasse. Fuming, I glared up into his hard green eyes. He hadn't shaved and a fresh stubble of hair sprouted from his firm jaw. His thick auburn hair stuck out at right angles and I had a sudden bizarre thought of women clamouring to smooth that glowing mantle.

"We are being followed, Miss Lavender, and the sooner we depart the better."

My head spun around, trying to determine whether he was deceiving me as I summed up our surroundings. The road beyond was a hive of activity. Bullock drays had already started their arduous day's journey northwards and several early morning commuters were walking in step with their easy pace. Several men trotted by on fine horses, heading no doubt for the gaiety of Melbourne. It seemed a reasonably calm landscape. I turned to voice my dissension but was interrupted.

"Hock was attacked last night. One of his unfortunate captors lies gagged in the stable; the other managed to elude him. After a persuasive interview he believes that Sanders had enlisted a few unscrupulous individuals to watch us in case we escaped, no doubt to ensure we do not interfere with his negotiations."

"Ridiculous. Why would they attack Hock?"

"He guarded our door last night so we could sleep. I assume you were too exhausted to notice."

I stood there for a moment with my mouth gaping, trying to register this information. Yes, I had been beyond exhaustion; my muscles still ached from that treacherous ride. As they say, a canon could have gone off my room and I would have slept through it. Well, this cemented my resolve to continue onto Melbourne alone!

"This is enlightening, Captain, but as you are aware this has nothing to do with me. If you would be so kind as to lend me the passage for Melbourne, I will be on my way."

"I have already enquired on your behalf, Miss Lavender. I for one, would certainly prefer if you were out of danger and removed from our company!" he said, rubbing the bridge of his nose as he spoke. I had observed this habit during the voyage; somehow it occurred when I or an errant seaman was in his vicinity. "From enquiries it appears that the best alternative is to proceed to Sandhurst and await your brother."

"But that is the other direction. Surely I can find a stagecoach heading south."

"Blame it on the gold, but all the coaches are full, north and south. They are demanding ludicrous prices to Sandhurst and are being paid it. Southbound, the bountiful miners have commandeered the transport. It is near impossible to get a ride from this small outpost. I have taken the liberty to pen a note to your brother assuring him of your safety and begging him to travel at his earliest to Sandhurst to escort you home."

I digested this information grudgingly. Thank goodness Alexander would learn my whereabouts. He would have been frantic yesterday and last night. I uncrossed my arms and capitulated. "Thank you. But I am not riding as your Indian squaw today."

A slight twitch appeared at the corner of his mouth, growing into a glorious smile. I reluctantly reciprocated in kind but stood firm.

"You will be pleased to hear I have purchased at a most exorbitant price a horse for your convenience, madam!" He bowed and gestured with a flourish towards Hock who was standing quietly beside a lovely saddled roan. "Viper at your service, No innuendo implied!"

"My goodness! How did you find a side-saddle out here?" I asked, moving quietly towards the pretty mare. She delicately nibbled and snorted at my extended hand.

"I can be persuasive at times and money talks," he replied, his eyes sparkling with mischief.

Running my hands down her flanks I turned to the Captain with a broad smile. "She'll do nicely."

He moved to her side and clasped his hands together. I grasped the pommel with my right hand and placed my left boot into the Captain's waiting hands before springing lightly into the saddle. "She suits you," he said wryly, adjusting the stirrup to fit my walking boot whilst passing the reins carefully to my gloved hands. The attentiveness of his actions was distracting. I stared down at him and blushed self-consciously. I wondered if I had been too harsh in my objections to Captain Sterling. His beaming open face was playing havoc with my feelings. Turning to his young bay, he grabbed the saddle and hoisted his manly form comfortably into place. He had a good seat and for my father, that was an important achievement. A pity he was such a rigid and irksome individual.

"Come, *Chippewa!*" he called playfully, before bounding forward into an easy canter.

≈✧✦✧≈

Kangaroos bounded across the landscape as we slowed to a walk along the plains. Their early morning feed was interrupted by the screech of parrots diving from flowered white box gum to feed below. Ears swivelling in watchfulness, they appeared gentle creatures. Grouped, it appeared, in family packs, they were reticent and fearful of our presence. The Captain rode beside me, mentioning they were hunted extensively by the miners and landowners for their tasty meat. I voiced my compassion for the elegant and endearing creatures.

"No more than deer in England," he declared in that matter of fact voice that infuriated me. He spurred his horse forward, his brow crinkled in thought as we climbed the rutted track. His thoughts were no doubt consumed by his precious ship and by Sanders. I pitied his second in command; I was positive the Captain would not be caught off-foot the next time they met. Giving up any further conversation with the Captain, I turned to Hock.

"You are unharmed, Hock. The Captain mentioned a disturbance last night."

"Thank you, Missy Charlotte. I am very well," he said cordially, his reticence obvious.

"You have known the Captain for many years I believe. The Willoughby family appear devoted to him," I stated pleasantly with a brief smile.

"Master Gab has brought great joy to the family, especially to old Master Willoughby," he conceded staring fondly at the Captain's back.

"And no doubt to you?"

"Whoever said the heart of tiny grass could repay the sunshine of spring's three months!" he said with a lovely lilting voice.

"It is about love?"

"Yes by Meng Jiao, about a mother's love for her son!"

"It is beautiful."

"Yes." His animated face transformed into a serene smile.

The Captain, who had been riding ahead, reined in his bay and turned in our direction. His face was little flushed. "Miss Lavender, a little less gossiping and a little more concentration on your riding! The Gap is our next resting point." he said sharply before spurring his horse forward. Hock gave me a conspiratorial grin and encouraged his horse into a canter.

I was glad of my battered bonnet by mid-morning. The sun shimmered on the dry dirt track as our horses kicked up a film of dust. The weather had obviously quietened the spirits of the travellers on foot. A raised hat or a wave was all I received during the morning. Maybe it was my rumpled but elegant attire freshly repaired by Mathilda, or that I was now well placed on a fine filly. I suppose straddling a mount with my calves on display was too wanton even in the outer regions of the colony.

Captain Sterling had acquired a pistol from some destitute miner limping back to the city and displayed it as a preventative measure on his hip. Everyone possessed a gun or rifle on the road. Whether they could use them was another matter!

"Aitken's Gap is ahead, We will rest the horses," Gabriel rumbled in his dictatorial voice.

I looked around and wondered how many other people he chose to command.

              ฅ๏ะﭏฝ

We heard the settlement long before we reached its outskirts. Located on a summit, it was a natural point for rest. Scores of drays and bullock wagons were scattered along the side of the track. The Gap's natural spring water was a blessing to the fagged beasts and the weary miners. Up close the noise was deafening. Drivers cursed, whipped and used a colourful array of blasphemies to spur their animals forward. The hulking bullocks shook their massive horns from side to side in dissension, reluctant to leave the sanctuary of the water. The sound reverberated throughout the countryside and made simple conversation strenuous.

A new establishment painted with bold letters on the side – Bald Hill Hotel – rose above the litter of shanty stores. Its verandah made a haven from the quagmire of ruts and traffic. I hoped they had a modest room so I could repair my toilette. I was famished and my legs ached from the previous day's endurance ride!

A young lad, barely twelve, took control of the horses and ushered us into the hotel. Captain Sterling's hand, firmly placed on my lower back, propelled me into the lounge. I was, however, this time comforted by his presence. My legs felt like jelly and the bulk of the patrons were men, their seditious eyes locked obscenely onto my female form.

The Captain protectively escorted me towards the back of the lounge where a middle aged woman had gestured. Mrs Suzanne Millet introduced herself and waved in the direction of her entrepreneur husband, George, who was busy tending the bar. Clearly, Captain Sterling's attire and his herculean size had impressed our hostess, because she was already bustling us to an intimate room reserved for wealthier patrons. Captain Sterling continued the fabrication that I was his wife and I allowed it willingly. I felt like a prize pig for the slaughter.

"Mrs Millet, do you have a room at your disposal where I may freshen up?" I asked. I was trying to avoid squirming; my warm corset was irritating my skin with the sudden change of temperature, no doubt in harmony with my perspiration soaked chemise.

"Aye, this way, Mrs Sterling!" Her eyes ran down my skirt and she made it clear by the expression on her face that my lack of petticoats was a little fast. "I'll get young Betty to bring ye some fresh water," she said with a disapproving tightening of her lips, pointing towards a closed blue door several feet down the hallway.

I smiled radiantly in gratitude, hitched my skirt and hurried down, eager to wash off the dirt caked on my flushed face and sore hands. My gorgeous laced gloves were in tatters. The reins had worn them to shreds and my hands were blistering underneath. I hoped Betty had a clean brush! And I needed my corset loosened.

⚜

Captain Sterling had been liberal with his order. I returned to buttered bread, teacake, fragrant black tea and a copious amount of scones. Stoneware bowls brimmed with fragrant jam and fresh clumps of cream completed the picture.

"Tea, Captain Sterling?"

"No, thank you," he declared, his long fingers tapping rhythmically on a glass of whisky, as he leaned back into the solid timber chair.

I shrugged and fell upon the scones. Resisting my hunger and the urge to indelicately scoff them down, I meticulously spread them with an indulgent amount of jam and cream. Closing my eyes, I relished their fresh and warm plumpness. Mrs Millett undoubtedly had a good cook. I suddenly remembered our other traveller and between mouthfuls came up for breath.

"Hock?" I gasped. Captain Sterling's amused green eyes rested on my face.

"I doubt whether any scones will be left!" he stated, reaching across with a napkin to wipe a piece of cream from my chin.

"Oh." I reddened, aware that his fingers lingered near my jaw.

"You have a fine appetite, Mrs Sterling!"

I pushed his hand aside and coughed. A ghost of a smile had provocatively accompanied his comment. "Stop teasing, Captain! I was concerned about Hock." I jiggled the teapot and attempted to avoid his gaze.

"The reality, Miss Lavender, is that Hock is a Chinaman, a Celestial, and at present that is sufficient to ban him from the hotel." Jaw tightening, he gazed out the window to some distant point. "Mrs

103

Millet — under duress and handsomely rewarded — has consented to send a tray outside."

"Oh." I said for the second time, lost for words.

"The influx of Celestials from southern China to the goldfields does not sit easily with the Europeans. They are oblivious to the fact that the Celestials have as much right to be part of the rush as any man. However, their curious ways and appearance create an easy target. Hock has informed me that the government is even thinking of imposing a landing fee of ten pound on each Celestial to ensure their numbers are limited. This from a government that persecuted the traditional people of the land." Gabriel watched the commotion outside grimly.

"I suppose you have a better understanding of their ways than most, but you can understand the curiosity of their presence."

"Curiosity does not worry me but persecution is another matter." His steady gaze levelled upon my face.

"Prejudice is a harmful card to play." I hesitated. "My father was one of the first Europeans to free his slaves in Jamaica. Although it had financial implications for our plantation, he believed that every man had the right to realise their dream, regardless of their colour. He was regarded as quite a revolutionary by other planters. Part of the reason why he wishes to migrate to New England is due to the littleness of society both in views and compassion." My revelation must have surprised Gabriel, as a puzzled frown played upon his face.

"He must be commended! However, in leaving Jamaica I do not think he will find Nirvana."

"Yes, I suppose you are correct. I think he hopes it will give our family a new start. We are tainted by the slave trade in the islands." I glanced down at my hands blistered and marked by the reins. A vision of bleeding and battered black hands toiling in cane flitted through my mind. Suddenly a pair of large tanned hands gently cushioned my wrists, breaking the image.

"Our first priority is a set of leather gloves for your hands, Charlotte." His touch was gentle and warm.

"No, our priority is to reach Sandhurst, Captain Sterling," I remonstrated, disconcerted by his tenderness.

"Yes, that too! I will speak to Hock and meet you outside. The crowd has thinned and you will be unhampered." He released my hands tenderly and rose with unexpected vigour. His tawny brows knitted in thought as he strode out towards the rear stable at a measured and decisive pace.

Refreshed and my hunger satisfied, I thanked Mrs Millet for her hospitality and joined the other patrons on the verandah. The view of the street was both overwhelming and exhilarating. Carts and drays swayed precariously, their heavy loads pilled recklessly high, the cattle sweating profusely under the burden. The noise was deafening! The air was sated with flies, the crack of whips, and the pandemonium of animals; dogs, horses, bullocks and cattle. I raised my hand to my nose as a most disagreeable smell assaulted my senses, the odour of sweat, manure and urine.

"My bloody oath, lookie there," cried a disgruntled bullocky, pointing towards the horizon. Shading my eyes, I followed his gesture. From the rise in the hill appeared a large group of men on horseback. As they trotted closer, I realised they were in uniform, brass buttons shimmering in the morning sunlight, sabres raised.

"My goodness, is it the army?" I enquired of the crotchety figure whose eyes were glued to the spectacle.

Disgusted, he spat on the ground. "No, missy. It's the goddamn gold escort; thieving bastards!" Turning his back on the procession he shouted at his team, causing an officer's horse to shy to one side.

"You there, bullocky. Mind your cattle or I'll have your hide, man!" yelled the annoyed young officer, attempting to quieten his steed. The other troopers tittered at the young man's misadventure. The escort was heavily armed with several packhorses loaded with saddlebags.

"Them's the gold, a fortune headed for the treasury!" said the bullocky, cursing under his breath.

"Gold! Do you mean from the goldfields?" I stared in disbelief at the bulging bags as the escort halted at the police station and gaol.

"They could pave the road in gold," he grumbled, adjusting the timber yoke on a pair of complacent charges. "Mind you, missy, between the troopers, the sly grog and the brothels, it's a miracle the miners have anything." Satisfied with the cattle couplings, the bullocky doffed his hat, raised his long whip and cracked it with precision over the back of his lead, calling out, "Move Apollo, come on, matey!" and the long column of bullocks moved languidly down the dusty road. A lanky offsider skipped skilfully alongside the paired cattle, a swarm of flies in hot pursuit.

"If it appeals, there is a bullock dray available to transport you back to Melbourne – Mrs Sterling?" Captain Sterling's voice boomed from my left.

I stiffened at his jest, and conscious he would be smiling at my annoyance, I reached for the proffered reins. Using the height of the verandah, I ably mounted my mare and adjusted my skirt. It was only when settled that I dared glance in his direction. His eyes were already on a party of restless men approaching the troopers.

"Miss Lavender, I think we have outstayed our welcome. Let us push on."

"But where is Hock?"

"Don't worry about Hock. He is able to fend for himself."

As he pulled his horse towards the Sandhurst Road, several shots rang out in the main street.

"The gold escort may have encountered some adversaries. Let's continue our trip before all hell breaks loose," he declared, rousing his mount.

Glancing back, I could make out the troopers armed and steadfast. Officers barked orders to their men as they handed the saddlebags systematically into the confines of the gaol. The scene appeared tense, with several men gesturing and yelling heatedly at the troopers.

My mare stumbled on the dirt track and I quickly turned my attention to the task of saving my neck.

The Captain pushed his horse into a gallop, my docile mount following suit as we distanced ourselves from the mayhem. The surroundings were a blur as I gave my horse its head. After Aitken's Gap it was a relief to be out amongst the quiet hills. The soft chatter of magpies was the only noise to reach my ears.

We eventually slowed our horses to a comfortable walk as the track descended. I had trotted Viper to the Captain's side and was full of questions. "Do you think the troopers will contain the crowd?"

"They are well armed and supposedly used to this type of disturbance. To some men it is easy pickings to rob the unsuspecting." His face was rigid as he scanned the road ahead; his green eyes veiled and distant.

"I assume you have encountered such a situation before?"

"Yes! Suffice to say, that it is a brave man that faces a desperate one," he replied, his jaw firmly set. "We will need to rest our horses at Gisborne and Woodend, or so the stable hands at the Gap informed me, but we should reach Kyneton by late."

"Thank you. Mrs Millet advised me in a most disapproving manner that Kyneton was a flourishing rural town and sufficiently large enough to accommodate suitable apparel for a lady, especially one considering the purchase of petticoats." I said, repeating her comments.

Gabriel guffawed. "Well then, it is Kyneton for petticoats," he said, kicking his mare into action.

<hr/>

We occasionally halted at a creek for our horses' benefit but we rode relatively hard for the remainder of the day. We had a unpalatable stew at Woodend before continuing our journey. It was our practice to quicken our pace when we encountered strangers on the road. The Captain was conscious of my security and uneasy about the surrounding wilderness. I put this down to the fact he was a seafaring man and anything on land was foreign to him. Overloaded carriages bearing the flourishing signage of Cobb & Co stampeded past at a breakneck pace. Arms, hats and gloves waved in a blur of dust. My face was stiff with grime and my eyes stung with the grit of the track. Tonight, I would insist on a bath and hopefully a change of clothes. My corset had been loosened as far as propriety allowed and I was conscious of a most indelicate odour from my chemise.

Stopping at a small stream, fortunately devoid of wandering miners, I allowed my mare to nibble at the surrounding grass. I dismounted clumsily and bent forward to run my hands in the rippling water.

"Charlotte, do not move!" Captain Sterling's voice boomed sternly from above.

Blast the confounded man, taking liberties with my name and now with my personal space. I was at this stage flustered, feeling the strain of the past few days. I slowly got to my feet, my skirt dragging the bank's edge.

"Captain Sterling, have I not mentioned on several occasions that my name is Miss Lavender?" I retorted impatiently.

"Charlotte, I implore you to be quiet and still."

"And in future, I would prefer the benefit of –"

My eye suddenly caught a movement through the edge of the tussock. A black shiny streak in the undergrowth, a stripped ripple of diamond scales, slithering on a pathway towards my voluptuous folds. I could feel the colour drain from my face. I detested snakes; in Jamaica there were racers, but the boa I abhorred.

"Charlotte, do not move. Do not scream. Stay perfectly still!" Gabriel said above.

My gaze was riveted on the reptile as it glided rhythmically through the grass, its black head pausing to decipher the vibrations from under its belly. It was beautiful in a terrifying way but I remained painfully still, my traitorous legs quivering. Suddenly, my horse snorted, its ears on full alert. It had smelt the danger and its hooves commenced a frantic dance. Holding firmly onto the reins, I judged whether I could leap up into the saddle, but my dress was too heavy and cumbersome. By this time the snake was alerted to our presence, its regal head raised high in anticipation. My mind screamed as I saw it surge forward raising its head. A loud crack rang out from beside my shoulder. As I watched in horror, its withering headless body fell to the ground.

I turned to one side and emptied the Keating Hotel's unpalatable lunch stew onto the boots of Captain Sterling. My body shuddered with every heave.

The mare, terrified by the noise and still fearful, tugged me unceremoniously backwards into the stream. Gabriel grappled for my arms, but it was too late, my clothes dragged me neck deep within seconds. Sharp and jagged river bed stones stabbed my thighs and gashed at my already sore derrière!

"Stay still, Charlotte!" he yelled in exasperation, removing his boots and coat.

"Do you envisage that I intend making a further fool of myself, Captain?" I grimaced, attempting to find my footing.

"For goodness sake, woman. Your skirt will pull you down further if you attempt to struggle."

Aware he was unfortunately accurate, I remained relatively still, using my arms gently to keep my body upright as the stream rippled past. My blonde hair billowed and curled around my face, conjuring up a fanciful depiction of Ophelia. It was somewhat soothing to be immersed, refreshing in fact! My bonnet dragged at my neck – I dared not try to undo the ribbons in case it drifted off or, worse still, sank. For all the commotion that had preceded my dilemma, it was pleasantly peaceful as I glanced up. The eucalyptus trees glistened in the mid-afternoon sun, their white trunks reminiscent of corseted ladies with arms swaying in the wind. I smiled. *What an absurd thought!* Maybe I was hallucinating in the heat.

"I am glad you find this amusing, Miss Lavender," growled the Captain as he tentatively placed a foot into the stream. He had stripped to his breeches and the sight of his half naked body made me gasp. Unfortunately, at that precise moment my foot slipped and I took a good dose of water.

"Please try not to drown before I reach you," he said as I coughed and wheezed, endeavouring to regain my balance. A sturdy arm darted out, grabbing my waist firmly.

"Congratulations, Miss Lavender. We are now both soaked to our skins," he grumbled, dragging me like a piece of flotsam, my face pressed intimately against his broad chest. He ranted about the perverse pleasure I received in creating a stream of misfortunes upon his head. I was far more happily occupied.

Within moments he had deposited me on the bank, his muscular arms clasped firmly around my waist. Two wet otters or should I say platypuses! Flushing, I pushed him away, attempting to adjust my bonnet. Had I complained about the heat and sweat of my clothes earlier? Now I was saturated from neck to foot. I attempted to squeeze water from the yards of my expansive skirt as best I could, considering my chemise and stockings were in no better condition underneath.

Nearly tripping with the weight of the fabric, I negotiated my way up to the track. Captain Sterling returned with my subdued mare and with one swift movement placed me upon the warm saddle. An herculean feat, considering I probably weighed twice as heavy wet! The mare shimmied to one side, obviously aware of this.

Fortunately, we spoke little before Kyneton. My mind was not disposed to make idle chatter after the afternoon's events. The day was a complete disaster, like the last few days! Gabriel set a scorching pace, and I was relieved when the banner welcoming us to the Gold Digger's Arms came in sight.

14

KYNETON

Mrs Byng eyed me dubiously, her hands crossed severely atop her ample bosom. As she rocked on her heels, her starched linen apron crackled with the motion. Her silver laced hair was pulled back into a severe tight bun, undoubtedly as inflexible as her personality. I must admit I would have been as sceptical as her if I had viewed my appearance of a mangled bonnet perched upon damp tangled hair, with wet underclothes dripping on her Persian runner. I presented a questionable figure of a lady. However, I was a lady and as such I demanded recognition. I held myself high and raised my chin, but before I could speak the Captain intervened.

"Your servant, Mrs Byng." He bowed politely, a winning smile plastered upon his face. "We desperately require a room and as you can see my wife is indisposed. The journey has been gruelling and we have incurred a few mishaps upon the way. Haven't we, Charlotte?" His smile was disarming as his brow arched in query. I nodded, too exhausted to reply or argue.

Plainly, Mrs Byng was sympathetic to our dilemma – or Gabriel's charm – because within minutes she had bustled me to a second floor suite, despatched a young coloured girl named Aurora to my toilette and placed a warm bath before the fire. I was in heaven. I lay blissfully soothed in the warmth of the water contemplating the morrow.

Sandhurst was within easy reach now. I would find a suitable hotel, purchase suitable attire and wait for the arrival of my brother. Finally, my life would settle back into some form of order and predictability, not this whirlwind of danger. The last few days had been dreamlike. I had been kidnapped, assaulted, nearly ravished, all but killed by some hideous reptile, and near-about drowned in some remote bush creek. Life with Captain Sterling was eventful! Sighing, I lifted my relieved body from the water, wrapping my hair in a stiff towel. Mrs Byng was certainly a stickler for starch. Aurora had kindly supplied a robe, one that had seen better days but was fresh and clean. Relieved, I relinquished my dress and chemise for a much needed wash before the morning trek. The fire crackled with warmth and I gradually succumbed to sleep, curled up in the slipper armchair.

What seemed like hours later, I was woken by a soft tap on the door. Anticipating Aurora, I went to beckon her in. However, the abashed face of Captain Sterling peeped around the corner. "Excellent. You are dressed," he declared, striding into the room.

"What!" I snapped, using my mother's most condescending voice.

"If I may remind you 'Mrs Sterling', this is 'our' room and I am disposed to having a bath. Whether you're present or not." His chin was firmly set in defiance.

"I cannot leave the room! I have no clothes except this shift." I declared, mortified, jerking to my feet. His green eyes ran down my stiffened form, taking in the body hugging robe that exposed too much of my legs and arms.

"I suppose you will have to close your eyes," he replied with a grin.

I squeaked and headed for the bed as he started to remove his coat.

"This is highly improper, Captain Sterling. My brother… Oh my goodness!" I choked as he proceeded to unbutton his breeches. I leapt under the covers of the large sprung bed pulling the blanket over my head. The audacity of the man! The bath water splashed and I prayed that none of this adventure reached my father's ears. I had a reputation to consider!

"Are you peeking, Mrs Sterling?" The Captain chuckled, resting his head back on the smooth rim of the tin bath. His hair wet and sleek, just like his body. Closing my eyes to a vision of latent virility I scooted wordlessly back under the woollen cover. "Being a seafaring man, I rarely ride these days! I forgot how gruelling such a ride can be! My thighs are… well the water is bloo… soothing. I must compliment you on your excellent horsemanship. Your skill in the saddle is commendable, Mrs Sterling!"

I turned my head from my burrow of blankets, to deliberately stare at the ceiling, avoiding any eye contact with the Captain reclining in my bath! I ignored his provocation and asked, "Do you think Hock will be able to track down Sanders?"

"If anyone can its Hock! He has a myriad of contacts on the fields. Quite a number of his relatives have braved the passage to travel to the Golden Mountain." The sound of splashing water reached my ears.

"Are you getting out?" I exclaimed in dismay.

"No! I'm too comfortable, even though the water is damn cold."

"Golden Mountain?" I repeated sleepily.

"It's the Celestial's name for the goldfields."

"It must be difficult and lonely for them?" I yawned,

"Keeping you up? Surprisingly they are a well-oiled team. They always travel in groups. I suppose it is sensible considering the animosity they receive from Europeans. However, each member brings a unique gift to his group. There is always amongst them, a farmer, an apothecary, a blacksmith, a cook and so on. Each member supports its own community. Something the Europeans sadly have to pay for. Charlotte, are you still awake?"

❦

My eyes shot open; someone or something was moving in the room. The Captain breathed softy nearby from his bedroll; the fireplace had stilled. Maybe it was only a few hours since I had drifted off. I remembered a brief conversation with the Captain regarding the Celestials and the Golden Mountain. The pungent smell of lemon myrtle and golden wattle drifted in on the early morning breeze.

Tilting my head slightly I could see the window, the curtains stirring. Was it my imagination or was the window wider? A creak of the board confirmed my suspicions. *God damn, what should I do? Scream and rouse Captain Sterling or keep quiet to surprise the intruder?* My ears buzzed in anticipation. Whoever it was they were obviously taking

113

their time and would be sorely disappointed with pickings in this room. No cash left after paying for our room in advance, no jewellery or fobs.

Another creak of the boards near my bed – I froze. Peering into the dark I could make out a slim dark form. Maybe it wasn't valuables he was after? I tensed with my senses fully alert and then the decision was taken out of her hands as a large figure leapt across me.

The Captain with one swift movement had hurdled himself across the bed knocking the figure to the ground. Screaming, I fumbled for the candle flint. The Captain's full weight remained locked over the wriggling intruder, one arm locked around a slender neck as he wrenched the knife from the assailant's grip.

"For goodness sake, man, stop wriggling," he bellowed, pushing his knee further into the attacker's back.

"*Ting xia ni shanghaile wo,*" cried a feminine voice in pain.

"Lord! Charlotte, light the candle!"

After several attempts the candle flared into life. The Captain pushed the black clad youth into the light.

"Captain Sterling, who is it?" I croaked, still attempting to wake up.

"I would very much like to discover that myself."

He promptly removed the black head scarf that obscured all but the intruder's eyes. Captain Sterling gawked at the vision before him.

"You are Captain Sterling?"

"I am."

"My name Ju. Hock send me," she stumbled in broken English, before bowing respectfully before him.

I calculated that she was barely thirteen, her fine bones and bearing not reminiscent of the normal Chinese I had seen on our journey. It was rare to see a young girl. Her complexion was pale, almost opaque, with translucent skin encased in a delicate heart shape. Luminous almond eyes peeped out of heavily fringed lashes. Her lips were a soft bow of red. Jet black hair, now ruffled from the struggle, lay in a limp plait that tumbled down her slender back.

I sidled up to Captain Sterling's side, hands crossed over my chest. "Well, Captain! How fortunate you now have two ladies to contend with," I smirked, arching a flaxen eyebrow in amusement at his stricken face.

Turning to the young girl, the Captain asked, "If you have been sent by Hock, why did you carry a knife into our room?"

I sighed in exasperation.

Ju raised her head, her eyes locked onto the Captain's bare chest, avoiding his gaze. "My brother Jian waits below." She stammered fearfully, "He not sure which room, so he gave me knife. Window just big enough for me!"

Pushing past the Captain, I reached tenderly for Ju, her pert chin raised a notch in annoyance. "All will be fine, young lady! Captain Sterling is quite the bully. Now are you hurt? Are you hungry?" I demanded, manoeuvring Ju to the fireplace chair. Turning, I glared, at the Captain's dishevelled and half naked appearance. "I am sure that Captain Sterling, when suitably dressed, will seek out your brother and treat us with civility."

"Bloody hell." The Captain grunted with annoyance, snatching at his shirt. "Jesus Christ," he swore again, the sudden movement obviously affecting his chaffed legs. Cringing, he declared through gritted teeth, "Hold the knife, Charlotte! I will be back shortly!"

"Miss Lavender, must I remind you... And I hope in a better frame of mind, Captain Sterling!" I shot back.

Peeking around the edge of the door, I was confident that no other guest had been disturbed by the antics. The Captain waited for a moment on the landing to allow his eyes to become accustomed to the early morning darkness before descending the stairs. The front door was bolted and he gingerly eased the iron bar. It seemed to take forever, but gradually the door gave way and he stepped outside.

Moving to the window with Ju at my side, I waited for the Captain to appear. The moonlight stippled the road below and there appeared to be no other movement. A family of possums scrambled across the tin roof scavenging for food and a distant frogmouth owl hooted in satisfaction. A few miners had camped out under the verandah below and were snoring softly in their inebriated dreams. Captain Sterling was now on the road looking cautiously in each direction. An ominous shuffling sound made me look to his right. A blur in the darkness leapt out towards him as he quickly lunged to one side. A flash of steel caught the moonlight. Kicking out with his left leg the Captain managed to connect with his assailant's leg. A muted moan rose to our ears. Captain Sterling grabbed a handful of dirt and wildly surveyed the night for a weapon. A pistol fired to his left and his adversary collapsed with a wail.

"Bloody chinky, nearly robbed me," bellowed a miner. "That will teach him not to sneak up on a McLeary. Who the hell is out there?" he ranted, as rustlings confirmed the awakening of fellow drinkers, grumbling and groaning at the boisterous exclamations.

Before he was shot by some intoxicated loony, the Captain sensibly called out, assuring the miners that he was a patron of the hotel. After what felt like minutes of haranguing, he was waved onwards. He strode quickly towards the verandah.

I should have been more observant of my surroundings. Ju quietly slipped from my side as a bag was placed securely over my head, the knife wrenched from my hand. Too surprised to scream, I was swung up and onto a broad shoulder. Recovering, I started to kick, but by then my kidnapper was moving swiftly down the narrow back stairs, my feet banging against the steep rough balustrades.

15

CHEWTON

Jin Xiong Camp, Forest Creek Goldfields

Something was terribly wrong with my foot. Well, both my foots, feet, whatever they were called! In fact, to be completely honest something was terribly wrong with my whole body. I lay nestled in a sea of colours, my nose assailed by the pungent smell of incense burning sweetly at the far end of the room. Ladies in white silk gowns danced in the air, their fingers weaving tenuously towards the ceiling. An evil bronze dog snarled at their feet as they gyrated in the breeze.

Peacocks and pheasants danced before my eyes embedded in a vibrant sea of blossoms. My eyes lazily observed a flurry of figures moving quietly within the space, their chatter the only irritation in my bubble of peace. Heads of black, dipping sluggishly in tune to the raised voice of a golden fox. *Goodness.* I giggled. Was that the moon sailing past pursued by a five clawed dragon? Mr Golden Fox glanced in my direction, his eyes on fire. I wriggled further into my soft haven enjoying the pleasure of my skin rubbing against the garden of flowers. Voices drifted in and out as I dozed.

"You told us Sanders to keep her subdued and out of the way. We have complied," stated an old monkey, waving his arms presumably to heaven and the gods.

"And Sterling, what has become of Sterling?" The fox said, frowning at the gilt tiger at his shoulder.

"He was lucky. The gods shone upon him last night."

"The gods – you idiots, he will be trouble if he finds you!"

"We do not appreciate such insults from white monkeys! Take the woman and go. We will deal with Sterling. We have paid your master generously. We expect an end to this business."

Nodding, the fox's mane touched the spinning lanterns. His fiery eyes moved towards me, lighting a path of flaming scrolls. Ju floated at my side, submissively bowed, her delicate features hidden in the action. "Miss Lavender, our coach awaits."

Firm hands raised me towards the heavens and a chariot of clouds carried me to the crimson mountains. I tittered, as his hot breath tickled my hairs and his golden mane enslaved my senses. My body floated on emerald coloured fields as golden fringes caressed my bare skin. Bewitched by the swaying light, I lay listlessly buried within the fields of lavender surrounded by the smell of whisky and tobacco. My mind travelled to happy and sad times with each inhalation; Papa and his Havana cigar in the evening; Alexander and his petulance for malt whisky; smoke from the burning sugar fields, the slaves black as Satan in summer. Figures crammed into my brain. I shook my head trying to force them out but they pulled at more disturbing threads.

The gentle rocking stopped. A hand tugged at my waist and suddenly I was upside down falling into the centre of the earth. My feet clung to the crevice edge. I screamed as a fist sent me flying into oblivion.

❦

My eyes, heavy with sleep, gazed up at enormous velvet curtains floating in the bright light. Was it afternoon or morning? Was I awake or asleep? My mouth tasted like burnt chicken and flowers. It was strange and unsettling.

"Awake at last, my jade!" The clarity of familiar sounds tinged my mind. A face moved within my foggy vision. Its face contorted into an abhorrent malicious grin. I squealed, realising too late that it was a mask. Whoever he was, the mask was a cowardly disguise! The intricate silk mask with its dark colours covered his upper face allowing his mouth freedom.

A kaleidoscope of images, of temples, dragons and lanterns swum somewhere in the recesses of my mind. I slid groggily to my bare feet, my senses dull, my reactions slow and muddled. My captor stood before me, his arms crossed and his mouth twisted in a sinister sneer. However, it was the reflection in the elaborate mirror behind him that caught my attention. I gasped! My face – heaven forbid, was it my face? It was covered in thick decorative paint, a spectacle of red, white, green and gold accentuating my eyes and mouth. A tufted plume of feathers glistened and sparkled upon an intricate headdress disguising my hair.

"They are resourceful, you must admit," he exclaimed, enjoying my reaction. "A perfect disguise to hide you from prying eyes!" His hand slid up to clutch my chin. "Funnily, I have fantasied bedding an opera star but you are uniquely Chinese."

"You bastard!" I kicked out reactively, missing his manhood by miles and connecting with his knee cap.

"You little witch!" He winced but his long powerful hands held me rigid. I lashed out once again without luck, my captive clasping me tightly to his powerful side.

"Feisty. We can do this two ways, my jade. With force or with obedience!"

Suddenly he slid the silk jacket from my shoulders, trapping my arms within the stiffness of the brocade. His hands moved skilfully but painfully over my body. His fingers pinched and taunted my flesh. My pained eyes were riveted to the mirror. Whatever they had dosed me with still coursed through my veins; my reactions were sluggish, my mind slow and dazed. My anguish and stifled cries were reflected by the luminosity of the remarkable application of cosmetics. The vibrant colours accentuated every facial expression, from distaste to horror. It was hypnotic and at the same time a distraction from what was occurring under the hands of my captor.

"You are quiet, my sweet, but not for long. I promise a most entertaining interlude." Bruising lips nuzzled at my neck before sliding to my nipples. I wriggled and squirmed, letting out a pained squeal. My head felt heavy and unresponsive. A voice screamed inside it as I quivered with fear and anguish. I could feel beads of perspiration on my forehead as I struggled with my sluggish mind. His voice was familiar, disguised, but deep and menacing. His body slim and athletic. It must be Sanders, the warped degenerate.

If I kept him talking, would help arrive? To my knowledge, Captain Sterling was still in Kyneton. Had he been apprehended as well? I had heard gunshots and yelling as I was hustled out the back door of the Gold Digger's Arms by my Celestial captors. Hock could be anywhere, and who was to say he wasn't involved in this latest abduction? Had not Ju lulled us into acquiescence by mentioning his name? Finding a sliver of clarity I stammered. "Why now? Why not seduce me at Keilor?"

"Aah! Yes, well, circumstances have changed," he smirked.

"Captain Sterling will have your hide! He will hunt you down. You…you… beast," I screeched between clenched teeth. A harsh slap reverberated along my jaw and my teeth screamed in pain.

"I doubt it! My industrious friends will handle the situation proficiently." His hand jerked at the fastening of my silk trousers. "Enough of this senseless talk."

I was running out of time and his lecherous smile implied that he was aware of my naive tactic.

"Now if you start kicking again, my little witch. I will be forced to reprimand you! Physically!" My pants ripped and my last vestige of decency was stripped before his eyes. Salaciously he grappled at my thighs, pushing me firmly back onto the crimson covers. "Oh! You will enjoy this," he crowed, unbuttoning the front of his moleskins.

Seeing him distracted, I lunged, kicking with all my might. But it was useless. My arms were bound to my sides and my body unbalanced. Gasping for breath, I pushed onto the bed. Maybe I could reach the window; surely it was open. The curtains still moved in rhythm to the breeze outside. I yelled and he chuckled.

"Save your voice, my butterfly. I have paid generously for this room. The landlord was most understanding!" Firm hands snatched at my feet and wrestled me backwards. "We are but newlyweds. A little rough play implied to a most discerning hotelier. Come here, my sweet."

I squirmed and strained, my fuddled mind suddenly aware of the deafening thunder of boots on the timber staircase. Then the ear-splitting crash of doors wretched from their hinges, followed by the startled screams and abuse of disturbed patrons. Steadily and methodically, one voice thundered down the hallway, oblivious to the ensuring mayhem.

"Charlotte. God damn it, Charlotte, make yourself known!"

The masked man cursed profusely. His parting gift was a sly punch to my jaw as his lithe body slipped through the open sash window.

16

CASTLEMAINE

G entle but muscular arms carried me. I murmured incoherently, lost in pain, clouded by a fever. My face tingled, my body ached with every long stride of my rescuer. Soft and comforting lips grazed my forehead as I floated in darkness. A soft pale light flickered near my eyes as soothing words from another land echoed in my ears. Warm and slender hands rubbed aromatic oil into my skin. The fragrance of lilies infused my mind as I drifted into a fitful sleep. Disjointed conversations floated within my battered thoughts. I could not wake; I did not wish to wake!

"She has many bruises, Captain. But the fever that now takes her body, I worry about."

The voice was undeniably Ju's. *The little Judas!* Confound it, why was the Captain listening to the impertinent girl?

"You believe the plaster will work?" the Captain queried.

"The Wu Yang plaster very good. Good for swelling, good for circulation! Kwan Loong will help pain and heal cuts. But fever... we will see," she replied calmly.

"Do your best, Ju. Hock trusts your skill, as do I."

Warm long fingers massaged the palms of my hand. *Trust her?* I called out in desperation but the words were unintelligible even to my ear. Surely Captain Sterling was out of his mind trusting this young girl? This young girl who had quietly lowered her head as I was unceremoniously bundled into a sack and thrown over some coolie's shoulder. This young girl who had administered an opiate that had kept me dazed and incoherent for days. I moaned; my skin felt damp and my temples pounded. *How had a whole brass band entered my head?* A scraping chair reverberated through my body. Someone had obviously sprung to their feet.

As they talked, I managed to pry one eye open. A blurred view of Captain Sterling dishevelled and pacing, popped into view. Oh God, of all people to see me in this condition. All I wanted was to curl up and disappear down the closest hole.

"Opium!" he rumbled, one hand rubbing his temple restlessly. His auburn hair usually falling in soft waves stuck out in odd angles giving him the appearance of a man deranged.

"More opium will harm her recovery." Ju's sweet voice sounded vexed and impatient.

"Mrs McGregor is prepared to source a nurse if you wish." He stopped pacing and faced Ju.

"Many white people do not understand the nature of my herbs. I nurse Miss."

"Is there anything else you need? Bandages? Fresh ointment? They have a large Chinatown in Union Street," he exclaimed, gesturing wildly outside.

"I have all my needs. Thank you, Captain. I will do my best"

"Yes, yes, but her face!" He groaned. "You rest now, Ju. I will watch her."

"Captain. *We should feel sorrow, but not sink under its oppression.*"

"Confucius, I gather," Gabriel stated as Ju nodded in agreement.

"I sleep, Captain, but call if heat worse."

"Agreed."

The Captain sank irritably into the chair opposite and my eyes shut instinctively. *But her face* – that eerie comment struck at my soul. I did not regard myself as an overly vain woman, but I was certainly aware of my charms. And the effect of those charms on the opposite sex. An attractive face, an elegant figure and a vivacious temperament were gifts my mother praised. Would two out of three be sufficient? I rolled over, annoyed at my affectation and narcissism.

Lightly, a moist flannel was laid upon my neck. The cooling effect sent me gradually into a fitful sleep.

ꕔ❦ꕔ

It was late afternoon when I was aroused by the sounds of movement. Although the curtains were pulled, I could hear the yodelling cry of the cockatoo's busy nesting. I woke to the soothing administration of an ambrosial cream upon my neck. Its sweet pungent smell reminded me strangely of carrots.

I opened my eyes. Ju smiled, her heart-shaped face radiant. "Miss Charlotte, you wake. You hungry?"

"Excessively!" I croaked.

Someone rustled a paper nearby. They rose and strode to my side. "Well, Charlotte, you have certainly given us a scare," Alexander declared, bending over the bed and grinning at my upturned face. Tears sprung to my eyes. "This will never do, Charlotte! Here you are weeping at my miraculous and timely appearance." He bent to hold my hand in affection.

"Oh, Lexy, it is so good to see you!" I blubbered.

"And you, my love. You had us worried. Wipe your tears; all is well." Embarrassed at my affectionate display, he handed me his well-laundered handkerchief.

"I'm sorry, Alexander. It has been a trial. I am so delighted to have you close by," I mumbled, squeezing his warm hand.

"No apologies necessary, I shall send for sustenance. Mrs McGregor bakes the most exquisite teacake. Maybe I will inform the uncivil Captain Sterling. The man has paced his way to the cellar."

"Mister Alexander, broth please for Mistress Charlotte!" Ju prompted.

Waving her protests aside, Alexander marched out of the door.

"He only teases, Ju. He is resourceful, my brother."

"I hope."

"Now Ju! Before the men return I want the truth and no holding back. I am appreciative of your kind attention but, young lady, you have been less than truthful."

Ju blanched at my accusation and nodded her silky dark head

125

in acquiescence. "Please forgive me." She emitted an agonising sob before sinking gracefully onto her knees.

Ju proclaimed her innocence and that of her twin brother Jian in my kidnapping. They had been instructed by Hock to find Captain Sterling and give him a message. They must have been careless because they had been followed. Her brother had been overpowered and bludgeoned before her eyes. The men, pigs from the Jin Xiong camp, had insisted she follow through with her errand. They had lurked below, holding her unconscious brother as ransom. Her only hope was to keep quiet and obedient. Captain Sterling had avoided capture but they had bundled me off to the Celestial camp near Forest Creek, to Jin Xiong's compound. The theatrical cosmetics had been his idea to ensure I was well hidden. She had been forced to administer the opium to quiet me.

"And the man who took me away from Forest Creek?" I asked.

"A golden haired man, from Melbourne; a sailor and trader for Jin Xiong."

"Sanders!" I spat, almost physically sick with disdain. "As you are here, I presume you were released by Hock or his confederates?"

"Yes, Master Hock paid Jin Xiong for us. There is bad blood between them, but Master Hock is good man."

"And Captain Sterling?"

At the mention of his name her gloomy and dejected face transformed into an exquisite bud of tranquillity. She truly was an exquisite child; one day she would be a Celestial Star.

"A most auspicious gentleman!" She blushed prettily. "He has been kind. Master Hock brought me here for healing when Captain Sterling found you."

"Oh."

I felt it best to drop the subject of Captain Sterling; it was not healthy for young girls to dream. "What were you applying to my neck?" I asked. "It reminded me of roast carrots."

Ju chuckled, her eyes sparkling with laughter. "It is cnidium from the book of Shennong Ben Cao Jing. It is a yellow flowered herb from my hometown. It will help with your skin. And yes, it smells like English carrot."

"How do I look, Ju?" I enquired, desperately needing reassurance.

Soft brown eyes appraised my face and exposed arms. Weighing her reply she gracefully replied, "The swelling has gone. But the bruises are the colour of the rainbow." She beamed.

"Well, rainbows are beautiful!"

"Yes, rainbows are beautiful and fortuitous." She smiled in her gentle way, hands fluttering like butterfly wings near my face. "We have been worried."

"Well, I can imagine my brother has torn strips off Captain Sterling."

Ju's shocked face made me add quickly. "Figuratively, Ju. My brother would have been displeased at the unfolding events."

Suddenly a raucous of sounds assailed our ears. The door jerked open after a perfunctory knock and the herculean form of Captain Sterling advanced into the bedroom. His blinding green eyes scanned my face and my enfeebled form. "You are awake!"

"Yes, as you see… famished and parched but awake!" I faltered in my reply, for my dry tongue caught on the roof of my mouth. Most unbecoming!

"Your brother has ordered a plethora of food. I hope you are up to the task?" A smile twitched at the corner of his mouth as he gazed at my tilted face.

Suddenly aware of my ghastly appearance, I blushed, embarrassed by his scrutiny. I suppose it was but another colour to add to my rainbow! "Thank you for your concern Captain Sterling," my voiced rasped, as I regained my composure.

"You had us worried, Charlotte – Miss Lavender." he declared sternly, crossing his arms. "Ju has worked tirelessly whilst I raced off to fetch your brother. It was a darn inconvenient distance."

At this point I was becoming angry. The man was sounding like my father! "Well, Captain, I appreciate the sentiments! I am most thankful that my brother is here to take care of my wellbeing and comfort," I said sourly.

He made some mumbling utterances, unfit for a lady's ears, and stalked over to the window.

Yes, he may have rescued me from Sanders but as this stage I was too fatigued to remind him that my present condition was due to his infuriating disregard for my welfare. Maybe 'disregard' was too harsh, but his obstinate insistence to find the *John Robinson* at all costs was certainly to blame.

"May I?" he enquired gesturing towards the heavy velvet curtains.

"Yes, sunlight would be refreshing," I said meekly, annoyed that he persisted in staying in my room. Ju fluffed up several of my pillows and, bowing, slipped from the room.

"Is there something you wish to discuss with me, Captain Sterling? You appear distracted."

The Captain lowered his arms and leant casually against the window sill. The sunlight wove its rays fondly through his unkempt hair, creating cinnamon and gold strands that shimmied and flicked in harmony. He had shaved and his clothes were neatly pressed. As always, the white of his shirt again made a startling contrast with his tanned neck and face. Those stellar green eyes of his were imperviously fixed upon my face.

"It is a delicate question. Maybe something you should discuss with your brother," he said, slightly uncomfortably.

"Have I lost my virtue?" I replied indignantly.

The Captain choked and stiffened at my bold words.

"Is that too indelicate for you, Captain?" I raised my eyebrows in defiance.

"It was – it was not my initial question, Miss Lavender." he remarked, crossing his arms in a most imposing manner, which nettled me.

"Oh!"

"I wondered if it had been Sanders?" he ventured, his eyes now wandering over my form.

"Oh!" I stammered again before regaining some composure. "To be truthful, Captain Sterling, I was so overcome by the opiates that my mind found it hard to concentrate. Real life was hampered by the hallucinations. Clearly, Sanders was at the Chinese camp and I have brief memories of him absconding with me to the hotel. Beyond that my mind is vague. Ju did her job well!"

"You were lucky, Miss Lavender, that Ju was there. Her quick thinking ensured our early flight!"

"Yes, I have thanked Ju and once again I thank you and Hock. Now,

Captain, this is tiresome and I am fatigued by this line of questioning. I release you from your duty." I closed my eyes as a hint.

Clearly wavering between compassion and duty, he mumbled something about other affairs and excused himself. Passing the bed he briefly halted. I dared not peek. In a hushed and vexed tone I said, "And for your information, Captain, and this is certainly is not something I share with the general populace – however, I value your discretion. I am in the eyes of God, still a lady."

Did I detect a sigh of relief before his brisk footsteps retreated?

17

THE EMPYRE

A forced cough brought me back to my warm room. Mrs McGregor, the brusque wife of the proprietor at the Empyre Hotel, sat perched on the edge of what was plainly a most uncomfortable cedar chair, her needles clicking in the quietness of the room. I grimly believed that her terse countenance was due to my indelicate circumstances and unseemly companions. Her displeasure was made evident by her numerous questions regarding my journey from Melbourne. I had been evasive, feigning exhaustion as a means to avoid further interrogation.

Good gracious, the woman was only a publican! I, however, smiled and simpered in imitation of my mother. I had felt the hostility in her voice – what unmarried woman freely embroils herself with Chinese healers and disgruntled sailors?

Ju had disappeared after sunrise, gently administering her herbal medicines to my injuries. Alexander would naturally not rise until after breakfast and then he would demand service. I had not seen Captain Sterling for several days, and dared not enquire about him again. Last time I had done so, Mrs McGregor had raised an eyebrow in reproach. I had the unsettling feeling that her good grace was conditional upon the size of the Captains money purse.

I turned on my side, staring at the elaborate velvet wallpaper. Its dark and morbid tones reflected my feelings of anguish and woe –

the room was suffocating to my senses. My thighs ached with every movement! I shuddered, remembering the ride, the mask and the fever. Ju knew little about what happened between the Midland Hotel and the Empyre. Suffice it to say, Captain Sterling had with Hock's assistance seconded Ju from the Chinese camp in Chewton to care for my injuries. Ju had promised to return at sunset. I was, therefore, in the dubious care of the obnoxious Mrs McGregor, who mumbled as she knitted, grumbling at the inconvenience.

A few tears blurred my vision as my head screamed with uncomfortable and disturbing images. I felt disheartened, but squared my shoulders – I refused to drown in melancholy! Fortifying my mind, I resolved to rise tomorrow and seek some exercise. Alexander could escort me. The outdoors would be restorative; this room and Mrs McGregor's company was stifling. I dozed.

Ju returned as promised, much to the dissatisfaction of my minder. "A treat from Hock!" Bowing she extended her hands, delivering onto my palms a lidded blue inscribed bowl. The smell was divine and inside was an assortment of little delicacies.

"Master Hock sends them with his most humble respect." she intoned. I popped one into my mouth, heaven!

"Pork? And they are still deliciously warm."

"Yes," She bent over and pointed gracefully from one little morsel to the other. "This one is *wan tan*, this is *jiaozi* or dumpling in English. During our Spring Festival at home we eat dumplings to show our respect and love with God. Master Hock sends them to show you his admiration and friendship, Mistress Charlotte."

I blushed at the compliment. Hock had always been a trifle reserved with me. I should feel honoured. "Well, you can tell Master Hock, that the gift was well received and delightful." I smiled between mouthfuls, offering the bowl for her own selection. Shaking her head, Ju reached for her ointments. Content, I lay back onto my pillows. Her gentle ways were serene and calming as she applied her tangy balms. The soft tones of a song in her native tongue sent me back into a deep restful and satisfied sleep.

I woke to the warm touch of fingertips upon my cheek, reminiscent of my father's. In spite of the ludicrous nature of the thought, I inwardly smiled. As I opened my eyes, soft candlelight shone upon the startling catlike orbs of Captain Gabriel Sterling.

"I have disturbed you. My apologies, Miss Lavender," he stammered removing his hand swiftly as if burnt. He appeared travel weary, his clothes crumpled and his general state in disorder. His fine dark morning coat was wrinkled and dusty, and his bristled chin indicated it had been several days since he had seen a razor. His unkempt hair fell forward upon his temple in a loving caress.

"Goodness, what time is it?" I yawned.

"It is the early hours of the morning. I have just arrived, myself. You were calling out in your sleep and I thought to soothe your demons! I apologise for the intrusion." He moved stiffly to rise, but I laid my hand on his lap.

"Stay, your company is appreciated, Captain Sterling, if I might impose! The company of Mrs McGregor has dulled my senses." I attempted to grin broadly but my face rebelled in pain.

"Your brother?"

"Lost in action. I feel that the sight of my injuries offends him. He means well but he is unsure how to proceed. He is reluctant to embroil the local commissioner in order to protect my honour. He is distressed and distracted with the whole affair. I am determined to travel to Melbourne, regardless."

"You?" he croaked uncomfortably. I stared at his unshaven face. My face still tingled with those soft, caring strokes. I bit my tongue, fearful I would burst into tears. "I will survive." I declared stubbornly. Feeling awkward, I pulled myself up into a sitting position. Voluminous yards of fabric draped from my shoulders. Mrs McGregor had certainly ensured my appearance reeked of chastity.

"As usual, Miss Lavender, you are not wholly honest with me!" A slow grin lit up his face. God, I wish he hadn't smiled, it was so darned disarming. Steeling my resolve, I raised my chin an inch.

"I admit the past week has been gruelling but it is imperative that we return to some form of civilisation, even if it is Melbourne."

"I have a proposition for you, Charlotte – Miss Lavender. In fact, I had been determined to speak to your brother in the morning."

"Yes, well! I suppose you have matters to discuss regarding our transport and your precious *John Robinson*." I snapped, cross at the uneasiness of the conversation.

"Well, the proposition was a far more enjoyable matter." He replied, clasping my hand. "I believe, and I am sure your brother will concur, that the most appropriate outcome from the last few days is for you to become my wife."

My ears started ringing. My eyes flew open in astonishment.

"Your wife?" Before I could rally my senses, Captain Sterling rambled forth with the reasons why it was imperative that we become husband and wife. "And lastly it is fitting that I marry you after the events of the past few days."

"You must be mad?"

"What?" He bridled at my tone.

"You must be mad. Are you insinuating that marrying you will protect my honour?" A laugh escaped my lips as the room spun. I lunged forward, my eyes on fire, my chest filled with an uncontrollable fury. I lashed out at his face. Oblivious to reason, I launched at him, my hands pummelling his chest. Grappling with my hands Gabriel pulled me against his broad chest in a smothering embrace. A flood of tears lashed at my cheeks as I sobbed violently against his dusty clothes that reeked with manly odours. It was strangely comforting. His warm long fingers stroked my head as he murmured soft foreign words close to my ear. Like Ju's, the sounds were soothing and tranquil.

The realisation that I had vented my anger with little provocation sent me into another fit of tears. How mortifying that I had succumbed to an uncontrollable level of conduct. A handkerchief was forced into my hand and, shaking violently, I attempted to extract myself from the Captain's arms. "I – I am so sorry Gabriel, Captain Sterling. Please forgive me," I said, sobbing between hiccups.

"Forgiven! However, that does not change the situation, Charlotte. We will speak again tomorrow. I have upset your sensibilities. You are exceedingly delicate at present and I will not put you under any further duress. Sleep and we will speak of this matter later." With that, he tucked me firmly under the bedcovers. His green eyes were unfathomable, his mouth set iron firm as he watched me with a quiet intensity. I was unaware how long he remained in the room.

Embarrassed, I had kept my eyes closed before eventually succumbing to the waves of exhaustion.

I woke to the laughing cackle of distant kookaburras as they welcomed in the day. I had become accustomed to their peculiar call, Ju informing me that they were a type of kingfisher that travelled in families, hunting small lizards, mice and large insects. She adored talking about the varied birdlife. I teasingly threatened that when I recovered I would seek out that family of kookaburras and tell them that early morning laugher was poor taste.

I lay back, lost in the garish beauty of the elaborate ceiling. Some tradesman enraptured with his mastery had decorated the suite with classical mythological scenes. Panels that were obviously imported from Italy were affixed to the ceiling, surrounded by leafy and Persian inspired borders. It was ostentatious but somewhat fittingly grand for a goldfield hotel. Figures of Diana and Apollo flew across the sky pursued by mythical beasts and gods. I lost myself in its vibrancy, reluctant to allow my demons to take over. The last few days had been trying and I had willed myself to prioritise. *Get better, get up and face the consequences.*

A knock at the door reminded me of the day's activities. I had requested Mrs McGregor to send up a maid at an early hour so I could enjoy breakfast in the dining room. Alexander had purchased several pieces of clothing and footwear for travelling, as well as undergarments. I would have loved to have seen him describing my size to the shopkeeper or seamstress!

Alice, a young woman from Scotland, assisted with my toilette. If she noticed my bruises, she kindly averted her eyes and refrained from comment. She chatted freely about her young and strapping husband Hamish who worked at the Forest Creek goldfields. So far, gold had eluded them, but it was a rich field and her husband worked hard. I was fascinated that the gold could be harvested from the creeks and not mined. No wonder it was a highly prized area, with gold running abundantly in the rivers and streams. It was refreshing to have someone chat to me without looking pitiably upon my face. Captain Sterling's conversation during the early hours and my reaction brought a shudder to my body.

"Am I hurting you, miss?" Alice asked, releasing the corset strings.

"No, Alice. Please continue." I felt my face blush in memory of the discourse.

It wasn't every day that a lady received a marriage proposal! A ridiculous one but still a proposal. I should be mindful it was done in good Christian faith.

Alexander's shopping expedition had been mildly successful. At least he had found a riding habit – one that appeared surprisingly half decent. It was gaudy, the dark jacket resplendent with brass buttons and soutache gold trim, but it was thankfully fresh and new. Given its elaborate matching round hat and veil, the dressmaker had obviously inherited the piece from Melbourne. Thankfully, it was cut for riding with the added benefit of matching slender trousers. The overskirt in the same black velveteen completed the ensemble. Reluctantly, Alexander had purchased at an exorbitant price a lovely tan pair of Northumberland boots for my benefit. They were a man's boot but the leather good quality and they were surprisingly comfortable.

"There, miss. You look very pretty," Alice exclaimed moving back to observe her work.

Very pretty did not sit well with my mood at present. The veil was a godsend; it camouflaged the icky yellow bruises that now covered my cheekbones. Several small nicks lined my mouth and eyebrows. Ju had assured me the bruising would fade with time. She had been initially concerned that my nose was broken, but thankfully the swelling had subsided to reveal my own pert beak!

Adjusting my hat, Alice led me down to the dining room. Alexander was already seated, perusing the local news rag. He rose, settling me carefully into a hideous moiré slipper chair. "Charlotte, you look splendid. I have ordered breakfast." He gestured to the waitress for more tea.

"What the dickens! If splendid implies a widow in morning, with a predilection for hessian costuming, well, here I am!" I exclaimed spinning slowly and pulling my ample skirts to one side as Alexander suppressed a smile.

"Now, Charlotte, the last week has been trying and I am the first to admit –"

"Oh Alexander, please refrain from being condescending. I wish to get back to Melbourne!" I said in frustration.

"Yes, well! I am mindful of your health and the best outcome would be that we stay in Castlemaine for another week or so to allow your bruising, ah, injuries to heal." He bent forward to squeeze my hand and, no doubt, to ensure his voice did not carry to our neighbours.

"Alexander Lavender, I will not and listen closely, I will not, stay another day in this, this, den of iniquity!" I screeched, oblivious to our fellow diners.

"Very well, Charlotte, we will leave this town but I ask your permission to travel via Sandhurst," he replied quietly, his hands raised in surrender.

"Sandhurst!" I exclaimed, fumbling for a handkerchief in my voluminous folds. Why was it that in the last few days I had become a waterworks of such large proportions?

We remained quiet as the serving staff deposited an array of dishes on the table. Alexander was a fine eater. I however, only selected a soft egg and a piece of fresh bread; my jaw still ached from the force of the blows.

"Charlotte, we will continue this conversation in the confines of your suite," Alexander said, his voice gentle and hoarse with emotion.

We ate our breakfast in silence, much to the disappointment of the other diners. My outburst had raised a fervour of conversation and shaking heads.

Alexander assisted me to the Grecian suite and instructed Alice to send up a pot of tea. My head was pounding as I gingerly lowered my frame into another gothic inspired mahogany armchair, its vibrant Grecian embroidery in unison with the ceiling panels above. The effect was gloomy and jarring to my disposition!

Alexander paced the room until the tea arrived. Pouring, he handed my treacherous shaking hands a cup of strong Darjeeling. Then, walking to the window, Alexander pulled the voluptuous curtain to one side. Bright light jumped into the room highlighting his fashionably trimmed locks and handsome features. Plainly, he'd been to the barber on one of his outings. Turning, he strode with purpose to my accompanying chair. "Charlotte, I am conscious that it pains you to discuss the past few days but I must be clear in my mind. God, I wish our parents had sailed with us!" Running nervous hands through his golden hair, Alexander stared at the floor. "Charlotte, did that man take liberties with you?" His voice croaked on the last sentence as his sorrowful eyes met mine.

Shakily I deposited my tea on the mother-of-pearl side table. "For goodness sake, why are all the men in my vicinity so consumed by my chastity? What about my injuries or my nightmares? Honestly, Alexander this is becoming tedious. Do you mean did – no, Alexander, fortunately, he did not!" My hands shook uncontrollably as I removed my hat.

"Charlotte! I have had words with Captain Sterling. Strong words, I must admit, regarding the imposition he created by embroiling you within his ridiculous plans."

"Alexander, he has been more than a gentleman towards me."

"Ha! A gentleman does not drag a woman through half the colony of Victoria chasing a lunatic. Over what? A stupid boat!" Alexander appeared to be whipping his emotions into a frenzy. I needed to take control and end this upsetting conversation.

"Lexy." I leant across and patted his clenched fists. "I will be fine. Let's journey back to Melbourne. Mother and Father will be expecting us to have located suitable lodgings and servants for their impending arrival. We will speak about this later." Ignoring my plea, Alexander leapt to his feet in agitation to pace the floor, his hands waving in irritation.

"I know what you are doing, Charlotte. Trying to placate me! I am sorry but after a heated conversation with that boorish man, I have decided to accept his offer. It is in your best interests and is the gentlemanly thing to do in such a delicate situation."

"Alexander!" I implored rising to my feet. Obviously my words were falling on deaf ears as he bluntly gestured for me to resume my seat.

"No, Charlotte! This is not your decision. This is a decision between gentlemen. Well, one gentleman and one barbarian." Striding to my side he lay his hand upon my shoulder. "It has been decided. You will be married in Sandhurst."

"What!" I pushed his hand to one side. "Of all the most annoying and despicable decisions, surely you could have asked my opinion!"

"Your opinion is clouded at present. I am your brother and this decision is in the best interest of the family."

"The family or me? You oaf!" I sprang to my feet, nearly tripping over the folds of my skirt as I stormed to the bed. I felt like ripping something apart in frustration, Oh. I wish Gabriel Sterling were here! The effrontery of him to think I needed to be rescued from society's prejudices. "I will not marry Captain Sterling!" I span around, holding a pillow to my chest – it felt decidedly comforting.

"Yes, you will, even if I have to drag you to the altar! Come, Charlotte, this is serious! We have talked of financial implications and your welfare. The fellow does have some substance, if I believe half of his word."

"Thank you so much! Your benevolence inspires me!" I shouted. Weakened by events I sank onto the covers.

"Come, Charlotte. Let us not argue. You are exhausted. Sleep and we will plan the details for our journey to Sandhurst!" Alexander moved to my side and planted a kiss on my forehead. "All is forgiven. A carriage has been ordered for noon. Rest now and we will enjoy a few days together before heading south." He was obviously happy with the outcome – coward!

Exhausted, I succumbed to his instruction and with a heavy heart drifted to sleep fully clothed, curled up around my comforting pillow.

18

INTERVENTION

North of Castlemaine

Captain Sterling waited beside the buggy, watching me descend the steps of the Empyre. His face was impassive as he swept off his hat. I was seething. Fortunately, a widow's veil covered my face but I was sure he could see the level of my disapproval by the rigidity of my shoulders. I flicked my skirt to one side, ignoring his hand, and hoisted myself into the buggy. I had been bamboozled into this ridiculous situation and I was not going quietly!

Our meagre ports were strapped on the back and as Alexander said his farewells to the McGregors, the Captain mounted his bay. I ignored the words he swore under his breath and gave an animated wave to Hock.

"Hock, I rely on you to give this to Ju. It is as promised, funds for her return to Canton with her brother." The Captain lowered a small leather pouch into outstretched hands.

"Very well, Master Gab." He bowed before moving closer. "She not pleased, Missy Charlotte?" His brown eyes twinkled as the words drifted towards me.

"Miss Charlotte does not see me as her knight in shining armour!" boomed the Captain indignantly.

"But, Master Gab, she does not —"

"Enough, Hock. I will see you at Lam See's this evening. *Yīlù píng'ān.*"

Hock stepped back, his voice soft, melodious with a tinge of sadness. I wondered whether he said the words in English for my benefit?

> *Here you must leave me and drift away*
> *Like a loosened water-plant hundreds of miles.*
> *I shall think of you in a floating cloud;*
> *So in the sunset think of me.*
> *We wave our hands to say good-bye,*
> *And my horse is neighing again and again.*

"Li Po?"

"Well done, your memory very good, Master Gab. You remembered! *Bǐ fú,*" Hock replied good-naturedly, bowing once again. Turning, he glided to my side of the buggy.

"Missy Charlotte, safe journey! And as one of our famous fathers said, *Wherever you go, go with all your heart, I will pray for you.*" His solemn words played havoc with my emotions. I could feel tears swelling up in my eyes. Reaching out, I clasped his small withered hands within my gloves.

"Thank you," was all I could croak before the buggy tilted and Alexander leapt in beside me. I wanted to say more. Thank you for rescuing me from Sanders, thank you for finding me and finally, thank you for sending Ju with her wonderful potions to my side. I released his hands and we bowed in unison as Alexander whipped the reins.

The Captain had signalled for us to proceed, advising Alexander that he had a quick errand to attend to before joining us upon the road towards Sandhurst. We chatted merrily for the first part of the journey, passing miners on foot and the usual bullock trains that rumbled northwards. The road or track, for lack of a better word, was savage. Giant potholes and scattered debris from ceaselessly migrating miners littered our path. We made slow progress and after an exhausting disagreement about the futility of my upcoming nuptials, I relented and allowed Alexander to concentrate on the road ahead. I sank into a pensive mood. Alexander and I rarely argued. Yes, we had spats like most siblings but we were close. This feeling of being railroaded into a marriage had us at an impasse.

It may have been the lacklustre appearance of the countryside, the drab overcast sky or crossing swords with Alexander that made me suddenly nostalgic about home and my parents. I recalled the vibrant tropical colours of our garden, the radiant azure sky, tea with Mother on the verandah…. my reverie was interrupted by the screeching of a flock of pink cockatoos and then by a booming voice.

"Stop right there, gov!" hollered a lean stick of a man stepping out from the dense foliage. His voice hoarse and muffled. A grubby red handkerchief obscured the lower part of his face. "Now hand over your purse and any valuables you have, gov, and that means the lady too." He waved a long rifle at our faces.

"God-damn," Alexander cursed pulling on the reins as another younger version of the stick man trotted up beside us.

"Get out and watch your step, gov, or I'll blow your head off!" The young man lounged defiantly over the pommel, his dusty old grey compliant and doleful. Alert brown eyes peeped over the edge of a triangle of patched cloth whilst two pistols were aimed squarely at Alexanders chest. I let out a groan! Our misadventures continued! And where was the Captain?

"I can assure you, young man, you will have small pickings from us!" I said sharply.

"Well, we will decide on that, missus. You certainly look and sound fine to me. And no foolish moves from the gov. Come on, get out." Our highwayman waved his guns towards the bone-dry track.

The older stick man had adeptly moved to our poor steed's side, grasping the reins and lowering his rifle. Alexander, inordinately quiet as he lifted me down to the track, released me abruptly and spun around extracting the small Belgian pistol he always had primed during our travels. Unfortunately our luck had abandoned us! A sharp and piercing shot rang out as Alexander swayed and crumbled to the ground. The pungent smell of gunpowder mingled with burning linen assailed my nostrils as I screamed and sank to his side.

"Now you've done it," yelled the older man, reaching over to whack his partner upon the hip.

"You brutes. You have killed him," I screeched, fumbling with the buttons to his superfine jacket. Alexander's face was devoid of colour, his cornflower eyes dazed as they focused on my face. He moaned, trying to rise.

"Alexander, be still. I need to stem the bleeding."

"Sorry, Charlotte," he gasped before falling into a dead faint.

The sound of pounding hooves interrupted the quarrel between the highwaymen. Thank God, it must be the Captain, but I was powerless to warn him of our predicament, as I pressed my handkerchief into my brother's wound.

Captain Sterling halted as the stick man raised his rifle. His face was thunderous as he summed up the situation. I sat unceremoniously on the dusty track nestling Alexander's prostrate figure in my lap. A miniature firearm lay discarded on the bracken verge and yards of my ballooning fabric rippled in the afternoon breeze sending withered leaves and dust skywards.

"Ballocks," he said with venom.

"Now, gov, we don't want any more bloodshed," exclaimed the stick man, his knobbly hands gesturing to the ground. "Lower the gun and get off your mount!"

"Gabriel Sterling, I curse you and this godforsaken land!" I cried defiantly, futilely trying to stem the blood from Alexander's shoulder injury.

Growling, Gabriel dismounted and moved forward.

"That's far enough, Mr Sterling! Throw the pistol on the ground!"

Reluctantly, he acceded with a grumble moving to my side.

"Now, as I said to the unlucky gov on the ground, hand over your valuables, mister, and we will let you go!" snarled the younger stick man, dismounting to collect the firearms.

"I have no gold, you wretch! You both can go to the devil!" The Captain's hands were placed on his hips, his back erect, head held high rebelliously. He looked every inch the hero! Bloody men!

"Well said, Captain Sterling! I suppose it is your intention for me to nurse two men with gunshots," I snapped, my hat sliding obstinately to once side, as I gave him an ill-humoured glance.

"Now, missus, don't you fuss. Your gov was too hasty! All we want is your gold and valuables," the older highwayman soothed.

An eerie peal of laughter escaped my mouth, making the old man jump. I was still cradling my brother as I wrenched at my veil, displaying my bruises.

"Blazes!" cried out the younger stick man, his eyes riveted to my damaged face.

"Gentlemen, in this past week I have been kidnapped, abused, robbed and suffered indiscretions no lady should speak of in company. But, this would have to be the most ridiculous! I repeat I have no money and no valuables." As I spoke my chest rose and fell, fluttering my bodice lace like some enraged black cockatoo. Alexander groaned at my movement.

Unsettled by the turn of events, the bushrangers moved to one side. Their masks fluttered as they argued once again. It was an absurd and laughable mess, except for the dire injury to my poor brother.

The Captain crouched to feel Alexander's pulse. I pulled back his wrinkled tweed jacket to reveal a bloodied patch spreading from his collarbone to his shoulder, his linen shirt singed with black powder.

"Thank God, it is relatively strong. It appears to be a clean shot, however when these scoundrels realise the futility of their ways, I will return you both to Castlemaine," he said calmly, green eyes riveted on our antagonists.

"Not so fast, Captain Sterling – Captain Sterling of the *John Robinson* I presume?" Stick man junior swaggered over his pistol butt pushed into the Captain's forehead. He flinched, cursing under his breath, fists clenched so hard that his knuckles were white. "Mister, you are coming with us. Some matey has a price on your head and we mean to collect it."

"I think you are mistaken. This is my husband and he certainly has no price on his head," I stated innocently, my blue eyes wide in astonishment as I stroked Alexander's forehead. "I strongly suggest you leave so we may find a doctor for my brother. Murder receives a far more brutal sentence than robbery!"

"He drew first," the young man said with a touch of animosity.

"It is in your best interests to release us and ride away."

"It ain't proper, missus. You haven't handed over your valuables, and if this is Captain Sterling, we mean to take him hostage." His chin was indignantly raised, pistols in defiance.

"Well, that is absolutely ridiculous!"

The older stick man raised his rifle and shot into the air. Screeching corellas and galahs launched into the sky, swirling overhead. Shaking his lank grey hair in disgust, he lowered the gun and extracted another pistol from his waist belt. "Son, stop listening to that woman's drivel and tie the Captain's hands."

"I ask for one service, gentlemen!" The Captain turned a concerned eye to my face. "That you assist the wounded gentleman into the buggy. My wife is delicate at present."

The son, after a nod from his father, half dragged poor Alexander to the buggy and dumped him in unceremoniously.

"You're, certainly not going to give into these, these, scoundrels, Gabriel – Captain," I said, shoulders braced indignantly.

The Captain shrugged and extended his large hands. The rope was firmly bound and by the disdainful look on Captain Sterling's face, a little too tight. Fumbling with the saddle, he managed to pull himself up onto the seat. The older bushranger grasped the reins and with a "Hola!" to his stead, leapt into a fast trot.

"Find Hock." Gabriel yelled back at me. I had tentatively taken hold of the reins and glanced up. He repeated the request again before the thundering hoofs drowned out his voice. I raised my hand in acquiescence and headed back to Castlemaine.

19

GOVERNMENT CAMP

"Captain Fawcett is in charge of the police force – if you can call that motley scum a force!" Mr O'Gregor ranted, shaking his sizeable head in distaste. "My apologies, Mrs Sterling, but some of those men are downright seedy. Ex-convicts, ex diggers, good for nothing low lives that see policing an easier task than mining. Feathering their nests with fines and bribes, the bast –."

His view, I soon discovered, was echoed by a large majority of the mining populace. "Well, I must seek immediate assistance, Mr O'Gregor, or my husband will be at the mercy of other unscrupulous characters," I replied, becoming agitated by his comments.

"Well, don't you worry your pretty head, I will escort you to their headquarters at Forest Street." Raising his voice to a bellow he shouted orders to his freckled stable boy, William, to saddle the horses. My own little beauty, Viper, rested quietly at the trough.

Mrs O'Gregor bustled me into the cramped kitchen, no doubt to probe me with questions. After deflecting several of her suggestive comments, I rushed down some teacake and a lukewarm tea she pressed upon me before escaping back to my brothers room. A stout gentleman was bent over Alexander, his robust form busy at his task.

"He was fortunate, Miss Lavender, or is it Mrs Sterling?" Dr Jones turned, grinning as he finished the knot around Alexander's exposed shoulder.

"Dr Jones. Yes, well, I am unable to elaborate at this time but I ask for your discretion," I remarked, stroking Alexander's slightly warm forehead as he dozed peacefully.

"Discretion is a doctor's companion!" he said soothingly, detecting the edge to my voice. "The wound?" I asked, staring at Alexander's handsome profile, his dishevelled flaxen curls spread out on the laced pillow.

"Luckily, a clean nick to his collarbone, but it will be mighty sore tomorrow. I have given him some laudanum for the pain. I will call this afternoon to change the bandages," he said, snapping his battered medical case closed. "If anything untoward happens, Mrs O'Gregor knows my residence."

"Dr Jones, one other question, if I may."

"Certainly!"

You are friends with the Willoughby family?"

"To a degree! My association is with Mr Trent Willoughby," he said, his thick brows tilted in query.

"As you are aware, Captain Sterling has been kidnapped. I wondered whether you would be so kind as to communicate this to the younger Mr Willoughby and ask for his discretion. It would be remiss of me not to inform his family of the situation!"

"Yes, of course, and I am at your service if you require it!" His amiable face revealed a cheerful smile.

"Thank you, Dr Jones. You are most reassuring."

"Until tomorrow, Mrs Sterling!" Bowing, he made a brisk exit.

With trepidation I left Mrs O'Gregor to sit patiently with Alexander as I joined her husband. My riding habit was stained and dirty from the confrontation with the bushrangers. However, with a little sponging I presented a reasonable picture. Thank God for black! Apparently, my dinner companion last week, William Wright of the Gold Commission, had set up a government camp at the converging creeks of Barker and Forest. I was thankful for Mr O'Gregor's company – a sea of men ranging from officers in English uniform, to scruffy dressed gold troopers through to clerks. Their bold eyes watched our slow progress through the camp.

Mr O'Gregor motioned to one of the dishevelled troopers seated near the official stew-pot. "Looking for Captain Fawcett."

With an obscene leer at my person the man pointed to a shabby stringy bark hut on a slight rise. Dismounting, Mr O'Gregor knocked loudly on the roughened timber. "Captain Fawcett, O'Gregor from the Empyre," he hollered.

A smartly dressed officer emerged from the humble hut. Brass buttons sparkled on his blues, an astounding contrast to his sparse surroundings. Removing his hat in acknowledgement of my presence, he bowed before placing it tightly upon closely shorn locks.

"O'Gregor." He dipped his head in acknowledgement. "What brings you to the government camp?"

"Might we have a word with you, sir? Mrs Sterling is distressed at her husband's disappearance and seeks your confidence."

I hoped I looked suitably distraught for a woman who had witnessed her husband's kidnapping by ruffians. Mr O'Gregor assisted me from my mount and escorted me inside, throwing our reins to a young private. Settled on a firm bench seat, Captain Fawcett listened intently from behind an imposing cedar desk. I decided not to divulge the entirety of the events but only those pertaining to Captain Sterling's kidnapping on the road to Sandhurst. Therefore, I gave a concise description of the men, the location and my brothers injuries.

"And Mrs Sterling, you believe your husband is being kept as a hostage for a ransom?" he enquired.

"Undoubtedly, Captain. He has the ability to raise funds which may appeal to unscrupulous men."

"An incredible story. Usually the bushrangers in these parts are slow witted, fearful of their scrawny lives. They have a predilection for snatch and run robberies. It's unbelievable that they would kidnap your husband and demand a substantial ransom," he replied, his expression dour. "There is nothing else you wish to share with me, Mrs Sterling?" His manner was pompous and condescending.

"I might add, Captain Fawcett, I am not accustomed to being interrogated by officers. My good friend Mr William Wright will certainly hear of this injustice. I simply wish to find my husband. If you are unable to assist my cause, I will seek assistance from Melbourne," I replied in a voice that suspiciously reminded me of my mother's!

The use of Mr Wright's name had, as I expected, surprised

my doubting officer. His features relaxed into a more sympathetic expression; his crisp moustache now framed an affable mouth. After taking pertinent notes, he explained all avenues would be investigated. He would personally lead a contingent of troopers to investigate the scene.

Thanking him for his kind assistance, Mr O'Gregor ensured I was swiftly mounted before escorting me back to the hotel. His furtive glances offered the only indication he was slightly suspicious of my actions. Judging by Captain Fawcett's inept manner and a further discussion with Mr O'Gregor I gathered that police intervention would be ineffectual. I desperately needed to find Hock. Alexander still rested; the laudanum a thankful pain relief!

Mrs McGregor had reluctantly pointed me in the direction of the Chinese stalls around in Union Street, her tone as usual disapproving, and her manner obstinately superior. Thanking her with undue courtesy, I plucked at the vast expanse of my skirt, until I found the wrist loop. No point in tripping my way down the congested street. Adjusting the strings on my veiled hat, I set forth in pursuit of information.

Fortunately, it was at the third stall in a row of haphazard structures that I located news of Hock. Amidst an abundance of fresh green vegetables and pumpkins, an enthusiastic young man greeted me with alacrity. He knew of Hock, Hock from Fragrant Sea! His dark queue swished with excitement, his hands pressed together in deference. His name was Chu and he prattled on good-naturedly in almost indecipherable English. Yes! Hock was presently at Forest Creek Diggings, nicknamed Chewton by many locals. Rewarding him generously, I promised with enthusiastic gestures and smiles to return with a message.

As I strolled purposefully back to the hotel, it dawned on me that Hock might not understand English in the written form. Plainly, my vegetable seller's grasp of the English language forbade an oral message. I had been toying with the idea of making the journey myself, as I felt obliged to Captain Sterling. Throughout our ordeals, he had studiously ensured my comfort even though I may not have agreed with his intent.

My incident with that bastard Sanders (which I preferred to keep at bay) had made me charitable in my opinion of the Captain. He had nobly overseen my recovery and, instead of bounding off after Sanders, had stayed at my side in a most sympathetic manner. Incidents Ju had shared in confidence. If anything, Captain Sterling was a gentleman!

Blast the man! I could not leave him at the mercy of those ruffians or that insidious scoundrel Sanders. Even now, his name affected my breathing, my heart racing uncontrollably. I glanced down to my hands; white knuckles clenched gripped my skirt in agitation. Taking a few deep breaths, I cleared my mind. It would take all my persuasive skills to bring Alexander around to my way of thinking.

On returning to the hotel, I took the coward's way out and scribbled a note of intent. I popped my head around the corner of the door to ensure he was resting peacefully —fortuitously the doctor was packing up his kit. I waited patiently just outside the doorway.

Closing the door quietly behind him, I confronted the good doctor. "Dr Jones, I realise this is a great imposition but I wondered whether you would be so kind as to escort me to Chewton?" I whispered.

"Chewton? Forest Creek Diggings?"

"Yes, the same. I must find Hock. Captain Sterling insisted I locate him."

"This is most unusual, Miss – Mrs Sterling. The diggings are really not fit places for genteel ladies. Especially beautiful genteel ladies," he said uneasily.

I was glad I was still wearing my netted hat. Close scrutiny of my bruised face might have changed his perception. "Yes, I understand, but this is crucial!"

"Let me get word to this Hock and have him brought before you, Mrs Sterling. That would be far more appropriate!" he declared, a frown lining his forehead.

"I thank you for your concern, but I must see Hock myself. It is important! The Willoughby family and myself would be incredibly grateful," I pleaded, ashamed at the pitiful figure I presented to coerce his sympathy.

"Very well. I cannot leave for the diggings until after three. I will call for you then. Is that suitable?"

"Perfectly. Thank you, Dr Jones."

Leaving detailed instructions with the disapproving Mrs McGregor and a letter for Alexander, I strode out towards the stables. I had secured Alexander's travelling pistol within the deep pockets of my habit. Feeling it hard against my hip lessened in my mind the danger of future encounters.

Mrs McGregor had viewed the arrangement as most inappropriate, pointing that fact out to myself and her husband who cowed in his wingback. Fortunately, her dialogue on the evils of the 'yellow devils' was interrupted by the arrival of the portly Dr Jones, followed closely by young Chu. I thanked them for their courtesy and bounded out the door with wings on.

Young Chu trotted tirelessly at my side. His sturdy shoulders supported a worn wooden stock that in turn held two intricately woven baskets. Plainly, my young Chinese man was excessively well exercised. Dr Jones, no doubt was accustomed to these scenes at Forest Creek but I caught him glancing surreptitiously at Chu who had set a graceful and rhythmic pace. The pot-holed road with its bullock ruts appeared well travelled, and some erstwhile traveller had painted on a wobbly sign 'Mt Alexander Road'.

The absence of trees and the multitude of tents welcomed us to the frenetic activity of the Forest Creek goldfields. Dr Jones pointed out the decimation of the forests from one hillside to the next. Chu in his affable way nodded in agreement. Timber apparently shored the new mines; the miners exhausting the streams had moved into the hills to find the source. Timber warmed their hearths, supported tents and created government outbuildings – all in the name of gold! The sea of tents was overwhelming; all pitched along the creek bank and winding up through the valley like an ant trail. Even the noise, the clinking of spades and the rattle of gold cradles, reminded me of an ant's nest.

As we descended into the town, a line of troopers approached us, Captain Fawcett in the lead. "This is most propitious, Mrs Sterling, I have been in Chewton questioning several leads. Dr Jones!" He bowed slightly, a forced smile plastered to his stern face. Ignoring my travelling companion, Chu, he informed me sadly that he had had no luck in discovering the whereabouts of Captain Sterling or his rogue captors.

"It is a mystery, Mrs Sterling. There has been little word on the fields. But be heartened, I ride for Sandhurst tomorrow, I will make further enquiries on your behalf."

"You are most kind, Captain," I said without enthusiasm.

Sidling his dark mount close to mine, he gestured to tell me something in confidence, lowering his voice to barely a whisper. "Mrs Sterling, I would be remiss if I failed to advise you that any association with Dr Jones would be seen as indiscreet. He is a known rebel on the diggings. The Chief Commissioner would no doubt inform you of his indiscretions."

"Thank you, Captain." I smiled sweetly, concerned that if I said anymore I would lose my patience and my tongue.

Touching the brim of his hat, he trotted on. His smirking troopers followed. As the last trooper passed Chu, he reached down and without provocation slammed his truncheon hard over the young man's shoulders. "On your way, you heathen!" he yelled breaking into a gallop. Chu collapsed to his knees, baskets crashing to the dusty ground. Dr Jones sprang from his saddle with the agility of a much younger man, cursing. Unfortunately, riding side saddle meant my reactions would have been clumsy and injurious. I could only watch in sympathy.

"Heathens, and they have the audacity to call the Celestials heathens!" he grumbled inspecting Chu's bruised back.

Several miners had stopped work and were staring at the doctor as he cursed.

"How is Chu, Dr Jones?"

"My sincere apologies, Mrs Sterling! The moment roused the beast in me," he replied shamefaced.

"To be expected – and Chu?"

"He's a strong boy and I am sure this is not his first experience of police violence. Come on, lad. Up you get and lets find this Hock." I grimaced. I thought I had left that type of mentality back in Jamaica. It was naive of me to consider that relocating to Port Phillip had miraculously changed society's perverse attitude towards non-English workers. Clearly, Chu was in pain but he nodded good-naturedly before balancing his apparatus gingerly on his shoulders. We rode on in silence until we reached what I surmised was the town centre.

The only stone buildings appeared to be the devotional First Church and the Red Bull hotel. A fitting tribute to Western hypocrisy! Due to the leering and ungentlemanly comments of the passing men, I stayed close to Dr Jones' side. I sent Chu off to locate Hock whilst dismounting with the kind doctor's assistance. A ragged ginger haired boy appeared from the shadows to stable our horses.

The Red Bull sat pleasantly on a gentle rise overlooking the energetic activity of the fields. Its rambling verandah was a haven for the miners. I had been informed that licences for grog were difficult to obtain. I wondered whether the Red Bull was built on the foundations of the sly grog trade. Dr Jones ushered me into the small reception. "The publican is a surly man but well respected, Mrs Sterling. The rooms are modest but clean. I will take my leave and call for you tomorrow morning unless I am advised otherwise. They know where to reach me."

"Thank you, Dr Jones. You have been most kind." And he had! With a flourish of his hat, and a bow from his ample waist he excused himself, joining a party of jovial miners on the front verandah.

The proprietor, a beefy mountain of a man with a moustache to match, peered over the counter in a most unsavoury fashion, assessing my dishevelled appearance and my lack of luggage with disdain.

"Good man, I have journeyed from Castlemaine to enquire about a friend. Unfortunately, the expediency of the meeting necessitated my urgent departure. My luggage is at Mr McGregor's establishment, The Empyre, with my sick brother. Do you have a room or do you wish to continue appraising me in that distasteful manner?" Two large bushy grey eyebrows shot up to meet a receding forehead. Pointing to the exorbitant tariff board, I duly paid. Gruffly, he turned and escorted me to a modest room at the rear of the main dining room.

"Lock your door, breakfast is at seven," he declared in an abrupt manner, slamming the door behind him. Indignantly, I scanned the space. It consisted of an iron bed and wash basin perched on a chipped marble topped chest. Otherwise it was serviceable. I decided to sleep in my clothes.

Exhausted, I collapsed on the edge of the bed, its cast iron frame creaking unpleasantly. Removing my bonnet, I rested my head against the grubby wall. Surely Hock would receive the message of my arrival from Chu. I had been convinced he would be prompt; he was devoted to Captain Sterling.

Just as my stomach had commenced rumbling, a dark plum pudding of a girl opened the door after a pitiable knock. "Father says you better have your dinner on a tray. Your pretty looks would create a riot in the front room." Curtsying with a snigger on her thin lips, she placed a tray roughly beside me on the bed. I barely had time to thank her before she scootered out, reminding me of a red Christmas bauble. Obviously the genes ran strong on her father's side. The hearty steak and kidney pie tasted surprisingly good, washed down with some form of stout. Mrs Plum Pudding was the saving grace of this establishment, I assumed!

Any rendezvous with Hock would be fraught with difficulty. If Mrs McGregor's attitude was any indication of that of the rest of the populace, I would be best to wait outside for my Chinese visitor. Rather than parade through the hotel, I moved briskly to the back courtyard and waited. After fifteen minutes of pacing and avoiding miscreant miners relieving themselves near the privy, I had propped myself on an old wooden crate out of view, my hand vigilant on my gun. My feet hurt and I still ached in places that made me blush with indignation. Chu appeared reliable and I sincerely hoped he had relayed my simple message. Captain Sterling may already be dead or in the hands of Sanders. My heart raced at the absurdity of the situation. I prayed that the Captain was holding his own. Of course, Gabriel Sterling may have already escaped. He was a force of nature, with his broad shoulders and natural agility. The man had been blessed with a physical presence rivalled by few.

I was roused from my thoughts by a movement in the darker confines of the unkempt backyard. It was Hock in a subdued dark grey outfit that was beautifully buttoned with butterfly toggles. He rushed to my side, his queue bobbing carelessly behind him and his seasoned face full of concern.

"Missy Charlotte, where is the Master Gab?" Crouching, he reminded me of an old cricket.

"That is exactly my question too, Hock." I proceeded to inform him of the unfolding events over the past twelve hours. With his piercing brown eyes locked onto mine, he gasped and groaned as the story unfolded.

My arms extended in capitulation, my voice rising to an unattractive pitch, I felt tears swelling. "Hock, I have no idea where they have taken him or where Sanders may be hiding." Patting my hand in a fatherly manner, Hock managed to allay my worst fears. When I had finished my tearful explanation, he placed his hands inside his sleeves and closed his eyes. His forehead was furrowed with worry as he muttered what I believed to be a prayer or incantation in Cantonese. Luckily, the miners' bladders had held out during our discourse. It would have caused an unpleasant scene if they had seen a Chinese man kneeling at the feet of a lady.

"You rest, Missy Charlotte. I will find Master Gab. You not worry. Go tomorrow. Not good place for ladies." His gentle brown eyes reflected the soft glow of the moon. As he turned to leave, I suddenly grasped his arm in determination.

"Hock, you must understand that I wish to find Master – I mean Captain Sterling – and ensure he is unharmed. I insist I accompany you."

"This is not done, Missy Charlotte. Master Gab may be in great danger. He would not agree. Too much danger! Too risky!"

"Well, Captain Sterling is not here and I insist!" I stood, my small frame rigid with determination.

Hock's traditionally shaven high forehead glowed in the moonlight, worry lines puckered with concern. as he gazed skywards, eyes raised in forgiveness or exasperation. He levelled solemn eyes on my face. "Very well, Missy Charlotte. I pray for our safe journey and protection. I will call in the morning. You rest. I find word of Master Gab."

"Hock, Dr Jones escorted me from Castlemaine and –"

"Do not worry. I speak to Dr Jones. We meet here as sun rises!"

20

BUSHRANGER'S HUT

Hostile looks had appraised our early morning departure from the Red Bull Hotel. It appeared from snippets Hock had acquired by sending his patriots through the night to various Chinese diggings that our erstwhile bushrangers were squatting near Mount Alexander. They had a reputation for robbing unknowing travellers on the Castlemaine to Sandhurst road and south to Kyneton.

We travelled most of the morning, stopping for a brief breakfast mid-morning in bushland north of Forest Creek. Hock delved into his brightly embroidered bag and cooked an exotic dish of dried fish and rice, covered in a tangy sauce. We sat in companionable silence around a simple fire. Occasionally, Hock paused and parroted some of the birds that perched overhead; it was amusing to watch his face and mouth contort with intense effort. What changes a week could produce! Here I was sitting cross-legged in the wilderness in the company of an elderly Chinese man, my escort and protector.

It was late when we reached the base of Mount Alexander and set up camp for the night near a sluggish creek – Hock laughingly naming it 'Weary Creek'. Our quarry was apparently but two miles beyond the gorge.

I lay in the morning quiet waiting for Hock to return from his reconnoitre. Rustling bushes and a soft curse in Cantonese alerted me to his arrival.

"Well!" I declared, waving Alexander's gun anxiously.

"Patience, Missy Charlotte! Please, the gun!" He gestured to my hand. "I think I teach you a few quiet tricks!"

Apologising, I placed the gun back in my pocket. "Tricks?" I exclaimed.

Foraging in his bag he pulled out a sheathed ebony handled knife. Bowing before me, he handed it to me with both hands reverently extended. "For you, Missy Charlotte! Now I show you how to use it."

He watched me unsheathe it and wave it frantically in the air. "Stop!" he yelled. "You must hold it firmly, like axe. I show." He started moving the weapon skilfully and smoothly. After watching his graceful demonstration, I followed suit. "It is not the force but the skill," he insisted, beckoning me to attack him.

Gnarly firm hands expertly intercepted my assault, twisting me artfully to the ground. I squealed as he yanked the knife from my hand. "That is unfair, Hock! No man would fight a woman so!"

"I not worried about gentlemen, only Sanders and his men. You must move at the last moment. Push knife down with your weight, like this! Understand?"

"Understood." I beamed as he returned my smile. His astute weathered head was shaking at my enthusiasm. "Let me try it again." This time I landed squarely on my posterior but with the knife still grasped in my hand.

"Very good, Missy Charlotte! Slow, smooth and deadly." He helped me to my feet. "Surprise is your best weapon!"

"Thank you, Hock!"

"Do not thank. Confucius say: 'By three methods we may learn wisdom; First, by reflection, which is noblest; Second, by imitation, which is easiest; and third by experience, which is the bitterest'!"

Frowning, no doubt at my lack of wisdom, he turned and moved swiftly towards the creek. "Come, but quietly and listen!" he beckoned. Silence seemed a strange instruction, considering that overhead budgerigars and lorikeets chattered endlessly in the big red river gums.

Huddled behind a large clump of swaying golden wattle we had observed the simple slab hut for over an hour. Unfortunately the wattle had a detrimental effect on my sinuses and I permanently had my nose buried in my handkerchief.

Hock's scrutiny of the vicinity had left us in no doubt that the house was the only possible hiding place for the Captain. He had inspected the precariously leaning bark shed to the west, its contents housing the bushrangers' scraggly mares – and, fortunately, Gabriel's fine bay. Unless they had squirrelled him away in some outhouse, we were relatively confident he was inside. Patiently, we watched, and our endeavours were rewarded. Busily carrying a water bucket and washing, a weather-beaten woman emerged. Her skirt dirty and tattered, she pulled her patched shawl tighter around her bony shoulders to combat the early southerly. Wisps of grey unravelled from her severe bun tightly pinned at the base of her thin and haggard neck. Hooded eyes darted over the landscape.

Jumping to action, I bounded to my feet. A task not so easily completed with nearly eight pounds of material wrapped firmly around one's narrow waist. Hock unceremoniously yanked me down.

"Missy Charlotte! We wait. We watch," he whispered urgently.

Opening my mouth to protest, I quickly quelled my reply as the worn timber door swung inwards once again. A dishevelled Captain emerged, his hands securely fastened behind his back, and a pistol rammed up against his shoulder. His face appeared bruised and bloodied, no doubt from several struggles. Indicating the creek, the junior stickman untied his rope manacles and shoved him forward.

Hock touched my sleeve, his bony index finger to his lips. Motioning that I stay hidden, he deftly crab-walked down to the water edge overhung with thick acacias. Adjusting my skirt, I shifted to one side to avoid my legs cramping. A feeding wood pigeon eyed my performance with contemptuous orange orbs. His ruffled head turned in mortification at the interruption of breakfast.

Falling to his knees, Gabriel stiffly cupped and threw the fast moving water over his blotchy and bruised face. One eye appeared slightly closed, puffy and raw. His morning jacket was torn at the armpits, the once pristine shirt slashed and streaked with blood. Otherwise, he appeared physically unharmed.

Removing Alexander's weapon concealed neatly in my deep pocket, I waited for Hock's word.

A faint bird noise pierced the morning air. The dulcet overtones were unfamiliar to my untrained ear. The effect, however, was different for Captain Sterling. Glancing at his captor, he slowly turned his head downstream and started humming. The humming escalated to a fine baritone voice, the song rhythmic, the words undeniably Cantonese. The older man promptly cursed him, instructing his son in no uncertain terms to retie the knots. Gabriel defiantly remained kneeling, his scrapped and bleeding hands tickling the surface of the stream. His full lips pulled back into a thin line; his square jaw rigid and uncompromising.

"Get up, you bastard," Stickman junior swore in frustration lashing out with his foot. With perfect agility, Gabriel twisted on his haunches, kicked the young man's legs from under him and threw him to the ground in one fluid movement. One powerful arm wrapped a strangling hold on the lad's knobbly Adam's apple, the other pommelled a few choice punches to his kidneys. It happened within a breath of the wind. The father stood motionless, his wife stunned, then she broke the silence with an ear-piercing scream.

The pounding of horses put an abrupt halt to activity. Hock had luckily remained concealed, and I froze at the sight of Sanders suddenly looming over the proceedings with a heavy armed group of men.

"Captain Gabriel Sterling, the very man! My, my, you have been busy!" Sanders stated, sitting arrogantly upon his horse. A sardonic scowl distorted his once amiable face.

Gabriel released the coughing boy and rose slowly to his feet, brushing off his clothes in an off-handed manner. "Haven't you gone to hell yet, Sanders?"

"Tsk! Tsk! Captain. You underestimate my resilience. As I must admit have I!" Turning to the older bushranger, he threw him a bag of coins. "You have been most obliging. The matter is settled." Sanders signalled to one of his cronies to dismount.

"What the blazes do you need now, Sanders?" Gabriel stood akimbo glaring up at the men. A powerful stance even from this distance.

"Yes well, plans have changed," Sanders replied, his voice slightly agitated.

Gabriel, aware that Hock was close by, raised his deep voice in defiance. "I have already signed over the ship. Go to hell, Sanders."

"Unfortunately, the delectable Miss Lavender has disappeared," Sanders exclaimed, chuckling as he saw the Captain flinch. "But I have something as desirable." He motioned the men to part and a bound Ju appeared, her lovely hands manacled in front, her poor slippers in tatters.

"God, Sanders, I will tear you from limb to limb, you bastard." The Captain spat out a few more colourful curses; he was out of patience, poised for flight. His commanding voice booming across the clearing in protest, hands flexing.

"Temper, Captain! Miss Ju has kindly joined our happy group for Sandhurst. However, I must insist you join us so we may formally complete the transaction!"

Gabriel kicked at the earth, his fists curled in fury. His battered red face blazed with rage. Finally, he turned to Ju, rattling off a stream of Cantonese. She nodded.

"Now, now, Captain. No heathen language, please! Miss Ju has been as yet untouched. I only ask you to accompany us to ensure she remains so!" Sanders smirked, stroking his small goatee.

"My horse is out the back. But I insist that Ju ride with me."

"Of course! Fetch it, Willis! I am not an unreasonable man," Sanders snickered, turning and firing off an order to an unsavoury individual who stroked Ju's ebony plait. "One other thing, Captain, your lucky knife – and gently does it. I would hate to harm Miss Ju."

Gabriel threw it defiantly at Willis's boots.

During this conversation I had remained riveted to the spot, thankful for the camouflaging effect of the golden wattle and my dark clothing within the shadows. The sound of Sanders' voice was debilitating; my body shook with rage but at the same time trembled with fear. Collapsing to the ground, I buried my face within my voluptuous folds. I was a coward, I could not face the man, could not assist the Captain. I was weak, too weak to even save Ju. Jerking at the feel of a warm arm upon my shoulders, I sank relieved upon the slight chest of Hock.

"Shh, Missy Charlotte! It is all good. Master Gab knows we are here!"

"We are helpless to assist with Sanders now commanding the situation," I said, my voice tense and quivering.

"Sandhurst has good Chinese town. It will be good for us. Good for Ju! We must go to our horses." Nodding, I gathered my skirt and followed Hock downstream, listening to the ominous sound of retreating horses in the background, as Sanders and his cohorts rode away with the Captain. Sanders – the deceitful bastard! To think that during the voyage I had enjoyed his company. I nearly threw up!

We had left our mounts hobbled at our bush camp to avoid any undue noise. I was relieved to see the noble beasts enjoying the wild oat grass.

"You fine now, Missy Charlotte?" Hock enquired, his wrinkled face frowning with concern.

"I am so sorry." I leant forward and hugged him.

"Master Gab be OK too. He is a not only born under the sign of the dragon but the auspicious fire element," he said reverently his hands clasped as in prayer.

I laughed impolitely. However, Hock continued, defiantly ignoring my pert attitude.

"Master Gab was born under the sign of the dragon, a most illustrious sign. He has what many white men call the Midas touch. I have heard this name from Master Trent. He possesses magical powers! The dragon is invincible and Master Gab will soar to the highest mountains through his life." I stared astounded, mouth gaping as Hock continued. "Unfortunately, being a dragon he also has qualities many people find bad. His power may make people fear him. Within his deepness, he has a big heart that sings with health and love." Hock beamed proudly.

Squirming, I immodestly snorted. "Yes, Hock. Well, dictatorial, stubborn and irritable are words that spring to mind as other dragon attributes!" Seeing Hock's confused expression, I patted his slender arm. "Let's go. I am sure we have a long ride ahead."

Manoeuvring Viper to a nearby paperbark stump, I mounted with Hock's assistance,

"Come, we will ride on the song of the fire dragon." He grinned and I smiled faintly in return, grasping my reins, Sandhurst bound.

21

SANDHURST

If Castlemaine had appeared prosperous for a country town, Sandhurst was excessively flamboyant. Large structures displayed the imminent and rapid climb of the town in social and financial circles. An impressive array of structures lined the main thoroughfare of Pall Mall. Striving for its identity, it had fallen into the usual colonial habit of naming its illustrious streets after English locations, plainly to elevate their station. Strangely, it left me a little cold, as it had in Jamaica.

I had grown to enjoy this country's strange and evocative local names, some from the black people, others evolving from circumstances. They rolled off the tongue with creative and amusing dexterity. Digger's Rest, Kangaroo Flat and Kooroocheang came to mind. The sun was blinking through the western stuccoed buildings as we entered Bridge Street late afternoon.

"*Wènhòu wǒ de péngyǒu,*" Hock yelled to the Chinese men lounging on crates or squatting in groups smoking. Their eyes were like saucers as they watched me ride by!

A plethora of merchandise lined the road – silks, tea, brooms and vegetables. No doubt the opium dens were concealed in the side alleys or hidden upstairs. The bustling atmosphere enlivened my senses. Although these streets were predominantly home to the Chinese, there appeared to be all manner of men in top hats to cabbage caps bartering and cramming the stores. The exotic sounds of a pipa or Chinese lute floated on the breeze whilst vibrant coloured flags criss-crossed the street fluttering in rhythm. Viper moved her head in annoyance as the buzzing crowd thickened and a steady stream of piled wooden carts raced past, their owners queues swishing with the effort. After Bridge Street we swung northwards, finally stopping outside a majestic red building with its beautiful golden motifs. Undeniably Celestial, its twin lions ferociously guarded the entrance on grand bluestone mounts.

"This auspicious temple is a safe place of worship. It belongs to the Chinese Masonic Society. A very English name do you not agree?" Hock smiled wryly and, pointing at the left vertical couplet, he translated the Chinese script. "*Righteousness conspicuously brightens heaven and Earth with its echo, penetrating deep and wide to all aspects of natural phenomena, and then to the right, Leaders amongst heroes are aroused to come for the great expansion of the good lodge.*" He chuckled, "Strong words for such simple people." Dismounting, he turned, "Please stay here, Missy Charlotte. I find safe rooms." Bowing graciously, Hock disappeared into what appeared a caretaker's residence, the chatter of voices and pots resonating in the early evening. My stomach growled; I was famished.

Our room was simple, but serviceable. I use the term 'room' loosely. Hock had acquired the back room from a distant second cousin who traded in various assortments of silk in central Sandhurst. Bundles of tightly folded materials lay stacked systematically against the timber walls. Surprisingly, the room was furnished with a decorative iron bed, its elaborate silk covers and pillows out of character with the drab interior; the bold feminine touches a stark contrast to s simple shopkeeper's store. My thoughts were interrupted by Hock bringing a simple meal of vegetables and noodles. The day had been tiring, and with Hock on guard behind the room's partition, I soon drifted to sleep.

◦❦◦

Hock had the lightness of foot of a man half his age. He moved quickly to the edge of the window and with ease slid over the sill. I lay quietly in bed barely breathing as his figure disappeared. With one almighty whoosh my breath caught up to my lungs, forcing me to gasp, as I swung my uncovered legs from the warm covers. Recovering my composure, I clutched at my chemise, pulling its folds around me for comfort and warmth. The cold floorboards were a chilling reminder that the temperature outside necessitated far more layers than I possessed. Guardedly, I leant against the sash window and peered into the darkness. A thousand stars lit the sky, a gibbous moon waning in the distance. The subtle light illuminated shapes and forms in eerie contrast. A shiver ran clean to my toes, but not before my eyes perceived the flash of light off a shiny braid as a small figure disappeared into the Red Temple. Furious at his lack of confidence, I stumbled in the dark, grabbing for my skirt and boots. He clearly had set up some type of meeting at this ungodly hour. No doubt it concerned Captain Sterling. With no time for stockings or the ministrations of tiresome buttons on my blouse, I wrapped my dark pelisse over my chemise and scrambled with little dignity through the open window.

Huddled against the timber braces, I waited for any movement on the road. Then, picking up my incumbent folds, I raced for cover amongst a line of silver banksias. My ears thundered with the sound of my thumping heart. Scooting past several flimsy tents that resounded with their occupants' snores, I headed uphill. The simple temple lay north of the cultivated vegetable gardens that surrounded the Chinese compound. Fortunately, the timber gates were ajar, the guardian lions threatening keepers, surreal and confronting in the dim light. Inside, the temple was peaceful, its flowing lines evoking harmony and contentment, although a single flicker of light glowed from under the caretaker's red door.

My toes ached, unused to the raw leather of my boots. Scolding myself for lack of foresight, I shimmied along the wall to the closed shutters. Voices drifted through the timber cracks. The tone of Hock's voice suggested he was displeased and agitated by his companions' comments and protestations. A few sharp barks from Hock and the light moved from under the doorway past the shuttered window until it appeared wavering in the darkness. Two small forms scurried into the adjacent building from what I believed was the main temple. Stepping cautiously to avoid a dunking in the ceremonial pond, I shuffled along the impressive red doors. Clouds scurried across the sky with the imminent breaks creating pockets of light that illuminated the simple oriental gardens. Pressed against the wooden panels of the entrance chamber, I was unable to detect any further sounds. Suddenly, the panel swung inwards, launching my body into the arms of my wiry companion.

"Missy Charlotte, you big bother," he snapped, adjusting his dishevelled jacket and untangling his queue that entwined my neck.

"You left me behind, Hock! I am able to assist with your enquiries!" I declared, puffing out with what was left of my self-esteem. Standing ill at ease on the earthen floor, I was aware of my shabby appearance. Behind Hock an elderly and wizened man puffed at his long pipe. His veiled eyes studied me nonchalantly.

"Master Gab do horrible things to me if you are damaged – hurt."

"Captain Sterling can go to hell! He pulled me into this fiasco. The sooner we have him back, the sooner I may return to my brother."

Hock chuckled, firing off a few words to the old man in Cantonese. Squaring my shoulders I prepared to launch into another torrent of words. Turning in disgust, the old caretaker shuffled away. Grabbing my arm firmly, Hock steered me past the door guardian and towards the main altar. "I have word of Master Gab, but first we pray for success," he whispered.

With remarkable speed, the old man lit the altar candles. A soft glow bounced off five bronze vessels. The centre bowl was decorated with sacred dragons twisted in harmonic unison, the sand inside littered with blackened stubs. Apples, cumquats and small flour delicacies graced the altar surface, and a gold emblazoned red cloth tumbled to the swept floor.

"We pray to the mighty Guan-Yu, the god of war and prosperity. He is our wise judge, guiding us through times of trouble, supreme protector of our simple lives and a provider of wealth. For men so far from their loved ones, the qualities of Guan-Yu are needed in this strange land." Hock reverently lit a slim stick, and holding it gently between his palms he brought it close to his forehead. With a bowed head, he solemnly moved forward, whispering an incantation before placing the stick within the ornate ceremonial bowl. Turning, he beckoned me forward.

I could imagine my mother writhing with indignation at this heathen practice. The auspicious bronzed deity indignantly frowned down upon my sceptical face. His red face glowed in the dim light; his warrior sword raised in defiance. I shrugged, and copying Hock I performed a similar ceremony. There was no harm in having a god, and a venerable one at that, on our side. The peace and sincerity of our offering somehow filled a spiritual void. I stared at the two sticks, the smoke spiralling towards the ceiling. It was at this moment I knew we would have success. Surely with Guan-Yu on our side we were invincible. With a slight bow to the caretaker, Hock gently clasped my arm and escorted me carefully back to our simple room.

☼❦☼

My head pounded and my mouth was exceedingly dry. It was early morning according to the angle of the sun. Its weak warmth washed the walls, creating dappled images through the lace curtains. The sound of carts and carriages bustling outside penetrated my fuzzy brain. I groggily pushed myself to a sitting position.

From what Hock had shared with me only hours ago, it appeared that Captain Sterling was detained in a warehouse off Bridge Street. From knowledge he had obtained from relatives, the Captain was still alive but detained by white pigs.

I rubbed my temples hoping to drive away the throbbing pain. A scratch at the door and an accompanying greeting ushered forth Hock, balancing a breakfast tray. "Up, Missy Charlotte, busy day," he declared, placing the piled tray upon my lap. The delicious assortment of dumplings, sweet buns and noodle soup stirred my appetite, and the tantalising smell of black tea revived my senses. Hock watched with amused detachment as I indelicately consumed the spread with gusto.

"Well Hock, what is our plan?" I mumbled, biting through a delicate pork dumpling.

Hock frowned. I knew he was displeased I'd insisted being part of the rescue party. He had said as much last night. However, I remained steadfast. Captain Sterling had been instrumental in my rescue and I vowed to be part of his! Hock no doubt would launch once again into a litany of reasons why I should not accompany his party.

"Please, Missy Charlotte. You stay here safely. My brothers have arms."

I chuckled. "Yes, well Hock, I too have arms." Raising my hand in protest, I continued. "I am aware of your strong attachment to Master

167

Gab, I mean Captain Sterling. However, on this point I stand steadfast. Now please take the tray so I may dress."

Hock looked displeased but did as I requested, shutting the door with a quick snap. When we had rescued Captain Sterling I would explain Hock's reluctance to drag me along. He was a dear, but terribly overprotective!

Dressing with purpose, I dispensed with the corset. I was truly thankful that the riding suit fastened at the front and it was trimmed with sturdy military style buttons, not with a frivolous line of pearls. I imagined that flexibility would be far more important than fashion. With no grooming set, I plaited and wound my hair into a tidy bun at the base of my neck. The past few weeks in the sun had streaked the blonde with platinum shades. Dark smudges lay under my eyes from lack of sleep and several cursed freckles sprinkled my golden cheeks. With a huff, I grabbed my hat and gloves. I was going to have words with Captain Sterling, very strong words!

22

Ares

Sandhurst Chinatown

The sun was barely above the golden wattle bushes on the horizon, but already Chinatown was abuzz with people and the frenetic traffic of goods. The explicit sounds of Cantonese punctuated the early hour with shouts, shrieks and the sound of haggling.

It had taken an interminable amount of time to find the building. Hock had insisted we inspect all escape exits before hoisting me up to the warehouse skylight. From my vantage point, I could see Gabriel lying on the floor, his hands manacled to an iron pillar in the centre of what appeared to be an abandoned wool merchant's shed. Remnants of packing crates were scattered on the timber floor. The rough kilned bricks glowed a vibrant iodised red in the morning sunlight. The window was fixed, and after several precarious moments on Hock's shoulders, I was able to ease the latch. Hock grunted and groaned below as he balanced on a water trough.

A slow growl punctuated by several explicit curses disturbed the quiet; it took me a few moments to realise the sound emanated from the Captain below. Roused, he untangled his bruised body and sat up. Sunlight streamed gloriously into the gloomy interior. Dust danced in the sunlight shimmering and sparkling like a Piccadilly music hall. Shaking his head, he glanced up at the roofline. Momentarily startled, he quickly recovered, a curse escaping his lips as he saw me hovering outside the skylight.

"Missy Charlotte, come down. You fidget too much," Hock whispered, buried in the voluminous folds of my skirt.

"Shh, Hock. I have found Master Gab, err Captain Sterling," I replied, stiffening at the entrance of Sanders and his two sidekicks. Gabriel had struggled to his feet, hands bound. His fine stalwart form was defiant and prepared. Sanders was agitated, pacing the floor and pointing accusingly at the Captain.

A muffled voice exclaimed from below. "Missy Charlotte."

"Shh Hock. One more moment!" The shoulders of my companion flexed and relaxed.

"Gentlemen," Gabriel bellowed, more than likely hoping that my face would recede with the warning. "I had wondered when you would be serving breakfast. I am famished."

"Shut your smart mouth, you cocksucker," boomed the man next to Sanders, his hairy hands clenched in anticipation.

"Now, now, Slatter, the Captain is but playing. Gabriel, this is tiresome," Sanders stated inspecting his long fingered hands in meditative thought, his slight frown the only sign of disaffection. "All this animosity would cease if you would be sensible and disclose the location of the opium. I still have the youthful Ju at my side."

"Look, Sanders, I have already signed my ship over to you. Why don't you go and search it, you bloody imbecile? If your cargo is missing, someone in your confidence has obviously absconded with it. If I had known it was on-board, it would be now seven leagues under the sea."

"Tut, tut, Captain. Language. The problem is, Captain, that I do not trust you." Sanders cold blue eyes were veiled and spiteful.

"The feeling is mutual." Gabriel stepped back to stretch his bound arms.

"I can only deduce that since our interview in Keilor you have somehow organised the removal of the cargo from its location. My men have pulled the ship apart. Unfortunately, your first mate O'Toole hampered our movement. Sadly, he will not be part of any future crew!"

"You are a bloody fool, Sanders. How long do you think you have before the authorities and my friends become suspicious about your activities?" Gabriel ventured a quick look skywards to my hiding place; his eyebrows pinched with concern – or was that anger?

"My point exactly, Captain. The quicker this matter is completed, the quicker we can move on. I have a generous group of travellers who wish a speedy departure after the goods are discovered." Walking to the far door, he turned. "I leave you in the capable hands of Willis and Slatter. Slatter, I wish the Captain conscious for a talk later. Confine your enthusiasm to below his neck. If you are not forthcoming this time, unfortunately, your young friend will suffer the consequences. Until later, Captain Sterling. Au revoir!"

The bastard sauntered out as if it were a social call, young Ju in tow. I wobbled on my perch, but kept vigilant.

Slatter's eyes seemed to vanish within his heavily sun-baked bald head and hairy brows. The burly sailor's thin lips were set in a grimace – or was that a smile? The anticipated punch landed squarely on the Captain's solar plexus. Gasping, he doubled over, winded by the sudden impact. Slatter had remained close, poised for the next punch, gloating over the Captain's pain.

Seemingly focused, balanced and calm, the Captain's leg shot out, the heel striking Slatter's kneecap with a crack. Before Willis could react, he grabbed the pillar, spun into the air and grabbed the mate's scrawny neck between his legs. Willis's arms flailed in terror as Slatter cried out, nursing his smashed kneecap. Willis quietened, his lips turning a ghostly blue as Gabriel released his hold. The sailor's body slowly slumped to the timber floor. Slatter had recovered sufficiently to move outside his realm. The burly man's eyes were aglow with fury and pain as he shifted backwards on his rear. Grasping one of Willis's legs, Slatter pulled him out of reach. The action confused me until the bastard extracted a large kris from his mate's hip. By this stage I could see the Captain's shoulders sagging. All this activity coupled with his obvious injuries was taking its toll on him. I was riveted.

Dragging his injured leg behind him, Slatter slithered forwards, the wave-edged knife raised menacingly. His eyes watched the Captain with malicious intent. Captain Sterling appeared to have only one choice – up. Grabbing the pillar in a bear-like fashion, he attempted a Tongan palm tree mount. This was not an easy task for a thirteen somewhat stone male in a depleted physical condition with gravity as an adversary. Sliding to the floor, the Captain braced himself for the onslaught. I imagined that Slatter would be far more cautious this time!

Slatter spun the kris vertically and, using the long blade as a crutch whilst holding the hilt, he struggled to his feet. His face contorted with the pain of the movement as his body flexed, no doubt with an adrenalin fuelled determination to kill the Captain.

The strain reflected in Captain Sterling's jaw line, rigid and unyielding. It behoved me to admit that Captain Sterling was a vital and magnetic man with irresistible herculean qualities.

The knife whipped out, slashing at his chest. Instinctively, he raised his foot. Unfortunately, Slatter was prepared, wielding the blade through his leather boot. A trickle of blood oozed out of the opening.

Coming to my senses and realising that Captain Sterling was now in mortal danger, I called to Hock. With a slight wobble, I was lowered to the ground and with my pistol in hand I sprinted to the street front, my band of warriors in tow!

☙❧

Sanders had clearly made an escape through the back office as we bounded through the entrance brandishing pistols and knives, with several relations of Hock yelling war cries. At our appearance, Gabriel, bloodied and bruised, braced himself beside the pillar before gracefully sliding to the floorboards, his weight dragging me with him. His lacerated face rested on my lap surrounded by the crumpled folds of my skirt. One iridescent green eye squinted as he broke into a ghastly lop-sided grin.

"Miss Lavender, you are a most exasperating woman. Why the blazes are you in Sandhurst? You should be safely on your way back to Melbourne with your injured brother."

"The feeling is mutual, Captain Sterling, and Alexander is quite well, thank you." I flushed.

Hock hovered above, deftly releasing the Captain's bleeding wrists from the manacles, his hands wringing in agitation afterwards. "Master Gab. It is a most unwelcome situation! What do you suggest?"

He raised himself to his elbows and surveyed the scene. "Summon the police, Hock. I will deal with them. It may be best if you remove yourselves to more salubrious surroundings – you know the authorities' view of Celestials fighting. Ju is locked in the store room. Please ensure her safe transport."

"And Missy Charlotte?"

"I will escort her to the Shamrock Hotel. Meet me there tomorrow morning, and Uncle, thank you." He nodded reverently.

"The man Sanders?" Hock spoke disdainfully, his mouth firm and cold.

"I have an idea on how to find that dog and the *John Robinson!*"

"Until tomorrow, Master Gab!" Bowing, Hock hurried from the room with his minions.

Agitated, I growled in an unladylike manner. I could not believe the man's audacity!

"It is your blasted boat you're still concerned about, isn't it? Of all the most contemptible things imaginable, you are still concerned about that stupid boat." I groaned, kicking out at his side and wrenching my skirt from under him.

"Ship, not boat," he managed to state before I slapped him squarely on the face – on, mind you, the unblemished side.

The Captain struggled to his feet, nursing his cheek with displeasure. "The events of the past few days have most likely unhinged your reasoning, Charlotte. The *John Robinson* is yes, important to me."

"Unhinged my reasoning!" I stared at him dumbfounded, my chest heaving with indignation. His battered body swayed with the effort to stand. Suddenly the wind burst from my chest as I was crushed into a vice-like embrace. The Captain's lacerated face hovered over my own, his green eyes flashing with a fiery intensity. His breath was ragged and uneven like mine, his arms relaxed, and his large hands started to stroke my back intimately. Furious, I started to utter my protest before in one crushing movement his lips descended upon mine. Warm and possessive, then soft and sensual. His body vibrated with the potency of our touch as my own responded in kind.

23

ERATO

I rolled over, my legs stretching instinctively, catlike, as the morning light peeped between the thick brocade curtains. Gabriel – he was Gabriel now, not Captain – lay on his back, his chest rising and falling, almost in harmony with my own. The bandages I had applied so carefully were now askew and loose from their knots. His auburn hair was ruffled and still damp from the bath last night. Resting gingerly on my elbow, I watched his breath ripple his muscles from the firmness of his abdomen to his broad chest. A long sinewy cantor of power in motion. I blushed. It was intoxicating and glorious.

Last night that body had moved within me and around me with a passion that had dissolved my inhibitions. His moistened lips were at peace now, so unlike last night as they suckled and caressed the length of my shapely form, travelling from the height of my bosom to the depths of my belly. Then, goodness, down to the fleshy and plump regions that ladies never discussed. His soft chuckle dissolved my abdomen into a quivering, shuddering jumble of pleasure. I had cried out in euphoria, my hips rising in release, waiting, yearning for him.

Shocked at my wanton thoughts, my treacherous body started to tingle with invitation and desire. As if in response, a hand shot out and grasped my chin, the thumb softly stroking the indentation below my lips. Intense iridescent eyes fringed with dark lashes locked onto my own. "Good morning," his voice croaked, still husky and gravelly from his ordeal. A beaming smile struggled to light up his features, restricted by purple bruising.

"Good morning," I whispered, embarrassed and tentative, fascinated by the hairs bristling on his jaw line. My mind was now dreamily enchanted by the sensuous movement of his fingers upon my face.

Last night I had not been prepared for the intense passion that had flared between us. It had been unrestrained and profoundly intimate. My body felt as if it would burst under his generous strokes and tender devotion.

⁊❦⁊

From Chinatown we had been whisked to the Shamrock, the authorities held at bay for a night only by the grace of Gabriel's commanding presence. In the confines of the suite, I had administered creams that Ju had entrusted to me. Gabriel's bruising was deep and painful. I grimaced at the extent, from his face to his abdomen. His initial obstinate manner in refusing my ministrations was laughable as I eventually badgered him into stripping and lying down. I bandaged his cuts and treated his abrasions, the massaging of the scented lotions an alluring catalyst to our lovemaking.

So here I lay, a wanton woman glowing under his gaze. My body now burning for his touch, as his hand moved down to…

The door rattled then a brisk knock reverberated along the ceiling. Gabriel swore, releasing me tenderly before leaping from the bed as he struggled into his trousers.

"Captain Sterling," a muted voice called through the red cedar door. "The constabulary are waiting in the foyer for you, sir." The tone was vaguely familiar; it must be the manager of the hotel, Mr Crowley. He had been excessively attentive to our needs, sending up a feast at a most inconvenient hour last night. Money talks in all languages.

Gabriel pulled up the covers abandoned on the floor and gently placed them over my nakedness and the tell-tale stains of our intimacy. A look of pleasure momentarily transformed his face. Striding to the door, he wrenched it open with annoyance.

"Captain Sterling, I apologise for the intrusion but Captain Fawcett from the gold police has arrived downstairs seeking an interview." Mr Crowley's heavily accented Irish voice was lowered in obeisance, or perhaps embarrassment at the half naked form.

Gabriel assured him of his compliance and thanked him before closing the door firmly. I peeked over the edge of the printed chintz. His herculean body filled my vision, the bed sagging from his weight.

"We have matters to discuss, Charlotte." The sombre and sensual timbre of his tone was at odds with the intense vitality that was Gabriel Sterling. Disconcerted and embarrassed by the change in his manner, I nodded, suddenly self-conscious.

"Dress and we will have breakfast when I return." Rising stiffly, he slipped into his clothes sluggishly, the bandages adding breadth to his vast chest. A gentle brush of his lips to my forehead, a lopsided grin and he was gone.

I languished for a moment still piecing together the events of yesterday. There was no use fighting the fact and it made no sense, but I was now resolved to assist Gabriel in finding his precious boat – damn, *ship*!

Sliding from the bed I sponged my body delicately, still feeling the soreness of my muscles from my adventures and the indulgence of last night. A smile stupidly played on my lips as I finished my toilette and dressed swiftly. I was a woman now, the potency of a man's body no longer an enigma. I shivered at my libertinism and salaciousness.

With my hair brushed and forming a low neat chignon, I completed the picture of respectability. I desperately needed to find a ladies' store; my chemise and undergarments needed replacing and I sorely required a new gown. The riding habit reeked of horse, perspiration (glowing, would insist my mother) and the dregs of my exploits in Chinatown.

A scratch at the door heralded what I assumed to be the arrival of breakfast. I was famished! Calling my assent, I swung open the hardware, gasping in surprise!

It was the brilliance of the dress that initially shocked my sensibilities. The sea of yellow, red, gold and black was mesmerising. Before I could scream, two firm hands bustled me back into the suite and deposited me unceremoniously onto the slipper chair. My sentinels stood unyielding at my side. As I attempted to rise, the imposing

Celestial raised his hand signalling my restraint. A hand whipped out from black cloth beside me and gripped my shoulder.

Dressed in what I imagine was traditional nobleman attire, my honoured guest's splendour radiated in folds of intricate embroidery. His apricot-yellow robe was ablaze with peacocks and celestial symbols, and a mystical dragon slithered down the front. The silk was exquisitely embroidered with gold-wrapped thread. Soft silk slippers moved his bulk surprisingly noiselessly across the polished floor, his attire complimented by the addition of a ceremonial hat in silk brocade, the crown some type of red twine and topped with a knob. The attire alone confirmed his standing, his wealth and his power. Lowering his ample form into the opposite chair, he assessed me uncomfortably through dark eyes. A bead of perspiration across his lip was the only sign of his discomfort.

"Miss Lavender," he stated in a high pitched effeminate voice, his beautifully manicured hands resting casually on his knees. Not even a nod or bow followed.

We eyed each other for a few seconds, before I opened my mouth to speak. Another slight pressure upon my collarbone. I closed my mouth and waited for his next move.

"We wait for Captain Sterling. Please indulge me!" Adjusting his tunic, my guest leant back and closed his eyes.

Cursing, I attempted to relax into the confines of my seat. I hoped Gabriel could clean up this situation upon his arrival. The present turmoil of my life was becoming hard to comprehend. Maybe it had something to do with my relationship with the Captain. Annoyance and boredom overcame my fear as I squirmed in my seat. I needed to create a distraction upon Gabriel's entrance.

"Miss Lavender, it is best you remain still or Ah Cow will administer a most unpleasant relaxant." Forbidding dark eyes watched my face as I relaxed reluctantly into my seat.

A light knock, and the door framed the lanky and formidable Gabriel Sterling. His fleetingly sensual smile suddenly became a hardened line. Even my signal of warning – tipping the walnut side table with its ruby etched lamp – did not rattle his composure as he purposely strode over to our companion. I could see the tension in his face; a frown just visible under his auburn cowlick. My heart did a ridiculous flip as he sent me a steely green wink.

"Shi Qi, I am truly honoured." Gabriel bowed before settling onto the Queen Anne sofa. The tautness of his frame the only indication of his displeasure. I was well aware of this trait – had I not been the recipient of it upon the *John Robinson?*

Shi Qi enjoined his minders to move back and turned to Gabriel. "Captain Sterling. It is I who is honoured." An artificial smile distorted his plump doughy cheeks. "This is what I think the English call a 'social call' to ensure you are in good health and you have attentive care." A chuckle erupted, then a suggestive stare rippled down my person in a most irritating manner. The big piece of blubbering whale would wear my boot if he continued to utter such lewd remarks.

"I am honoured by your concern," replied Gabriel, his fingers creating a thoughtful cage under his chin. His emotions were concealed behind an impassive face.

"If you should find yourself in need of a friend, Captain Sterling, please send word. Our community is close-knit. My tentacles, as they say, touch all!" With a dismissive gesture, Shi Qi rose, his regalia a kaleidoscope of colours as he departed, a band of black at his rear.

I heaved a sigh of relief, my shoulders aching from my intruders' pressure. "Well, you could have at least defended my honour," I exclaimed, massaging the crick in my neck as Gabriel stared at me in deep thought. His face was stony.

"It was not a matter of your honour, Charlotte. It was a threat from Shi Qi!" Rising to his feet, he held out his large hand, "Breakfast, Mrs Sterling?" he enquired as a devilish grin swept his features.

I brushed aside his hand and rose, angrily. "But who is Shi Qi and why the clandestine visit?"

"Let us have breakfast first, I am ravenous." His eyes twinkled.

"And Captain I do not appreciate your double entendre." I strolled past regally, a devilish smile escaping my lips.

Whilst feasting on a gigantic pile of steak and eggs, Gabriel brought me up to date with the morning's events. The gold police had not been overly concerned about the attack in the warehouse. Relieved he had escaped any further questioning or harassment, Captain Fawcett was duly convinced the dissidents were after money. He had not elaborated on his kidnapping, giving the essential references to ensure the police report reflected the danger to his wife and servant. A bold distortion of the truth, but apparently essential at present without a proper police force in the town. Gabriel no doubt wished to handle the situation in his usual high-handed manner. Throughout the account his eyes flashed with annoyance, adding an agreeable iridescent sparkle.

"And Shi Qi?" I enquired, nibbling daintily on a cold piece of toast, as I admired his energy.

"Shi Qi is but a big fish in a small ocean!" he stated, nodding in appreciation as I poured another cup of tea. "A lowly Chinese nobleman who has risen to untold heights in the goldfields, his line being intimidation, procurement and opium!"

"But how do you know of this man?" I ventured, summoning the young waitress for a fresh pot. Gabriel lowered his voice as several male patrons sidled past; their inquisitive stares were disconcerting. I pulled my collar higher and straightened my back. A twitch of his lips was the only indication the Captain had noticed my discomfort.

He continued, "Hock has used his services and I have met him previously. In fact, Shi Qi was instrumental in discovering my whereabouts."

This information surprised me, I could not imagine Hock dealing with such a perverse being, but I had noticed stranger alliances than these since leaving Jamaica!

"So! The social call?" I mumbled thoughtfully.

"Shi Qi is definitely annoyed. There may be another intrigant attempting to move into his territory or disrupting his trade. It is but a guess. Hock has voiced a similar concern. My feeling is that the *John Robinson* is embroiled in this travesty. Similarly, Sanders is but a lackey, the mastermind behind this is far more ingenious" Leaning back in the chair, his arms folded over his chest, he looked a formidable character.

"So where do you go from here? Back to Melbourne?"

"No! Not Melbourne! I have another meeting with Captain Fawcett at noon and I propose to pursue certain avenues."

"And they are?"

" I am obviously an important link in this conspiracy and to find out why, I must hunt down Sanders! You, Miss Lavender, must return to your brother and head south at the earliest." He leant forward to whisper the last sentence insistently. His large hand clasped mine in a gentle caress.

It was a logical deduction but somehow it did not sit easily upon my shoulders. I had vowed in my heart to assist Gabriel in finding the location of his precious ship. Retreating to Melbourne in my mind declared defeat, and a Lavender certainly did not succumb easily to intimidation. Gabriel's hooded dark green eyes scrutinised my face for my assent.

My decision was not due to the fact that he was the most infuriating individual of my acquaintance, or that he had risked his life to rescue me, but that I now felt a vestige of allegiance to him and Hock. He would not be happy, but here I would stay. What man didn't need a woman to champion the path of reasoning?

"I am aware of the danger, Gabriel. However, I feel compelled to assist. Hock has been an able companion and protector." The reference to 'protector' was a slap in his face. His jaw tightened in annoyance, a scowl transforming his previously congenial countenance.

"Charlotte!" he said sharply through clenched teeth, his voice barely audible above the clatter of morning plates. "You will leave today and travel back to the Empyre. I insist!"

Gently removing my hand, I drew myself up to my full five foot five inches. "I am truly sorry, Gabriel, but I stay!" Raising my chin in indignation and quivering with emotion, I glided out of the saloon, my handkerchief to my eyes – a fitting picture of the scorned wife! Well, he had left me no choice; the morning room no doubt would be abuzz with the unfolding events. Being manipulative was not morally part of my character but I needed to end the conversation. Gabriel was a force of nature, and if I had not diffused the situation, I would have been physically bundled into a carriage. Therefore, if my womanly wiles had given me some breathing space, I had succeeded. A fleeting vision of Gabriel's flashing eyes and tight jaw spurred me on! I had to find Hock – and quickly!

24

SHI QI

It had become abundantly clear to me that if we were to discover the whereabouts of the *John Robinson*, I must pursue the theory that there was a new player in the market as Gabriel surmised. Naturally, the best person to assist me was the effeminate Shi Qi. Being a mere woman in his Celestial eyes, I needed the assistance of Hock. No doubt my elderly companion would be close to the Shamrock. I therefore badgered the young girl, Dawn, to make enquiries outside on my behalf. It wasn't long before she returned to the room, her freckled face shining with willingness. I should add that I had acquired a new room from the Irish proprietor, John Crowley, after I had dramatically broken down in tears in his office. No doubt he would hear about the marital dispute at breakfast. I needed my wits, and any dalliance with the intimidating and if not charismatic Captain Sterling would be a hamper to my resolve. The tears I must admit were dramatic and unladylike, but necessary in these dire circumstances.

Good to his word, Hock waited patiently on the verandah of the Shamrock, avoiding a zealous grey haired porter who was sweeping the dust and clay left by the diggers' boots from the frivolity last night.

"Missy Charlotte, this not a good idea! Master Gab has asked me to watch you while he sees the gold men," Hock said after I requested his assistance.

"Yes, well, Hock, in a way you are watching me!" I responded, moving deftly to his side with young Dawn in hand, kindly seconded from the obliging Mr Crowley.

No self-respecting lady could walk the streets of Sandhurst without a suitable escort at her side. Unfortunately, the appearance of Hock invoked the customary rude and prejudiced language from unsavoury persons.

Hock shook his head in contrition but walked a few feet in front, weaving his way through the early morning traffic. Shamrock was situated on the corner of the main thoroughfare of Pall Mall and the bustling street of Williamson. Dawn had indicated that a store called Craig Williamson and Thomas would be most suitable to procure items for a lady. Having pacified Hock and sent him to secure an appointment with Shi Qu, I walked confidently into the newly erected draper's, the smell of fresh haberdashery a welcome treat. It was a delight to immerse myself in the world of silks and ribbons after the past few weeks of drama. The store manager, Mr Thomas, was exceedingly attentive, if not obsequious at times. Dawn enthusiastically assisted with the numerous purchases – a ready-made chemise (my present one was disgustingly inadequate after all my travelling), a duck blue silk nightdress from France (I dared to remember how many times I had slept in my day clothes) and a new pair of sturdy tan boots. I revelled in the purchase of hose, pantaloons, and finally a crinoline, a necessary lady's accessory.

After selecting a leghorn straw hat trimmed with fashionably wide gold silk ribbons, I sent my purchases to the hotel, charging the account, of course, to my 'husband' Captain Sterling. The cashmere jacket, over an imported marigold surah silk blouse with a matching Indian shawl was a last minute indulgence.

"Missy Charlotte!" Hock materialised from the shadows of the verandah as the draper's bell tinkled on our exit, his demeanour cautious, eyes darting into the passing crowd.

Taking his sinewy arm, I progressed down the street, oblivious to the stares. Dawn gasped at my intimacy but fell in behind us, obviously resigned.

"It has been arranged, but it is dangerous game you play. You are but a fair and colourful bird amongst the hawks." His wise head shook in concern.

"Yes, well this bird must ruffle some feathers and it seems logical that Shi Qu be our first prey. He would be remiss to harm an English lady considering the tide of public opinion at present. I must change, Hock, I will join you within the hour."

Dawn's attentive and deft administrations had my toilette completed in no time; my battered riding attire was replaced by a glamorous morning outfit. The marigold blouse set off the colour of my hair and the matching jacket with epaulettes accentuated my corseted waist. I had decided that if Shi Qu wore his investitures as his badge of honour and coveted position in the community, I would also display my rank as an English lady!

Fortunately, Dawn had a bulky but compliant Yorkshire lad as her beau, and I had enlisted his services along with Dawn's for the afternoon. His daunting appearance was an added bonus considering my motley array of companions. Therefore, with my trusty entourage in tow, I took an hackney from Williamson Street to Bridge Street, the hub of Chinese activity within Sandhurst. Hock had directed the cab to an inconspicuous store; its shopfront squeezed between two prosperous vegetable stores laden with fresh morning produce. Silks and cottons spilled out onto the walkway, and tassels, ribbons and coloured lengths hung precariously from the simple rafters of tin and timber.

After paying the driver an exorbitant fee, Hock bowed before the wizened proprietor who sat cross-legged on a dusty packing box. His dark eyes were astonishingly alert, sunk within a crinkled and weathered face. Dressed in a simple traditional brown tunic, he gestured dismissively to the rear of the establishment. Following in Hock's wake, we skirted the bundles of fabric, making our way through a simple potato sack covered doorway.

The opulent cave we entered was no doubt Shi Qu's; it reeked of his grandiose level of egotism. Chinese lanterns that hung randomly created a subtle intimacy. The shimmering luminosity reflected off the rich fabrics that draped from the tent-like ceiling. Resplendently placed in the centre was a stylised red chair with dragon armrests.

The room was empty of people, and I assumed that in his perverse way Shi Qu wished to make a grand entrance so I remained standing. Dawn and John whispered covertly behind me whilst Hock stood pensively at my side in anticipation. As expected, Shi Qui was ushered in by his minions, his silks striking and opulent. Symbols of the sun were intricately embellished on fine silk; an orange peacock embroidered gracefully down one side perched on an axe. Impressed with the lavish display, I instinctively curtsied. Surprisingly, Shi Qu bowed – well, I believed he bowed, for his expansive stomach bent slightly. He motioned to the simple chair placed by his servant. Once settled, his dark ebony eyes scrutinised my person, taking in my finery.

"Mrs Sterling," he exclaimed, "a pleasure. How may such a simple man as Shi Qu assist?" A tranquil but cheerless smile appeared on his doughy face.

"Shi Qi, I thank you for your audience. I believe that I may assist you!" I smiled agreeably, and paused for effect to remove an elaborate handkerchief from my purse. Dark puffy eyebrows quivered in surprise.

"Continue!"

"No doubt you are aware another party is at present attempting to monopolise your activities." I paused, watching his features harden. "In pooling our resources we may discover the perpetrator." Hock mumbled unintelligibly beside me.

"And, Mrs Sterling, why would I choose you?" Shi Qu leant forward, his massive body rolling precariously.

"You have little choice, Shi Qi. The present Celestial prejudices limit your endeavours. An English lady is something of an anomaly in the goldfields. I can tap into – dare I say – certain areas that may not be open to your enquiries."

"Does Captain Sterling approve of this rashness?" A sneer played on his mouth as he watched my reaction.

"Captain Sterling is, as we speak, enquiring with the local gold commissioner regarding perfidious activities."

"And, Mrs Sterling, why do you wish to be involved?"

"To assist my husband, of course!"

I had no idea what Captain Sterling was doing at present. However, his meeting with the Gold Commissioner doubtless had something to do with his precious boat. I needed a clue to the whereabouts of Sanders and then hopefully a link to his nefarious leader. Shi Qi had not disputed my claim of another syndicate pushing into his line of work. I hoped my confident demeanour and his need to eradicate opposition had turned the tide in my favour. I was creating aspersions that were not concrete – skating on thin ice.

Shi Qi leant back into his sturdy chair closing his eyes. The quiet allowed the buzz and bustle of Chinatown to disturb the sanctuary. His cheeks wobbled as they strived for breath.

I remained quiet, my heart beating uncontrollably as my sweaty palms gripped my handkerchief. I was completely and utterly out of my depth and Hock knew it! A rasping intake of breath alerted me to my companion's scrutiny.

"Mrs Sterling. I have asked and I have been advised!" A slow sardonic gaze settled on me. "Yes, I will assist but do not believe that, as you English say, 'it will be a stroll in the park' – my adversary is cunning!" Gesturing to his closest minion, he rapped off a few words. The diminutive individual retrieved a box from a draped hidden shelf. Shi Qi removed a small wooden tablet engraved with a single gold symbol and handed it to me. "This symbol is a sign that the information or the person has been sent by me. Goodbye, Mrs Sterling!"

He waved us away. I rose to utter another question, but Hock grasped my arm and propelled me into the street.

"Miss Charlotte, it is done. He will be in contact! Now we must confer with Master Gab. You have brought great danger to your door," Hock whispered as we moved steadily down the street. Bemused, Dawn and John hung respectfully behind as we conversed.

I shrugged my shoulders. "I have been besieged by danger in the last few weeks. This time it is on my terms!"

"Master Gab will not be pleased." Hock's head shook with despondency.

"But Hock, how long will it take for Shi Qi to contact us? It is crucial that we find the whereabouts of Sanders and ultimately the *John Robinson*."

"Be patient, Miss Charlotte. Shi Qi wishes for this to end as much as you!"

We reached Pall Mall in no time and duly the Shamrock. The past hour in Chinatown had taxed my sensibilities! I was famished and, after thanking my obliging couple with suitable compensation, I retired to the front parlour. Hock had already excused himself, mumbling about Master Gab and retribution.

It was late, so most of the male guests had eaten earlier. As steak and eggs seemed the main fare, I opted for eggs, followed by some refreshing tea with buttered fresh bread.

A tingle down my back should have been a warning. Then a firm hand touched the base of my neck. Long fingers moved caressingly into my curls. I froze, my cerulean blue tea cup poised at my lips. My body humming with the intimacy!

"Charlotte, I hear you have had a busy morning." His low mellifluous voice was disarmingly personal.

Lowering my cup, I tilted my head to see a pair of amused green eyes assessing my discomfort.

"Yes, you have been busy! New clothes, new shoes and new friends!" Gabriel settled into the chair at my side, his smirk suggestive.

"I suppose you have spoken to Hock."

"Indeed."

"Well, how goes it with the Commissioner?" I asked, refusing to meet his eyes.

"I have a few leads, but please, tell me how your day progressed." His rich baritone voice was clipped and terse.

"Would you care for tea?" I suggested, motioning to the waitress.

"Yes. And with it, answers."

"Oh, very well! No doubt you have heard Hock's version." I told him about the unfolding events of the day. The brief dialogue, covered my shopping expedition with Dawn and my meeting with Shi Qi.

"You realise you must depart for Port Phillip? I cannot have you in danger!" His catlike eyes watched me intently, his fingertips stroking my gloved hand.

"Captain Sterling, I may be using your name, but you are not actually my husband. I will do exactly as I wish!" I said quietly, my temper rising with every utterance.

"For your own safety, Mrs Sterling, while you are with me you will do exactly as I say!"

"Safety. Huh, when have you been able to keep me safe!" The fiery words were out before I could even contemplate what they implied.

Gabriel's face blanched and his full mouth disappeared into a thin harsh line. Rising, he bowed at my flushed countenance and said, "I will escort you to dinner at six."

25

THE GOLDEN TABLET

The single tap reverberated throughout the modest room. Collecting my gloves and purse, I moved to the door. Captain Sterling's tall solid body lent nonchalantly against the frame. His new collared shirt accentuated his handsome tanned features which were offset by yellow bruising around his cheeks. His dark face was impassive and sombre.

"I am sorry," I declared self-consciously, my expectant face raised as my eyes scoured his stony face. I had been mulling over our previous conversation and was ashamed at my bluntness. Gabriel had been attentive to my safety but circumstances beyond his control had torn that fibre of our trust. I suppose deep down I was angry and hurt. Some perverse idea drove me now to find Sanders; it somehow would right the balance in our problematic relationship. I dared not think of our future. Tilting my chin a notch, I asked breathlessly, "Am I forgiven?"

One firm hand grasped my waist protectively, the other pushed the door shut with a resounding thud.

"Forgiven!" His knowledgeable mouth nipping at my exposed lobe and sliding sensually down my nape. I was lost, my body yearning for his touch, as deft fingers moved to my laces.

Snuggled within the covers, I drifted out of a deep and satisfying sleep to the sounds of joviality and caterwauling outside. The theatre attached to the hotel had no doubt closed and the miners were suspended in a moment of euphoria brought on by the absorption of a great deal of whisky. Shortly, the gunshots would start, waking the general populace. Grumbling, I attempted to roll over, my body hindered by a muscular arm resting over my ribs. A deep resonant breath sounded comforting and warm to my ear.

Through the open window I could see lanterns moving in a haphazard pattern down the street. The moon was low and already the chill of the early morning had descended into the room. Sighing, I moved carefully onto my back and a puff of gentle air tickled my nose. Tilting my head, I could just make out his face in the dark. High cheekbones a little discoloured, his masculine contours at odds with those full lips, relaxed at present in slumber. It was a strong and powerful face. However, I had grown to know those green eyes gave away his secrets! They vacillated in colour and vibrancy depending on his mood; at one moment solemn and thoughtful, the next emotive and vital. Last night they had been unguarded and sensual.

I had barely closed my eyes when a slight movement from the doorway raised my alarm. A figure stepped out of the dark shadows and moved stealthy towards the bed. Before I could scream or rouse Gabriel, my mystery visitor raised an ancient wooden tablet. The gold symbol shimmered as it reflected the first precious slithers of light. Catching my breath, I gazed in fascination as with quick movements the messenger placed the tablet and a small note on the side table. His slight form was swathed in black from head to foot. With a curt bow, he retreated quietly. My saviour angel was content to dream at my side!

My curiosity piqued, I inched to the edge of the bed, attempting to slip gently from Gabriel's hold. What had Shi Qi discovered? Plainly it was of immense interest; the gold tablet would not have been idly or casually issued. I dared not hope it was information regarding Sanders' whereabouts. Shi Qi had spies in all corners of the goldfields. Hock had mocked my innocence at the workings of the Chinese crime lords. I wondered whether I had unwittingly stepped beyond my own level of comfort. Well, in hindsight I had done that as soon as I'd stepped onto the *John Robinson*.

I eased one bare foot onto the rug below and shifted my hips to rise. My movement was unceremoniously checked by a hearty tug at my waist as Gabriel energetically tumbled me back into his firm arms. Buried against his chest, my muffled protest was ignored as he distractedly wound his long fingers gently through my dishevelled hair. Recovering, I wriggled and pushed my way upwards to confront his irritatingly smug face.

"I was mistaken!" he stated, grinning from ear to ear. "It is not my formidable presence that makes me irresistible to you but my sorrowful circumstances." I shook my head in exasperation.

"You are decidedly the most irritating man I have ever met."

"And you love it!" he declared his green eyes twinkling with virile intensity. "What news has Shi Qi ?"

Momentarily bewildered by the 'love' word, my befuddled brain realised he had been aware of our anonymous and exotic messenger. My mouth agape must have prompted a further comment.

"Surely, Charlotte, even in your enticing arms I must remain vigilant!" He grinned, his eyes pensive as he leant gracefully over my body to retrieve the message. Indignantly, I shifted to a sitting position, adjusting my chemise as it wantonly slipped over my limbs. Fluffing up the pillows Gabriel hoisted me to his naked side. I schooled my countenance into an inscrutable expression, intimately aware of his broad chest rising and falling but inches away!

"Here, Charlotte, I presume Shi Qi's missive is for your eyes," he stated seriously, passing the note to my hands. Surprised by his amiability, I folded back the note; it was penned in English. The fluid strokes in black ink were almost box like in their structure, the words elegantly and smoothly brushed over the mulberry pressed paper.

The man you seek camps at Emu Point with a Long Song.

"Well, that is annoying, Hock has mentioned Emu Point but what on earth is a Long Song? Plainly it is a code!"

A throaty noise broke loose from my companion, his chest heaving with constrained mirth. Raising his hand to fend off my protestations, I slid off the bed to stand indignantly, hands on hips. Another chuckle nearly undid me as I rummaged for a shawl.

"Obviously you are aware of the meaning, but as usual you intend to exert your superiority and leave me floundering. I would prefer if you left, Captain. I will summon Hock, a far more pleasing individual." I turned my back and proceeded to gather his garments strewn on the intricate hewn rug; a disquieting reminder of our intimacy last night.

Powerful arms scooped me up and deposited me squealing onto the covers.

"Forgive me, Charlotte, but it is hard to resist, when you present such a charming picture."

Disconcerted, I attempted to sit up but gentle hands caressed my toes, before weaving their way up my exposed legs. Sensual catlike eyes riveted upon my upturned face. "A most charming picture!"

Shi Qi's message was lost within the blankets.

⊙❀❦❀

Bereft of his energy, the room sadly appeared unpalatable and drab. Rummaging on the floor for the note, I read it out loud, hoping that the intonation would jog my memory. It was then I noticed that Long and Song were capitalised. Foolish, foolish girl! If I hadn't been so hot headed, I would have deciphered it logically. It was a name! A Chinese name! Hock had referred to Long when in Chewton; my memory was so dazed at present with the confounded events. It should have dawned on me after Gabriel's unusually hasty intimacy. Plainly, he knew the identity of this Long Song. Hurriedly, I dressed, annoyed at the early hour and Gabriel's subterfuge. My corset was loose but without a maid it was useless to persevere. The bodice fitted snugly and I was thankful it buttoned to the front. Pushing aside the crinoline, I settled on the dark riding slacks and their accompanying skirt. It was probably more appropriate than a full skirt. Conscious of the dusty conditions on the roads, I changed into boots, my stockings well tied. There was a slight chill in the air but no doubt the day would warm up so I seized my pelisse. Bonnet on, I briskly headed for the kitchen.

"This very bad, Missy Charlotte. Long Song very powerful lord. His family most illustrious in southern China! Shi Qi must make mistake. This is not right!" Hock shook his head in disbelief, his hands waving in agitation.

"Well Hock, there is only one way to find out and that is to visit Emu Point and find this, as you say, distinguished lord!"

"Master Gab has —"

"Yes, I can imagine what Master Gab, Gabriel I mean, has requested. I will not stay at the hotel whilst Sanders wanders loose. From prior experience, I feel he will most probably require our assistance, anyway, Hock!" I grinned, placing my gloved hand lightly on his shoulder in companionship.

"You make me a very bad person, Missy Charlotte," he stated, but his dark eyes twinkled.

"Wonderful. Please inform the stable that we will require horses."

After a hasty breakfast of — you guessed it! — steak and eggs, events had made me excessively hungry! I met Hock on the sweeping verandah. The Shamrock stable mounts were sadly pitiable! Their poor backs were bent with age and misuse. Hock shrugged; it was the best he could conjure up at such short notice. My own lovely mount Viper was missing in action. Sighing, I took the reins, the old hag watching me with a wary eye.

Although it was early, Sandhurst was already bustling with a pulsating energy. On the opposite side of Williamson Street was a hotch-potch of buildings. Tents, timber slab shops, and occasionally a red brick frontage, lined the dusty thoroughfare. Their rough canvas signs billowed in the early morning breeze. It was hard to imagine that only a few years ago this area was overrun with sheep and the closest to civilisation was the lowly shepherd! Mr Crowley had boasted yesterday that the region now exceeded forty-thousand people, no mean feat considering that the town of Melbourne prior to the rush catered for just over twenty-thousand!

The amazing addiction of gold! It was a wonder that any ship sailed or retained their crew with such statistics. No wonder Gabriel was desperate to locate the *John Robinson*. It was his livelihood but he was also beholden to his loyal core of men who were obviously held on board.

Hock assisted me in mounting, our unusual camaraderie receiving unflattering comments as our mounts manoeuvred past several cheerless men smoking and gossiping on the uneven street. I raised my head a trifle higher as we broke into a laboured trot heading northwards.

Emu Point, Hock informed me, was the Chinese camp we had

frequented during our dash to rescue Captain Sterling. It was located on the northern end of Sandhurst and surrounded the Red Temple. Long Song was from the province of Kwang Tung and had travelled to the goldfields with a band of loyal men and a vast crew of Celestials. He was said to be blessed with Imperial favour and status. Long Song headed one of the older societies that nurtured, oversaw and assisted Celestial workers on the fields. The society lent funds to its members for prospecting, assisted with the gold, and maintained order within the Chinese community.

As we trotted past the Red Temple, Hock came to an abrupt halt, slid from his old hag and, moving within earshot, calmly whispered, "We are nearly there, Missy Charlotte. Long Song, illustrious man! We tread carefully!"

For a camp littered with simply constructed and humble tents, the silken banners looked out of place. Waving majestically, they were pitched regally outside a roughly hewn slab hut. Several hefty young men in dark tunics reclined on wool bales, smoking incessantly whilst playing what I believed was fan tan – a game that Hock and most Celestials were addicted to. As we arrived, the men paused, turned their heads briefly then recommenced their game. We had been seen and noted.

Sliding from my ancient steed, I handed the reins to Hock, adjusting the ribbons on my broad straw leghorn.

The purple banners were glorious, gold thread depicted a two clawed dragon with flashing green eyes and a green beard bursting from watery depths. At the virescent edge, serrations were intricately embroidered with symbols such as butterflies and flowers. To complete the effect, five purple ribbons fluttered in the breeze at the base.

"The claws show the rank of the official, Missy Charlotte. Five claws for the Emperor and four for a prince." Hock gestured respectively with a gentle flourish. "Long Song ranks as an illustrious official with two. Please wait here while I request an audience."

Hock disappeared into the hut and a young Chinese boy led our ancient charges to a trough.

Clasping my purse to my waist, I strove to quell my nerves. If Long Song was aware of Sanders' whereabouts, why would he share his knowledge with me? Surely a man of Long Song's standing would not require the services of such a person as Sanders. He had immense influence within the Chinese community and to dally with European theft and murder seemed inconceivable. It was a quandary and one I hoped to solve soon – if only Hock would return!

The dark tunicked men chattered incessantly over their gambling, occasionally raising their heads to observe my movements. One in particular, his queue cut off to his shoulders, watched me incessantly, his dark fringed eyes hard and steady.

It was already mid-morning and the sun beat down relentlessly. I strolled over to a lone scraggly paperbark tree, thankful for its meagre shade. Marauding flies pestered my mouth and eyes, a simple boned fan helpless against their assault. Thankfully, Hock appeared in the doorway beckoning me forward. Obsidian orbs followed my progress. Clasping my elbow, Hock ushered me into Long Song's presence. Subtle red lanterns dangled overhead. The room, unlike Shi Qi's, was not grotesquely opulent but elegant in its utility.

Long Song's reception room contained a heavily lacquered dark chiselled desk and chair placed to the left of the entrance. On the intricate panels that probably divided this room from his private quarters were rows of shelves laden with inscribed tablets. The dirt floor was covered in surprisingly simple Chinese rugs.

As my eyes adjusted to the dim light, I was aware of a majestic gentleman sitting to my right, resplendent on a rosewood sofa. His handsome and youthful demeanour was a surprise! Atop his sleek dark hair sat a magnificent blue silk hat, its segments glistening with mirrors and topped with a red threaded tassel. Behind him guardian dragons peered solicitously from the wooden head rest, their counterparts embellished in gold embroidery upon the plum silk of the wearer sitting. Two claws were raised in defiance.

"Welcome, Miss Lavender, we had grown impatient!" voiced the illustrious one, sweeping his hand towards a low austere bench. If he had planned to intimidate me, he had certainly succeeded. His English and awareness of my maiden name suddenly made me nervous.

Sitting, I arranged my skirt discreetly, biding time to gather my thoughts, it was then I noticed Gabriel! A squeak escaped my mouth.

"Now, Miss Lavender, Lóng zhī xīn, has shared a most interesting story with me. It is only fitting that I hear yours. However, before we start formalities, let us have tea!" His voice was sweet-toned and harmonious. He clapped and a young boy appeared from the dark confines of the room, bowing before shuffling out in haste after Long Song had fired a few crisp words in his direction.

Gabriel sat motionless in a heavily ornate chair, his lithe form unreadable in the poor lighting. Spinning around, I attempted to make sense of the occasion. Hock crouched obsequiously at the entrance whilst several of the men from outside stood gladiatorial in the semi-darkness.

The minutes ticked by, the mood oppressive and menacing. Long Song watched me as a hunter watches his prey, his dark eyes intelligent and intimidating. I had plainly made my entrance whilst Gabriel was discussing the matter of Sanders with the illustrious one. I felt suddenly small and insignificant. An English lady in a situation that was certainly unfamiliar and definitely overwhelming, I wondered what story Gabriel had imparted, I suppose the truth was the only option. I hope Hock had our escape planned!

A rustle from the door heralded the arrival of tea. It was placed reverently to my right.

"Miss Lavender, will you do the honours? Tang is our master of tea. He has prepared an Oolong Tea. It is immensely palatable and especially excellent for the skin. If I may suggest it, a little brown sugar will nourish the stomach." Long Song's articulate English voice was unsettling considering our surroundings. However, the ritual of tea was something every English lady was groomed to host.

The cups were exquisite; small and fragile in princely colours, lotus leaf symbols floating deceptively beneath the surface. Tang handed the tea carefully with both hands, delivering first to Long Song and then to Gabriel. As a lowly servant, Hock was not worth serving.

About to sip the fragrant drink, I caught the flash of Gabriel's eye, his head tilted towards Long Song. Pausing I lowered my cup – clearly, ladies did not take precedence.

"Delightful! Thank you, Miss Lavender. Lóng zh⬚ x⬚n has been most complimentary of your skills and beauty. He has not exaggerated!"

Long Song's smile transformed his previously menacing face into one of sweet charm. His bowed mouth revealed immaculate white teeth hidden behind refined cherry lips. It was his eyes, however, that drew my solicitous appraisal. Soft lustrous almond eyes, exquisitely framed by thick dark lashes stroking soft cheekbones. His slim, tanned limbs previously poised were now casually draped against the headrest. *Beau idéal!* I must have sighed because Gabriel let out a snort as he recrossed his long muscular legs.

"*Lóng zhī xīn?*" I questioned, fumbling with my delicate carmine cup.

"My apologies, Miss Lavender! Gabriel to your beauteous ears! Lóng zhī xīn to us humble ones." He bowed slightly, his voice soft and intimate.

"Oh!" I declared spellbound.

A growl erupted from my left.

"To be grammatically correct, I suppose I should say my brother-in-law. My esteemed sister's husband!"

"Brother-in-law?" My hands unconsciously trembled.

"More tea?" he asked, his cherub smile overshadowed by a savage glint to his eye.

"No thank you! I apologise for my intrusion. As Gabriel has surely related the facts of the previous few weeks, it is only fitting that I leave you gentlemen to your discussion." Rising, I wobbled unceremoniously to my feet.

"Sit," Gabriel boomed. Long Song raised his immaculately groomed eyebrow. Spinning to face my treacherous lover, I gawked in an unladylike fashion, my face heating in distress!

"Charlotte, please sit. Long Song has a most indelicate habit of baiting his prey. Patience!" he said soothingly.

Patience? *I needed the holy trinity!* Reluctantly, I lowered myself with as much dignity as I could muster to the bench. Tang passed me another refreshing cup of tea. I nodded my thanks, my hands still quivering with anger.

"My apologies, Miss Lavender! I was unaware you were not privy to Gabriel's dark secrets. He has a most colourful background."

"Shut up, Ayan!" Gabriel growled irritably.

"Long Song to you, brother," he whipped back with venom. "Take care, I have guards who would be delighted to impose great suffering upon your person."

"You forget yourself, Ayan. This is an English protectorate, not China. English law is administered and English gentlemen have considerable powers!" Gabriel enunciated each word threateningly.

"You mock me!" Long Song rose threateningly, his imposing presence diminished by the cold sardonic force that was Gabriel.

"I point out the obvious!"

Enough was enough. What past event had created this bullring mentality overshadowing the whole proceedings? I wanted to know where Sanders was and where the *John Robinson* lay. Then I would be out of this mess, this toxic web of intrigue. Raising my gloved hand, I addressed them both.

"If you both intend on clashing horns, please allow me the convenience of leaving. I have only come on an errand to find Sanders and Gabriel's precious *John Robinson*. When you both feel up to the task I can be located at the Shamrock!"

Dumbfounded the men halted their pernicious assault. I rose and swept from the room, Hock close on my heels. Long Song's last utterance catching the wind.

"She is magnificent!"

26

RAMIFICATIONS

I should have stayed and confronted him! I should have swallowed
the bile that rose from my stomach and threatened to choke me.
Married, the cad! Well, that was that. He could find his *John Robinson*
and I hoped it was burnt to a cinder. My mount swung her head from
side to side in agitation. Plainly, her soft mouth was made sore by my
dispirited handling of the reins.

Hock remained quietly in vigil beside me, his head hung in
deep thought. Silently, even my complacent companion received my
contemptuous and hostile scorn. All these days on the road and not a
word that Captain Sterling was a married man, My blouse reeked of
perspiration as I sulked towards the Shamrock – or was that the stench
of adultery?

Alex, poor Alex, I had led him a merry chase and abandoned him
without a thought in Castlemaine. All for my blind and immature
actions in assisting Gabriel Sterling. What had Alex once said? *A wife
in every port* – the comment rattled me to the core.

If I had not been so overwrought and lost in thought I might have
seen the attack unfold. Sadly, it happened so quickly that I had barely
time to scream. Uncommonly strong hands lifted me from above in
one crushing hold. One minute I had been lamenting my situation, the
next I was swinging precariously above the ground. My left leg ached

as it had been pulled severely from the side saddle pommel. Hock swung out at my assailant to no avail. He was roughly dragged off his horse by a group of darkly dressed Celestials. Although his hands and feet moved with great agility and mastery, his opponents too were uncommonly skilful. Finally, they overpowered and bludgeoned him to the ground. I cried out, bucked and swore in a most unladylike manner, but the beady-eyed youth from Long Song's camp held me firm, his iron arms tightened across my back, eliciting a screech from my throat. Bundled into a crude wagon that smelled unpleasantly like a night cart, I was roughly restrained. The vile smell was slightly compensated for by the sweet smelling gunny sacks that suffocated my body.

"Let me out!" I screamed as rough hands gagged my mouth. I squirmed and wriggled trying to break free but my activity was quelled by a swift punch to my solar plexus. My captives had remained quiet during this whole exercise, the sound of distant rifles and cheering alerting me to the goldfields nearby. The burlap irritated my exposed face and arms as the cart bounced along. My gorgeous leghorn hat was squashed beyond repair.

Here I was once again paralysed, about to face my adversaries and all my mind craved was vengeance. I positively wished Gabriel Sterling immolated. The cart idled along for what seemed hours before I was unceremoniously hoisted like a rag-doll into a ramshackle slab hut. It was a bushland location from what I had briefly glimpsed, and musk lorikeets chattered conspiratorially in the encroaching acacia's. The gurgle of a nearby creek reminded me I was hot and parched; my saliva caked unattractively onto the tight cotton gag.

Shaken, I rolled over on the dirt floor, resting on my side. My back ached, not from the perilous cart ride but from the mishandling of the villain who'd hoisted me aloft from my mount. It was mid-afternoon if my calculations were correct. Sunlight still trickled through the western gaps in the stringy-bark slabs. The green hewn timber shimmered as the trickling golden sap glistened in the setting heat. Brown bark cockroaches scurried in the semi-darkness of the floor, luckily keeping their distance as they laboured in the undressed grooves.

I must have dozed off because raised voices and scuffling roused me groggily to awareness. Abruptly the door was sent crashing against its humble leather hinges as a stumbling male form was roughly pushed into the darkening space. His normally vibrant green eyes were now glazed and listless as he collapsed unconsciously into the dirt.

I remained staring at his body for a few minutes, making excuses in my mind why I should avoid him. His long lashes lay limp against his cheekbones, his chest rising at an alarmingly slow pace. His once pristine shirt was ripped and stained, as were his morning trousers. His legs stuck out at odd angles as he remained in a comatose state.

Thankfully, my jailer had removed my gag earlier, placing a jug of water and a bowl of rice at my disposal. My sanitary needs would be met by but a stone urn! I cringed, hoping that Gabriel remained out cold as I made use of the rough latrine.

Using the lining of my riding skirt, I tore the cotton into irregular strips. Inching closer to Gabriel I squeezed the water soaked rags above his face. The water trickled tenderly down his high cheekbones to partly open lips and over his uncompromising bristled chin.

"You are resolved to drown me, Charlotte?" my nemesis murmured in the growing darkness.

"The thought had crossed my mind." I uttered flatly, pulling my legs to my chest. All the pent up vexation dissolved with the sound of his voice. "Damn you, Captain Sterling!"

"Will you let me explain?" he mumbled, his voice distant and unsteady.

"Is there much to explain? I think our present circumstances preclude sentimentality." I rose to my feet and peered through the cracks in the door. "How many do you think there are?"

"Sufficient numbers to make our life difficult," he grumbled.

"Do you think it is Sanders?"

"No doubt. Is there any food?"

Feeling in the dark, I located the covered bowl of rice. "I'm afraid there are no utensils." I declared in a detached manner, passing the bowl into his outstretched long fingers.

"Will you join me?"

"No, I haven't the appetite!"

"Mmm, is that a reflection of Long Song's disclosures?"

"Maybe, but more so of my own naivety and stupidity."

"Charlotte, it is simply not –"

Before he could finish his sentence, a kick resounded on the threshold and a flash of a lantern alerted us to our visitor. Sanders' glaring face appeared at the door with two men, his eyes harsh and sinister. Devoid of his jacket, Sanders was dishevelled. His usual immaculate condition was reduced to a grubby shirt and crumpled pants. In one unsteady hand, he held an oil lantern, in the other a mug, I presumed of whisky. Motioning towards Gabriel, the two black clad Celestials moved into position, watching my companion with open hostility.

"Now, Captain! As in the past any misbehaviour on your behalf, will sadly affect the lovely Miss Lavender. Please follow me!"

Frustrated and angry at the perfunctory disregard for my condition, I moved forward. "Mr Sanders, I insist that you permit me to talk to your superior." I declared, my chin at a determined tilt. "Is it Long Song or Shi Qi?"

Plainly taken aback by my forthrightness, his face transformed into a knowing leer. "Miss Lavender, you delight me with your innocence! As you say, 'my superior' is far more adept than some yellow devil nobody!" Warming to the subject he swung his mug pointedly towards me. "The darn chinks have their uses but they couldn't organise a pig fair." Snickering, he took another swig from the mug.

Enlivened, I stepped forward. Sanders' inebriated state had strengthened my resolve. "So am I to ascertain that this bullying and coercion has been instigated by an Englishman?" My voice was full of malice. Sanders sudden silence and cocky pose answered my question.. "Stand aside, Mr Sanders, I wish to speak to this criminal personally, not to some drunken lackey."

Furious at my words and the blatant insult, Sanders lurched forward. I, however, was ready for him. With one swift stroke I lodged my beautifully carved knife to its hilt. With a piercing cry, Sanders dropped the lantern and clutched at his side. My hand shook and my dissembling legs began to quiver as I slowly moved towards the entrance. Several grunts and bumps alerted me to Gabriel's struggles.

Within moments, a familiar hand clasped my arm and steered me roughly into the night. The camp appeared relatively quiet but for a few muffled voices echoing up from the stream.

Finally, Sanders recovered his composure and voice, screaming for assistance. Skulking around the hut, Gabriel watched for sentries, then, convinced all was clear, bundled me headlong into a medley of acacias. Shots rang out from the camp as our desperate assailants attempted to stem our escape.

"Thankfully, it is evening but they will be after us at daybreak. We must put some distance between us and them, quickly!" Gabriel softly rasped, dragging me blindly through the undergrowth. My skirts were as usual a hindrance as they snagged on the varying obstacles of this alien landscape.

"You could relax your grip!" I protested through clenched teeth as we corralled along. His hand obstinately clenched mine even more firmly!

Thankfully, the moon remained morosely cloud bound, its limited light a blessing in terms of cover, but woefully inadequate for navigating the terrain. Once or twice we tumbled, tripping over camouflaged logs, Gabriel attempting to cushion the blow as we crashed onto a dry and inflexible bushland floor. After our third mishap, I wrenched my arm from his grip and sat sullenly on the track.

"Gabriel, I must get my breath! For goodness sake, do you have any idea of our direction?" I panted. My heart pounding, my head spinning with Sanders' disclosure.

Chuckling, Gabriel hoisted me up. "Charlotte, it may come as a surprise to you but I have sailed ships in the dark!"

Prickling unnecessarily at his sarcasm, I lashed out at his face with my open hand. Surprisingly, it connected directly upon his bristling jaw. No sooner had it occurred than I regretted my actions. Even in the dark I could feel his rigid and bridled posture. Exhausted, I collapsed in a heap, tears pouring down my cheeks. They call it delayed trauma! Placing that knife in Sanders' stomach had unravelled my mind. I loathe violence but the arrival of Sanders had driven me past any sense of reason. Strong arms pulled me into a gentle embrace as long fingers stroked my hair and lips glided caressingly over my brow. We sat entwined for ages as my emotions calmed. His soothing and tender words were disarmingly potent.

"I apologise. It has been a trying day and without your daring assistance – which I will duly reward at a future date – we would not be so advantageously placed. It is no mean task to wield a knife!" Wiping my cheeks, his fingers gently traced a path to my jawline, his eyes flickering in the wan light. "To use it is fearless."

Raising my chin tenderly, he placed a brief kiss upon my lips. "Now then, Mrs Sterling, let us proceed with haste." Nodding, I pulled my billowing skirts into a bunch and with his assistance stumbled to my feet. His hands were reassuringly steady at my waist.

For the remainder of the evening I stumbled and shuffled behind Gabriel. The air was tantalising. Lemon myrtle, touched seductively by the advent of dew, wafted through the crevices and branches of the bush, its invigorating fragrance conjuring the spirits of the land. My nanny, a Jamaican half-caste, had believed in the spirits of her ancestors. She had often talked about their presence and the undying connection with her forbidden land. I wondered whether the natives who walked this land had the same bond.

The night was alive with eerie sounds, Gabriel's hurtling pace pausing occasionally as a piercing squeal reverberated from above. Then the scurrying of paws revealed a group of red eyed possums intent on their evening meal or the enigmatic hoot of a barn owl. It was certainly an experience – a trifle unnerving at times with all types of mysterious animals scampering in our pathway, from flying foxes to what Gabriel pointed out as fuzzy bandicoots scurrying in the darkness.

By dawn I was exhausted, and even my companion was showing signs of weariness. Gabriel had followed the edge of the stream for a good part of the night, not only for the refreshing water but also as a guide to the colonial settlement. Just before dawn we headed south along what Gabriel believed was Bendigo Creek in the hope of reaching Sandhurst from where we had been forcibly removed. The sound of horses soon had us frozen and we sheltered behind a pile of rocks high on the bank.

"We must find somewhere secure to hide for the day. Charlotte, please stay here whilst I scout the surrounding land." He placed long fingers on my lips as I opened them to protest. "It will be easier." Resolved to my fate, I leant back upon the creviced rock, annoyed I had left my battered leghorn behind. The morning sun was already beating down; the rocks shimmering with the first lustre of sunlight. As I waited impatiently, several small lizards popped their heads out from under the slate and scurried away at my presence, except for a fat black scaled one that lumbered onto the warm rock, his blue tongue flashing out in protest at my intrusion. He observed me with distaste as the morning light sparkled and glowed on his shiny back. Lizards did not worry me greatly; Jamaica teemed with them. In fact, I had chased umpteen during my youth – green, brown, grey ones, and even a croaking lizard that infested our home. It was the snakes that bothered me! At home in Jamaica there had been large boa snakes slithering in the trees; they were harmless but unnerving. We had been warned about the reptiles in Port Phillip; they were venomous, brown, black and deadly. My encounter on the Sandhurst road sending shivers down my spine, I drew my pelisse tighter.

A soft movement on the rocks and a disarmingly attractive smile announced Gabriel's return. "We are in luck. Nestled on the north side of the bank is a shepherd's hut. It is adequate and well concealed." Coaxing my stubborn and weary legs to rise, I followed his lead.

It was ideal – musty but reeking of lanolin. A simple, well used cot was pushed up against the slab wall whilst a fireplace had been left piled with kindling. Gabriel entered first, inspecting the hut to ensure we had no slithering visitors. Once convinced that all was well except for a few skinks, he removed my pelisse and laid it across the bed.

"Sleep, Charlotte. I think it is best to take turns. We can't be too careful."

With barely a protest I curled up on the cot and fell into an exhausted sleep, not even Gabriel's close proximity disturbing my sensibilities.

It was my stomach groaning that eventually woke me! Gabriel was resting against the rudimentary door, his head flopped forward in sleep. His vibrant auburn hair was streaked with the golden sunlight that peeped through the cracks, and his sprawling legs dominated the space as his arms fell peacefully into his lap. I watched his chest rise and fall for several minutes, fascinated by his ability to remain upright.

Stretching, I dragged my protesting legs onto the dirt floor. My stomach rumbled once more and this time Gabriel peeked from under hooded eyes.

"The sound of hunger!" he proclaimed, shaking the sleep from his long legs whilst ruffling his hair in a most appealing manner. "I am a woeful sentry; I must have dozed off!" He struggled to his feet.

"Remind me to sleep with one eye open in your presence!" I declared, and his eyebrow arched at my comment. Flustered, I concentrated on the arrangement of my skirt.

"I fear our hunger will have to persevere until dark," he said. "I dare not light the fire and from what I have found on the shelves, we have only flour, salt and a little tea."

"Hallelujah, tea!" I moved over to the rough shelf.

"There is watercress in the creek. That is edible. If the fish bite, we may be lucky for supper."

"You have been industrious, Captain!"

"Captain?"

"I believe that is your title!"

"God damn it, Charlotte, this is ridiculous. I must explain!" His hand ran distractedly through his hair.

"There is nothing to explain, except that you are a philanderer."

"Philanderer! Balderdash! Just like a woman to jump to preposterous conclusions. I can assure you emphatically that I do not normally consort with my women passengers!"

"Liar!"

"Your assumption is illogical and unfounded." His face flushed crimson as clenched hands quivered at his side. "I am completely faithful."

"To whom? Your wife or to your perverse code of conduct?" I said sharply, my face feeling drained in comparison to his that was red and flushed. "You violated me, you, you, adulterer!" I threw back with vengeance.

"Violated you! Bah, you, I, we both found it pleasurable! But wild elephants wouldn't drive me to do it again!" he yelled, his shoulders shaking with rage.

"You will never get the opportunity again. You, you bounder!" I said, quivering uncontrollably.

A piercing whistle from outside shocked us into quiet. It was followed by the lively sound of livestock bleating and stumbling through the bush.

"If I am not mistaken, our shepherd has arrived!" Gabriel pulled me to the back of the door, his breathing still rapid as he attempted to control his temper. I, after all those stinging comments, was deflated.

The door burst open and a robust man with astounding full grey whiskers strode in, swinging a gun at Gabriel's chest!

"Blazes, I thought the place was full of bears. There was enough noise!" Lowering his gun, the man deposited his commodious saddlebag onto the cot.

"We apologise for the intrusion, but we were desperate for sleep and shelter." I stated solemnly.

The shepherd turned, his weather-beaten face, summing up our level of dishevelment and discord. His clothes were baggy and well-worn and washed. Mending stitches traversed his jacket sleeves and elbows like spider webs. His wiry grey hair and those impressive whiskers framed what appeared to be a friendly face. Hawk eyes watching us with interest.

"Should have guessed ! Married?"

"No!" I stated stupidly.

"No, not long." Gabriel interrupted.

"It gets worse! James Liston at your service. Hungry?"

"Famished." My stomach as if on cue rumbled disconcertingly.

Our shepherd laughed and pointed to the saddlebag. "I suggest you open the side flaps. There is a fresh loaf and cheese from the station. Not many folks come this way. All head for the goldfields!"

"We have had bad luck. We are heading towards Sandhurst," Gabriel replied, his alert eyes riveted to the gun.

"When you say bad luck, you don't mean dodging a band of blood curdling chinks scouring the bushland?"

I paused my hands began to tremble.

"I will double their reward, if you see us to Sandhurst !" Gabriel clenched his jaw, shifting his green steely eyes to Liston's face. "We have funds available in town."

"Who to believe? It should make good entertainment!" grinned our shepherd. His gun sat steady in his hand. "OK, tell me the tale."

Gabriel settled down at the roughened table, its seats but sawn off tree trunks in an assortment of heights. Liston sat opposite as I unwrapped the doughy bread and gooey cheese. The smell was intoxicating! Liston listened to Gabriel as he munched on lunch, his pocket knife stabbing at the softened cheese. Whistling at times, he motioned for me to join them, his hand gun now lying cocked beside his hand.

"Bloody hell," he shouted when Gabriel mentioned the *John Robinson*. "Knew you by name alone, Captain Sterling, but your reputation proceeds you. Worked on the Water Witch myself as watch captain. Now that's a clipper! Sharp lined, built for speed and using her sails day and night, through fair weather and foul. A beauty she was and fast."

"An opium ship I have been told. Is it true she was rigged with skysails and moonrakers?"

"Yep, her lee rails dipping in the water as we raced the devil himself!"

They both laughed, Gabriel's eyes shining with passion as he listened to the notorious and enthralling tales about the *Water Witch*.

Clearing my throat, I interrupted their discourse. "Excuse me, gentlemen, but may we return to discussing Sandhurst?"

Liston turned, viewing me through watchful eyes, saying, "My commiserations, Captain!" before continuing his colourful dialogue of his adventures. Shamed and a little despondent, I munched at the fresh bread and obligingly listened in silence.

Eventually, Liston shared with Gabriel his day in detail. After packing up his saddlebag and collecting his trusty mule, he had driven the sheep south of Ravenswood Run Station, heading for greener pastures. His intention was to stay overnight at this Bendigo Creek hut and then drive the sheep to pastures within Mount Alexander. Not one hour into his trip he had been overtaken by a band of Celestials headed by a blonde European. They had offered a reward for our carcasses! Liston's word not mine!

"Anyway, Captain. They have long gone. The head man seemed injured. Your doing?"

"No, my wife!"

"Jeezes." He whistled through gapped teeth. "Remind me to sleep with my pistol!" He chuckled, his eyes crinkling with delight, as his head shook from side to side. "I think the missus deserves a rest and I need to check on my lovelies."

I settled down on the cot, my head once again heavy with tiredness.

Was it minutes or hours later that a gentle shake to my shoulder roused me? My eyes flew open. It was dark and Liston smiled his toothy grin. "Supper?"

"Oh my goodness!" I stammered self-consciously. My eyes darted around the room in search of Gabriel.

"He is outside, ma'am! Your trusty sentry! Lamb stew? I have only two plates so you will have to share with the Captain," he announced as if reading my thoughts.

"Thank you, Mr Liston. You have been most accommodating." I attempted to rise gracefully but nearly fell head first over his saddlebags. The room was stifling! Liston whistled enthusiastically as he pottered around the humble hut.

"May I help, Mr Liston?"

"No, ma'am. My speciality!" He chuckled as he slopped the pot's contents onto dubiously clean tin plates.

The stew was delicious, even though I had to share alternate mouthfuls with Gabriel. His long expressive hands passed me the spoon after each mouthful. The hairs prickled provokingly on the back of my neck as he brushed my hand with his every move. I had initially proposed to eat after the men but my grumbling stomach won over my good manners.

"Yep, Bendigo Creek, named after old Bendigo! He has long gone. Shot through to California after hearing the news of the gold rushes in the forties. Poetic justice, really, considering that ten years later they tripped over nuggets in the creek. The goose must have been blind. All those years with the gold at his feet as he shepherded and watered the flock. Old man Myers thought it a big joke. Poor bastard probably died penniless in that heathen land."

"Is it far to Sandhurst from here, Mr Liston?"

"No, ma'am! Captain Sterling knows the way now. Myrtle will get you there. She's a homer, my pretty."

Myrtle was the old mule and companion of Mr Liston. Gabriel believed that our best option was to head off in the early hours of the morning. It was barely two hours by foot to Sandhurst, and following the creek would take us straight to the heart of the town. Gabriel had promised to leave the mule and supplies with the Bridge Street smithy, giving his word as a Captain and gentleman. Reassuringly, this was all that was needed by the besotted ex-sailor.

After dinner I volunteered to wash our utensils in the stream, under the watchful eye of the Captain. The water was surprisingly cold, and after putting aside the clean plates I dipped in my handkerchief. The coolness was revitalising to my flushed face and weary neck after the heat of the day. Strolling back inside I removed my pelisse from the cot and assured Mr Liston that I was well rested – he deserved his bed and a good night's sleep. Thanking him for his kindness, I retreated outside, his breath deepening into a loud and sonorous snore. Another reason to escape the confines of his humble hut.

Gabriel rose and followed me outside. I rested gingerly on a wobbly wooden bench gazing up at the stars.

"It's the Southern Cross."

"What?"

"The constellation that can only be seen from the southern hemisphere. It is called the Southern Cross. You can see its four main stars." He pointed out the configuration before carefully lowering himself to the seat. "A little precarious this seat." We both jiggled as the seat teetered under our weight.

"Story of your life, Captain?"

"Touché!"

For several moments we both stared at the night sky, reluctant to broach the subject that divided us like a canyon.

Gabriel broke the spell. A soft sigh reverberated from his chest.

"She was eighteen when we met. I was a besotted young man of twenty. Her life was one of privilege, mine one of hardship and struggle. She was visiting the Hong Kong wharves to farewell some English friends when her party was attacked. I had been supervising the loading of the Willoughby's clipper, *Fragrant Waters*, when I noticed the disturbance. Unthinkingly, I threw myself into the fighting and eventually with her loyal staff repelled her attackers. She parted the luxurious silk curtains and stepped from her private sedan chair. I had never seen anything so beautiful. Poets often scribe the virtues of alabaster skin; none had seen Yehonala. She was a fragile porcelain doll, wide brown eyes swimming under dark fringed lashes. I was totally smitten!"

Although the conversation disturbed me, I let Gabriel continue. His face was gaunt and thoughtful in the moonlight.

"Her father refused my suit. However, we continued to see each other secretly. Her brother Avan eventually persuaded to be our co-between. On my twenty-first birthday, I eloped with Yehonala. It was against her better judgement but I am a persuasive man, as you are aware, and she relented. Old man Willoughby took pity on us and housed us within his Hong Kong island compound. He had not been pleased with my behaviour, but the deed was done and he cared for her. As you can imagine, her father was furious. He questioned Avan and discovered his part in the scandal subsequently banishing him to an uncle in Beijing. He never allowed the family to speak or communicate with Yehonala again. Her mother was unable to assist or comfort her even as she lay dying in harrowing labour. The tears of sadness consumed her soul!"

The air rushed from my lungs, choking my voice, I had instinctively leant forward and captured his hand in mine. It trembled this time, clearly due to sadness, not rage. As he continued, his green eyes fixed on a distant point somewhere in the Milky Way.

"My immaturity, my stubbornness and my youthful disregard for her family, had brought my wife to the brink of desolation. She had loved me but she was also consumed by regret. Her family had disowned her, refused to answer her letters. She was dead to them, and in many ways that started the sadness within her heart that eventually let her succumb to the rigours of birth. You, Charlotte, of all people, are aware of my shortcomings!" He rested his catlike eyes upon my face and raised an eyebrow, I nodded in acknowledgement. "At that time, I was full of confidence. I did not see her heart breaking until it was too late. I innocently believed that in time her parents would relent. That we would stand as one. Unfortunately, my wife was but a beautiful flower, groomed for a privileged life, dependent on her family and overwhelmed by her husband. I felt like a bloody cruel fool. I still curse my insolence!"

"And your child?"

"He too died. It was a day that still haunts me."

"Gabriel." I squeezed his hand in sympathy. My eyes rimmed with tears.

"This tale was not for your pity, Charlotte!" He extracted his hand from mine, calmly but briskly. "Avan, or Long Song as you know him, started this conversation. I only wished to give my version of the story. It is not something I am proud of."

"Would Long Song seek to punish you for the past?" I bent my head, those eyes were now unrelenting and hard.

"Avan was aware how much his sister loved me. It has been many years now. I believe Long Song, although bitter, would not seek revenge. We were like brothers!"

"Does it not disturb you that we were both attacked after our meeting with Long Song?"

"I have thought long and hard on the subject. It is not Avan's way. He would have been decisive, dealing with us there and then. What disturbs me more is that someone wanted us to have the impression that Avan was involved. Someone wishes him implicated and I believe I am missing some vital clue."

"Well, I suppose our best course of action is to return to Sandhurst and question Shi Qi. It now seems ludicrous that he pointed us towards Avan when there is so much history between you."

"Shi Qi is but a peacock, with questionable ethics. The man we seek has a vendetta on me and subsequently you."

"And Sanders?"

"But another pawn. A very unscrupulous pawn."

"I am truly sorry for your loss."

"It is history! Now rest. My shoulder is at your disposal." He shrugged before relaxing against the raw sawn timber of the modest hut. His eyes closed, whether in painful reflection or tiredness I could not say. He was an enigma, curt, bombastic on one hand and compassionate and playful on the other. I leant comfortably against his arm. My mind span with his words.

27

MYRTLE

She was the most determined and stubborn beast I had ever encountered. I was positive that James Lister was laughing senseless at my misfortune. She fought, she bit and she kicked, and by the time she had settled down after some coercive therapy, I'd decided to walk!

Gabriel had long given up hope and strode ahead, his long legs making it difficult for mine to equal his pace. Mind you, I was hampered by the array of fabric that billowed from my waist snagging continuously on the bracken and tussock!

"You realise that in some Asian cultures they believe in the reincarnation of one's self as an animal! Would you ever consider a mule?" Gabriel grinned, a halo of sunlight bouncing off his auburn mane as his eyes sparkled with a mischievous intensity.

I chose not to dignify the question with an answer and continued dragging Myrtle.

"I am prepared to lead Myrtle and mount you!" The double entendre stopped me in my tracks. Myrtle bared her stained teeth! Gabriel held his hands up in mock surrender. "It was innocently meant! I apologise once again for my lack of social manners!" he stated, his face contrite.

"The problem, Captain Sterling, is that when necessary you are most gentlemanly but at present I do believe you are enjoying my discomfort," I said, tugging at the brute of a beast as it butted its velvety nose against my hip

"Does that mean you will allow me to intervene?" he asked, falling back to our slower pace. His hands crossed in a most irritating manner as he raised one auburn eyebrow in query.

I looked from Myrtle to the condition of my skirt. Raising my chin I nodded, conceding defeat. Attempting to conceal a smile, his firm hands spanned my waist and plonked me ungraciously on the worn saddle. He motioned to Myrtle and whispered sweet words in her elongated ears, after which our pace increased dramatically. Traitorous animal, she was obviously swooning from his endearments. It dawned on me. "James Liston told you how to handle Myrtle, didn't he? All this time you have been watching me struggle with this cantankerous beast and you knew exactly what to say!" In a huff I placed my hands crossly on my hips, nearly somersaulting backwards.

"If I remember correctly, you did say, 'I will handle Myrtle!' and then continued with a barrage of insults concerning my landlubber skills with cattle!" His mouth twitched at the corners.

"Point taken! Well, in the future I would appreciate some cooperation."

"Would you have listened to me earlier this morning?"

"Probably not!"

"Well, Mrs Sterling, cooperation is a double sided knife."

I swayed gently on Myrtle. "She was abominable!" I declared morosely.

"You were both abominable!" he laughed with such abandonment that I could not help but join in.

⁂

We had left at sunrise, the morning clear and balmy. By seven o'clock I'd realised it would be a hot day. I had fashioned and torn a piece of my skirt into a scarf and was thankful for its protection. Gabriel's tanned face turned at intervals to check I was still upright – or perhaps to gloat at my atrocious appearance.

An hour later he pulled our party into a small clearing near the bubbling creek and tied Myrtle to an ironbark tree that sagged precariously to the ground. "Breakfast?" he asked, pulling off a woven dilly bag.

"Yes, please. I am famished."

I threw my crumpled pelisse down as a rug, surprised at the ease of my movement. Four weeks ago I would have been aghast to sit in the bush let alone use a part of my clothing as a picnic rug!

Cross-legged, Gabriel divided the last of our precious bread and gooey cheese. The sun was warm and acted as a restorative to my aching back. I stretched my arms, enjoying the soft breeze off the creek. In the dappled shade, a blanket of mauve flowers waved in unison, their chocolate perfume intoxicating. A honeyeater hummed in the adjacent bushes, its wings barely touching the purplish-pink cluster of buds as it hungrily feasted. Distractedly, I nibbled on the stale bread.

"Penny for your thoughts?" Gabriel said, pulling at stems.

"I was thinking of birds."

"No diabolical thoughts concerning our captors or me?" Gabriel titled his head to one side in interest.

"No, surprisingly, just birds! It may surprise you, Captain Sterling, but I do have interests other than travelling through the countryside pursuing wayward men whilst attempting to escape others."

"Enlighten me!"

"You mock me?"

"No. I am not mocking you, Charlotte!" His intent eyes fixed upon my piqued face.

"You are mocking me! But I will indulge you. I was thinking of the birds in Jamaica and the similarities in this colony. And you?"

"Nothing so light-hearted! Charlotte, I must raise an issue that will no doubt be distasteful to your ears. Especially after last evening." I tensed, running my fingers down my skirt as a distraction. "You realise we must at some stage face the reality of the past few weeks. My high-handed and unthinking endeavour has breached – as your brother most delicately pointed out – certain social rules!" Gabriel stared out towards the horizon, his eyes giving me a cursory glance.

"Marriage?" I mumbled, gloomily contemplating the folds of my battered skirt.

"Yes, marriage! It is the way to preserve your honour and, Charlotte, you are certainly worthy of that respect." I cast a furtive peek in his direction. "I have acted reprehensibly and with little regard for propriety," he continued, the dappled sunlight caressing his amber locks as blazing eyes demanded my attention.

"Respect, honour, it sounds conventional, Captain Sterling. Something I thought you weren't!" I stated, raising my head in defiance. My voice was harsh even to my ears!

"I may have deficiencies regarding the rules of polite society but a lady's honour is paramount. I may not have acted as a perfect gentleman, in your eyes but I bow to *bienséance*."

"And was it propriety that seduced me?" The words popped out without thought.

"Honestly! No!" He paused, leaning forward. "That was far more pleasurable, but decidedly premature. However, as we are to wed, such indiscretions may be overlooked." He ran one calloused finger down the smoothness of my cheek, his gossamer touch stopping at my tilted chin.

I could feel the heated blush rise from my toenails to the tip of my head. I fumbled for my handkerchief buried within the folds of my skirt. I had never in my life spoken with so little regard for decency or been so affected by one man's touch. His presence played havoc with my emotions.

"If I might test the boundaries of our friendship, and I believe we are friends, Charlotte, after travelling these many months together! We are similar in many ways. Obstinate, driven and passionate!" He flashed a wry smile.

"And those characteristics equate to perfection in matrimony? It seems you have not learnt from your past! Surely another imprudent marriage would be indelicate," I remarked, lowering my eyes to gaze at his dishevelled neck tie.

Gabriel unwound his long legs before rising to his feet with the grace of a cat. I imagined my own performance would not be so charming. Grabbing hold of his powerful arm, I rose with a decorum of dignity. However, before he released my hand he bent and placed a feather-like kiss on my palm.

"I believe we would rub well together. Please consider my proposal, Charlotte. That's all I request!" With those words he bounded off to fetch Myrtle. Dispirited, I watched his lithe form retreat, long legs striding through the undergrowth. His broad shoulders slightly hunched as if in thought. If matrimony was based purely on the physical suitability of one's partner, Gabriel Sterling would be high on the list of prospective suitors. Real life was, unfortunately, not so naive. I bustled what was left of our frugal supplies into the dilly bag, collected my pelisse and followed the Captain, hoping Myrtle had acquired some manners during her rest.

The remainder of our journey was uneventful, although we did at one stage circumnavigate a party of miners busy at their labours on the outskirts of Sandhurst. I doubt they would have heard us – the racket of their shovels and cradle were deafening. Gabriel explained the technique in his deep rolling tone as he coerced the obstreperous Myrtle into a faster pace.

The prospector's most important commodity was a type of cradle in which he would systematically deposit sand and soil into the top called the hopper. Apparently, the larger rocks remained lodged in the top whilst the gold fell through the mesh. By rocking the cradle, the miner allowed the sand to peter away and leave the heavier gold to catch in the lower riffles. On a good day a fortunate miner may even discover an elusive gold nugget in the hopper. The poor alternative was the pan, laborious but cheaply acquired. The miner need only squat at the edge of the stream scoop soil into the pan whilst gently agitating it in the water. The gold would irrefutably sink to the bottom of the pan. The sparkle of gold after these endeavours must be bewitching and addictive.

Gold prospecting held little interest for Gabriel. He appreciated the process but his cursory description was to impart his general knowledge rather than due to a desire to participate. Clearly, battling the seas was a far more appealing inducement than labouring in the bush.

By lunchtime I was ensconced in my civilised if not simple room at the Shamrock. If my appearance was less than appealing, Dawn did not venture a comment, but assisted me competently with my ablutions. She had been sensible enough to request that Mr John Crowley retain my room for a few days. After my clandestine meeting with Shi Qi, John, her Yorkshire beau, had called at the Bridge Street store but had been refused entry. The arrival of poor Hock in such a forlorn state had persuaded Mr Crowley to seek assistance from the authorities and the gold patrol of Captain Fawcett.

"John created such a hoo-ha in the street that he nearly started a riot, ma'am!" she exclaimed proudly, brushing my damp hair. "It almost turned nasty before several troopers intercepted. My John was taken with you, ma'am, and declared that no chink – excuse my language – would interfere with him. Luckily, Captain Fawcett was aware of your husband's robbery and said he would look into the matter. But thank goodness, here you are!" She raised her hands heavenwards.

"Thank you, Dawn. You have been most helpful. Please convey my regards to John. He is to be commended. Any word on Hock?"

"Captain Sterling is with him as I speak. And may I say a handsome and gentlemanly husband you have ma'am," she rattled on, brushing my hair with long strokes, "if not a bit bedraggled at present! Poor Mr Hock has a nasty bump on his head. Cook gave him some chicken broth. The poor love! He was strange for most of yesterday. Kept on speaking in that funny language, repeating 'too long' and 'she'. Not much we could do, ma'am." She pulled tightly at my laces and I grimaced as she put her heart and soul into the task. "We did tell him not to worry, that we would have you back in no time! I do hope Captain Sterling can make some sense of him!" With an exaggerated sigh, she gave my corset a final tug and tied the laces. Maybe it was the erratic pace of life at present or the meals I was consuming but I believe my waist was two inches narrower than it had been.

A niggling thought had entered my mind whilst listening to Dawn babble on, but I was reluctant to acknowledge the prospect – maybe an informative discussion with Hock should be on the cards. Clearly, Hock was ranting about Long Song and Shi Qi in his distress.

Washed and dressed in a cheery morning dress of soft merino

lavender, I felt uplifted. My face had received a good dose of sun in the past few days and glowed a most unattractive crimson. Luckily, the minor scrapes and cuts were hidden by my full skirt and the Indian shawl. My hands still stung under the smooth velvet gloves, courtesy of an errant mule!

Before I joined Captain Sterling, I despatched a brief note to my brother in Castlemaine stating my whereabouts and assuring him of my safety. Guilt ridden, I followed Dawn downstairs.

Hock was a pathetic sight! His already withered and diminutive frame lay clearly in pain, and his eyes were vacant and dazed. His silken coat was in tatters, caked with dried mud and blood. Some kind soul had applied a poultice to his head. Mr Crowley had allowed him to convalesce on Cook's verandah and Gabriel's large form sat cross-legged beside Hock's makeshift bed. A quiet and soothing dialogue of rhythmic Cantonese from Gabriel lulled Hock's eyes to droop. I stood to one side, conscious of the intimacy between the men. Gabriel had not changed his clothes. His shabby torn coat lay to one side, frayed shirt sleeves askew as he clasped his hands tensely. The rigidness stood out in contrast to his soothing voice. My stomach quivered in disturbing flutters as I observed his tenderness. Hock nodded occasionally but soon drifted asleep, oblivious to the commotion from the kitchen.

"Laudanum," Gabriel quietly mouthed in my direction, before rising to his feet. Motioning towards the dining room, he clasped my elbow and propelled me up the stairs. "I have sent a message to Avan and Shi Qi requesting their presence. This charade has gone on for far too long. Hock could have been killed last night. I want answers now!" He growled and a passing maid nearly dropped her tray in alarm.

"Captain Sterling, I understand your concern, but upsetting the hotel staff is not conducive to our plans!" I wrenched my arm from his firm grip.

It took several seconds for his blazing eyes to register my comment. "I apologise once again for my ill-mannered behaviour," he declared through tight lips. "Excuse me whilst I change! Hopefully, I have some shred of clothing left!" Turning on his heel, he stormed out of the room, nearly colliding once again with the unfortunate maid.

Motioning for tea, I settled down to await his reappearance. As on other occasions our tiff had turned heads and murmurs rippled down the room. I removed my gloves nimbly, avoiding any eye contact before pouring the hotel's Ceylon tea in a ladylike manner. My unobstructed view to the street made a welcome distraction.

I realised that Gabriel was hurting. The past few weeks had taken its toll on his normally energetic and resilient character. No doubt he blamed himself for Hock's injuries, and, of course, the jeopardy he had unceremoniously placed me in. Contrition was an area of Gabriel's character he kept at bay. That's not to say he was a heartless individual beyond remorsefulness. Simply that the exuberance and energy of his temperament coupled with his unfavourable background had precluded the necessity for dwelling at length on such matters. Life was too short to dwell upon negatives. If anything, he was a realist, meeting challenges head on with cyclopean strength!

I smiled briefly, remembering our time with Myrtle. He was a most annoying man!

⋯⋯

Gabriel's return spurred another round of murmurs in the dining room. Thank goodness he wore a clean shirt, the necktie hurriedly tied. Shaved, clean faced, and with his unfashionably long hair slicked back, he pulled down on the hem of a sombre grey waistcoat.

"Mr Crowley's?" I stated, running my eyes down to his hastily brushed pants and splattered boots.

"A passing merchant's no doubt. Dawn seconded it from the closet. A resourceful young woman! You have won a heart there." He grinned, sliding his lanky legs into the seat at my side. I blushed, not from his comment but from the proximity of his sinewy hand that rested softly upon mine. With a quick squeeze, he released his hold and delved into the steak and eggs that miraculously appeared. Glancing up, his eyes sparkled devilishly into mine. Taken aback, I fumbled with the teapot. Yes! Dawn was perceptive. He was an extremely handsome man!

28

The Dragon

Pushing several sensual images aside, I picked up my cup, determined to concentrate on the matter at hand. "The meeting with Shi Qi and Long Song will take place where and when?"

"I have insisted on a meeting this evening at seven!" he proclaimed, a trace of tension about his jaw.

"But will they come?"

"Oh yes, they will come!" He smirked, beckoning for coffee. The tone of his voice was unusually menacing.

"May I attend?"

"By all means, but I ask for your discretion. In this meeting I must have full autonomy," His piercing green eyes levelled upon mine. "I do not wish any harm to befall you, Charlotte."

I briefly bowed my head, unsettled by the caress implied in his melodious voice. "Well, I shall leave you to your thoughts. I will check on Hock before I organise a few pressing matters." I rose unsteadily and Gabriel assisted me graciously from my seat, his hand lingering possessively on my waist.

"I strongly suggest you have a rest as well, Charlotte. The past few days have been trying. Any pressing matters will surely wait. I will knock on your door at the appropriate time."

Scooping up my gloves, I made a decidedly awkward exit as I

attempted to avoid those penetrating feline eyes.

Hock appeared comfortable, his body curled up in a clean ball of cotton. Laudanum still kept him drowsy, and his face was slack with weariness and discomfort. He partook of a little water before collapsing once again into a restless sleep. Dawn sent me on my way, promising to rouse me if anything changed. "Captain Sterling will no doubt arrive shortly!" I said, stumbling in my speech, my tongue reflecting my exhaustion. Once in my room, forgoing propriety and comfort, I sprawled across the iron bed with little thought to the covers.

ഇൻ

I must have dozed for hours, for upon waking my mouth was excessively dry and fuzzy. My half-closed eyes happened upon the shut window. Cursing, I raised my pounding head. Gingerly, I extracted myself from the pillow and shifted the casement window, allowing a gust of fresh air to invade the stifling space. Once I'd fully parted the curtains, light streamed across the seal, its reflection slashing a sundial beam across the shimmering floorboards. Slumping onto the edge of the bed, I contemplated my next move. It was late afternoon if I was not mistaken; the angle of the sun a firm indication. I contemplated the meeting this evening. I wished and hoped that this saga of the *John Robinson* would be solved. I needed normality in my life, time to reflect on the last few weeks and its impact on my life. I was not naive enough to believe that things would revert back to pre-Gabriel. I had been irrevocably ruined in the eyes of society, and those consequences now weighed heavily on my heart. Swallowing, I steeled my thoughts. Today was but one day; tomorrow was hours away. Rising, I observed my reflection. Still the same girl on the surface. Changing my bodice, I attempted to give some order to my unruly locks. The armour of a lady was her ability to appear unflappable in the most trying situations. A visit to Hock was nonetheless in order, I reached for my purse and slipped quietly into the corridor and out of the main door.

Pall Mall in the late afternoon was packed with dusty miners completing their town endeavours, stocking up on stores or haggling with gold buyers. Dawn had mentioned that the storekeepers also added to their profits by acting as unofficial gold buyers. Some were notorious for greasing their scales so the fine gold dust would adhere to the pan, using tampered weights or stealing small nuggets with their crafty long fingernails. Then they had the audacity to charge exorbitant prices for their goods! It was a den of vipers for the simple miner. No wonder so many of them barely made ends meet with their digs.

In the dusty quadrangle behind the main hotel, Hock held audience. Dawn, with her beau John, sat to one side on the kitchen verandah whilst Gabriel listened intently to his uncle's slow, quiet chatter. Hock beckoned me forward with a weak gesture but continued a steadfast dialogue with Gabriel. I stood to one side observing their intent conversation.

"He has been jabbering on for the past hour, miss. The Captain has been a right nursemaid, miss, feeding him broth and applying cool compresses."

"Thank you, Dawn." I instinctively stated, remaining riveted to the spot. My hands fidgeted in the folds of my skirt. I wished I understood Cantonese; Gabriel's intonation varied from embitterment to irritation. Hock remained calm but insistent. After a few minutes, Hock closed his weary eyes, and, with an impassive gesture, waved us away.

Gabriel untangled his manly form from the floor, his green eyes hooded and unfathomable. His face wore the look of a much older man. His jaw was rigid and his manner distant. He had clearly not slept.

"Is he in much pain?"

"The cantankerous old coot is slowly recovering, thank you!" he said ungenerously.

With a firm hand he clasped my elbow and steered me towards the main hotel rooms. "The dining room will be serving soon. May I suggest we have an early tea and discuss the upcoming meeting over a drink? You look well rested, thankfully." He glanced hesitantly at my face, his mollifying temperament unsettling.

"Come! Captain, it is not like you to be diffident when it comes to my feelings?" I jested, flouncing through the door.

"Impertinent miss!" he growled quietly, motioning towards a secluded table. His darkened eyes disturbed me.

The staff were surprised to see us so early but obliged with a pot of tea as we waited for our – no doubt unappetising – feast of mutton. Gabriel requested whisky, ignoring my raised eyebrow. I would have thought he needed all his faculties to engage our opponents. Whatever had transpired between him and Hock had clearly unsettled his sensibilities. He downed two glasses of some obscure Scottish blend, one after another. He chose to disregard my irritation.

"Is it something I have said? Or has Hock rattled your cage, Captain?" I snapped, watching a displeased frown travel across his brow.

"I apologise in advance for my incivility, Miss Lavender." He gestured towards the bottle. This was not good! I could not remember when he had last referred to my maiden name.

"Captain Sterling." I could be as obtuse as the next person! "If you intend on getting slowly inebriated may I remind you we have matters at hand. Your clarity of mind is important for this evening."

"Doesn't matter. It doesn't matter at all!" He gestured with an air of despondency before pouring another dram of whisky into the tumbler.

"Have you gone mad, Captain? What in heavens is the matter?" My nearest hand brazenly reached out instinctively for his arm.

Shrugging it off, he stared gloomily outside. Something was incredibly wrong. In all my travels with Gabriel, I could not remember once when his mood appeared so dark or desolate. Yes, he was an obstinate, exasperating and uncivil person, but he was also honest, courageous and fair. This despondent side was one that did not reflect well on him and one which he would not normally embrace. Reaching across, I grabbed the whisky bottle from the table and motioned for the waitress.

"Thank you, that will be all this evening." I deftly handed the half empty bottle to a bewildered freckled-faced girl. Rising, I bent over and whispered ominously into to Gabriel's ear. "Whatever your provocation, I will not sit and be insulted by you drinking like a common drunkard." My emotions were at breaking point. Turning on my heel I moved past his chair not before a firm hand whipped out and held me at bay.

"I will meet you on the Pall Mall verandah at seven. I suggest you bring some protection," he commented, signalling for another bottle. Furious, I grasped my skirt with dignity and exited, very much wishing to stomp unladylike from his presence. Glancing back, I was shocked to see his face slump into his hands.

"Mrs Sterling!" Surprised, I turned to find, Mr Crowley extending a folded message in his hand. "This missive arrived earlier. My apologies for not passing it on immediately."

Nodding, I thanked him before scurrying back to my room. Thoughts of Gabriel were prominent in my mind. It was probably for the best that I had retired; it allowed him time to consider whatever plagued him. Clearly, the conversation with Hock had created this despair. I was reluctant to query Hock – he appeared too fragile to browbeat at present and I valued our friendship. Sighing more with indignation than sadness, I lowered myself onto the corner of the rumpled bed. Contemplating the envelope, I was intrigued to discover the sender. Mysteriously it was addressed to Mrs Charlotte Sterling! Alexander would not receive my message for a few days. It certainly was foreboding that my name was linked with Gabriel's. But by whom? Tearing the seal I hesitantly opened the letter.

My Dear Miss Lavender,

I trust you are well, and enjoying your sojourn in the goldfields. Gabriel has kept me abreast of his undertakings and pitfalls. This has led me to delay business arrangements in Port Phillip and travel post-haste to assist you in your endeavours.

I am concerned regarding Gabriel's state of mind and request your discretion in a private audience this afternoon. I apologise for the abruptness of this missive but will explain my concerns upon your earliest attendance.

Yours sincerely,

Xavier Lawrence Willoughby, Esq

My goodness! First Hock and his mysterious reticence, Gabriel's despondency, and now old man Willoughby rushing to the goldfields. Whatever was afoot, it would be refreshing to engage in a discussion with Gabriel's adopted father and mentor. The past few weeks had been so overwhelming that a fresh set of eyes and ears would be greatly appreciated. Clearly, Gabriel had kept him abreast of his situation, which sounded incredible, but then again, Xavier Willoughby was a rock of society. Gabriel trusted him implicitly. I read the address and glanced at the small desk clock. I had over an hour before I met Gabriel.

Maybe I could persuade Mr Willoughby to join us in our clandestine meeting. With bonnet, gloves and purse in hand, I dashed down the servants' exit to the rear of the hotel. Hock still lay motionless, oblivious to the pandemonium of activity surrounding him. A nuggety Chinese lad lounged on the edge of the polished verandah, smoking. His sombre brown eyes glanced at me briefly before he returned to his pipe. It was with relief that upon scooting past the stables I managed to hail a hackney. My heart pounded in my chest! The impertinent driver ambled down the expansive but dusty Pall Mall turning west over Bendigo Creek before increasing his pace north towards Creeth Street. The shabby interior reeked of spirits; the once oiled leather was frayed and torn and mud caked the floor. I sat bolt upright, attempting to quell the bile rising in my stomach and thankful for my sturdy calf length boots. Finally. I gathered my skirt closely to my person, avoiding the ensuing filth.

"Apologies, missus, for the bloody mess!" the scrawny cabby exclaimed as he whipped the drowsy mare into a trot. "Needs a good drenching!"

"Undoubtedly!" I stated, gulping for fresh air. Keeping my face into the wind I blindly fumbled in my purse for a handkerchief. The scent of the cotton enabled my stomach to settle a little.

"Not far now, missus. Should I wait?" the cabby asked quietly, looking furtively towards the imposing building. His grin exposed dark crooked teeth.

"No, thank you," I said between shallow breaths.

Stopping with a jerk, I launched myself from the cab to the ground with little gentility. Handing over the exorbitant fare, I spun around to face the Long Gully abode. My cabby cackled as he retreated with a flourish of reins and a whirl down the sun-scorched track.

Set on a slight rise, the impressive home had sweeping views down the gully to Sandhurst. A lovely verandah graced the front, its bay windows beautifully adorned with classical inspired stained glass. No doubt they would look spectacular from inside; the colours were dull in the shade. An imposing cast iron fence lined the perimeter, its new bronze number blazing in the afternoon sun. A most pleasing abode. Following the meandering path, I stepped onto a tiled verandah.

The glazed tiles were a charming rush of colours, the edges trimmed beautifully with the Greek key. The home spoke of wealth and elegance transported from the streets of London. An unusual image was moulded into the brass name plate attached to the porch façade, its fluid script oriental in appearance. An unsettling shiver traced its way down my spine. Surely not! My head started spinning with an overload of thoughts and images. A memory, a figure, a smell, a voice swirled in my mind as I battled my panic.

29

SHÉ

"Welcome, Charlotte! It has been far too long!" a familiar voice purred from the doorway.

His long elegant fingers clutched my arm and pulled me into a tight embrace. His mouth descended hungrily onto mine. Surely this was a terrible, terrible nightmare? I was paralysed into submission as he indelicately ran his lascivious hands down my rigid body as his harsh kisses bruised my exposed neck. My breath increased in rapid spasms as I struggled for air – my darned corset!

"Breathless for my touch? Come!" he declared huskily, propelling me into the dim hallway. "I see you were sensible enough to come alone!"

The blazing sunlight was dwarfed by heavily carved cedar doors that lined the hall. At the end of the corridor a pool of light lit up the vibrant Chinese rug that adorned the polished floor. Images and watercolours of traditional Chinese landscapes decorated the walls.

Although I had prepared myself in that brief moment, it still came as a shock. The space was elaborate if not decadent. Full-length mirrors intricately framed in gold leaf hung intermittently around the room. Figurines swirled and danced in intricate detail on the walls as heavily embroidered curtains reflected the movement with explicit scenes of debauchery. A large carved bed encased in silk cushions of vibrant hues stood erotically as centre stage. Soft lantern light illuminated its sensual covers. Fighting the nausea that now erupted in my belly I spun to confront my jailer. Venom spilling from my lips! "It was you all along, you bastard. Not Mr Sanders, but you! How could we get it so wrong? Gabriel suspects but Hock knows, doesn't he?"

"Tut tut, my fair butterfly. Wasted energy on such trivial matters."

"Why?" I screeched through clenched teeth. My face was hot with indignation!

"It's of little importance at present. I propose that you divest yourself of that cumbersome corset and slip into something silken!"

"I will not! You can go to hell, you bastard," I spat, attempting to weave past his taut frame.

"You are a witch, but I have always enjoyed a woman with passion." He lunged, clasping my face in his hand. His nails dug into my soft cheeks and I cried out as he pulled my face closer to his. "You know the consequences, my little one. This time I will not be so lenient!" he said, shoving me towards the bed.

Winded, I pushed myself to stand and confronted him once again. *Think, Charlotte, think.* Neither Hock or Gabriel had seen my departure so there was little hope of a quick rescue. The note had cleverly alienated me and covered this bastard's tracks. Maybe more talking would delay the inevitable and allow an opportunity to present itself. My knife still sat nestled in my boot. A blessing from Hock!

"It's jealousy isn't it? It's not wealth because obviously you have that, but pure jealousy," I voiced, spitting out the words with vengeance.

"You are testing my patience, but…." He waved me on. "I do love the fire in your eyes." His gaze locked onto my rising bosom. Crossing his arms, he leant languidly against the wall.

"I saw the look in your father's eyes when Gabriel entered the room at Fragrant Water. His face lit up with pride and admiration."

I watched and waited. His sardonic expression was unfaltering except for a slight twitch of his right eye. *Got you, Trent Willoughby! Maybe by losing control he would show a chink in his armour.* "He was the golden child when you were growing up. The chip off the old block. The son who favoured his adventurous streak, not the one content to push numbers around on an abacus." I was clutching at straws, but keeping him angry and off-kilter was my best solution at present. No other plan had formulated in my befuddled mind.

"Go on, I am all ears!"

"The stealing of the *John Robinson* was not some nefarious plan by the Chinese community on the goldfields but down to your jealousy. An opportunity to bring Gabriel to his knees."

"Wrong, my sweet! But good try! Now where were we. Yes, I remember! No more talking, let me enjoy this moment. Last time you left me decidedly high and dry. Start with your bodice," he stated, moving towards the elaborately carved armchair.

Well, that had failed miserably. Maybe my best course was distraction. It would enable me to loosen my ridiculously constraining corset and hopefully to extract my weapon. I was not prepared to succumb to his lewd advances without a good fight and this time I was armed – not the naive and drugged girl from a month ago trapped in that ghastly Castlemaine hotel.

"I will make you a deal," I said.

"A deal! What may I ask have you to bargain with?" He laughed scornfully, distorting a face I had once admired as appealing and refined.

"I will willingly abide by your wishes if you share your motives. For interest's sake." I crossed my hands demurely in front of my skirt.

"I am not averse to violence as you are well aware. I am capable of taking you at any time!"

"But if I were willing and obedient to your wishes?" My stomach lurched with the words. I felt dirty and sick and lowered my eyes.

"Mmm. Obedient! Willing to abide by my every request?" His lasciviously rose to the fore. He leant forward his eyes wild with eagerness. How on earth had I thought this man was attractive? He was disgusting!

"Yes," I stammered.

He laughed. "Very well, remove your bodice and I will share my strategy."

Bracing myself, I undid the small pearl buttons at my ruffled wrist and then the larger ones that graced the silk ruched bodice. I slowly let the garment flutter to my feet. The hairs prickled on my exposed arms and my stomach rolled with disgust. "Well?" I pouted, attempting to appear composed.

"The clever and gifted Gabriel Sterling has been trafficking opium!" Trent smirked and pointed to my skirt.

"Gabriel – I mean, Captain Sterling – would never traffic in opium!" I gasped, untying my skirt.

"Gabriel has many faults but his largest is his insane trust in his crew! Money talks, and in the case of Sanders, it was yelling profoundly." He brandished his hand towards my crinoline.

Hock's weapon was small and I needed Trent close to have any impact. He was muscular, not dissimilar to Gabriel in height but leaner and far more sinewy, although no doubt just as strong. "So this is about opium and your jealousy of Gabriel!" I stared dumbfounded, my small blade humming in my boot.

"It is a neat package! Payback for my gullible adopted brother plus the necessary blend of demand and supply. Sanders – the fool – misplaced our shipment, but luckily for him it has resurfaced. This has been a mere hiccup! Gabriel is unfortunately collateral in this situation. I certainly would have preferred to continue the enterprise with Gabriel innocently unaware of his cargo. However, Sanders has taken the situation to an untenable position. Sadly, many men meet their death in the wildness of this country! Father and the girls will be distraught. The prodigal son discovering the maimed body of their beloved Gabriel – a most touching story!"

"You wouldn't dare!" I seethed, twisting the petticoat strings and stepping out of my crinoline.

"I wouldn't dare," he mimicked scornfully. "You promised me obedience. Remove your corset, slowly."

Stalling for time I issued another challenge. "And, may I ask where I lay within your diabolical plans?"

"Well, Miss Lavender, you are a delectable distraction. Gabriel's declared attraction piqued my interest. Regrettably, Castlemaine was a debacle."

"You are disgusting and certainly no gentleman!"

"But you are no longer a lady, Miss Lavender!" he smirked, his chin cradled by his fingertips.

The impact of his words shot straight to my heart. I could hear my mother's words reverberating through my being. *Charlotte, if you will not listen to your mother's advice at least be assured that if your actions do not improve you will no longer be called a lady. Once ruined no young woman is deserving of the title of lady.* Clearly, I was beyond saving. I focused on the thought that Gabriel had been attracted to me and his disclosure to his friend had been innocent. Willoughby watched me with amusement.

"I need assistance to loosen the lacings," I snapped, pivoting to display the rear of the hour glass corset and its woven lacing.

"I thought you would never ask!" he replied gleefully, rising to his feet and grasping my waist. He leant forward, his breath smelling of whisky, as he smothered my neck with kisses. Unexpectedly, his teeth gripped the nape of my neck in a savage bite.

"Beast!" I groaned in pain as I suppressed revulsion. *I must stay calm and concentrate on my next move.*

"Hold still!" he growled, pulling randomly at the laces. As the corset loosened, I bent forward and, with one swift movement, extracted the hidden blade from my boot. Holding its smooth handle firmly – a difficult task considering that my palm was hot and sweaty – I wrenched it backwards and upwards towards his stomach. The movement felt stilted, not smooth and balanced as practised with Hock. Maybe it was my clammy hand or that he stepped back but the knife unfortunately lodged deep into his coat jacket and pierced his thigh. Damnation!

"You bitch," he screamed collapsing to one knee.

Pushing him aside, I ran from the room. I prayed that the front door wasn't locked and bargained on his inflated ego that no one had followed. Luck was on my side – it was unlatched. Unfortunately, as I attempted to pull the massive door inwards, a muscular arm jerked me back sending me crashing to the timber floor.

Whoosh! The wind burst from my lungs as I lay prone.

"Get up, you witch. You will pay for this," he snarled, his voice sinister, as he held the small knife in his right hand, gesturing towards the back room.

Well, at least I may have stopped his lustful tendencies for the present. No sooner had I regained my composure than pandemonium broke loose.

The grand front door exploded inwards sending shattered timber splinters spinning in the air. Shards of coloured glass speared into the plaster and parquetry as Gabriel Sterling made a dramatic entrance.

Trent recovered surprisingly quickly and half dragged me into the shadows. My ornate knife was poised threateningly at my exposed neck.

"Leave her be, Trent. Drop the weapon!"

I had seen Gabriel angry but at present he was seething. His eyes were a molten green. His jaw was set tight and his whole body quivered as taut as an archer's bow.

"Back off, Gab! The lovely Miss Lavender has been a most entertaining and willing partner."

Gabriel's eyes swept over my dishevelled appearance. I was clothed simply in a transparent chemise. His eyes moved menacingly towards Willoughby. "Release her and you may make your escape, Trent. I give my word." His voice was modulated but lethal.

"Your word! God, you can be so pompous, Gab. Where would be the fun if I released Miss Lavender? I have grown to appreciate her finer qualities and curves." If Willoughby intended to goad Gabriel, he was doing a fine job. Gabriel shuddered with pent up rage, his fists opening and closing to release the tension. "You have been a infuriating thorn in my side for far too long, Gab! Stand aside and let us be on our way."

"You know I can't do that, Trent. Release Charlotte and I will give over my horse to you," replied Gabriel, inching closer.

Willoughby let out a low irritated snort. "A horse for Miss Lavender! Your chivalry disappoints me, Gab. I would have imagined a far greater trade for such a prize." He chortled, tipping my chin upwards with the tip of the blade. "As you can see, she is rather fetching."

Tears pooled in my eyes as the knife broke my skin.

"God damn it, Trent, What do you want, you bastard?" Gabriel stood transfixed, watching the blood weave a gossamer path slowly down my neck. The warmth created an unwelcome caress on my skin. "The *John Robinson*, I will sign over the *John Robinson* to you," he declared vehemently.

"But I have the *John Robinson* already, Gab, presently in port awaiting my instructions." He sniggered, releasing his hold a touch.

"Legally! Isn't that what you want? To see me penniless and broken?" Gabriel stated, his voice breaking with pent-up emotion.

"Yes, it is a temptation but so is Miss Lavender."

"Take no notice of him, Gabriel, he is playing a twisted game. He has already threatened your life and nothing will appease his inflated ego," I said.

"Miss Lavender finally speaks. Yes, unfortunately, Gab, she is correct. Your demise is the only outcome I seek. Then my family will revert back to their true order. I will be my father's only son, unhampered in my exploits and my lucrative trade from the East."

I was startled at how deep his resentment ran. *Trent Willoughby was deranged!*

"Well then, brother, let us take this outside. You are armed, I am not! Is that not a fair bargain for you?"

Willoughby watched Gabriel with hooded eyes, his mind clearly evaluating the outcome. He was no fool and Gabriel was a daunting man in a fight. Willoughby would be aware of his skills. I thought of our previous dinner conversation – it seemed months ago when he had commented on his zodiac sign. *Snakes tend to act according to their judgements, even while remaining private and reticent. They are determined to accomplish their goals and hate to fail.*

I shaded my eyes. The late afternoon sunlight lay deep and warm within the eucalyptus trees. The sound of lorikeets screeching in their evening nesting aroused me from the lethargy of my mind.

To my amazement, Hock stood to one side his bandaged head a crown of woven splendour, his normally immaculate plaited queue sprouting out at right angles. Dark eyes met mine with a touch of regret. I wandered cautiously over to his side to hold his hand. I could not vocalise the feelings churning in my soul. That bastard Trent needed a serious put down.

The brothers eyed each other like two warring Greeks: Hercules and Antaeus.

Trent had removed his jacket and circled Gabriel in a catlike movement, the knife flashing in the afternoon blaze. Gabriel held his hands high in what I believed was self-defence, one hand wrapped tightly in his removed waistcoat.

My feet were transfixed to the dirt as I watched a parry of legs and arms smacking against muscle and flesh. It was a symphony of movement, defence, attack and lunge. My brother had once demonstrated the gentleman's sport of boxing from the London Prize Ring. This, however, was far more graceful and deadly. Every part of the body had become a weapon! From the subtle play of the hands to the effectiveness of their feet, the movements were deadly. To the untrained eye they appeared evenly matched, except for the obvious weapon of Trent's. They were of a similar height and similar age, although Trent had a far leaner physique whilst Gabriel had broader shoulders and chest. They circled each other, assessing each other between tentative moves, dark eyes flashing, bright green veiled in concentration.

As Gabriel was tripped and thumped into the ground I let out a cry; blood spouted into the air from his mouth and blood oozed from a nasty slash to his shoulder. Trent's hand was poised once again. However, the power of Gabriel's arched back sent him rocketing into the air. Hock turned to me and chuckled. "Master Gab learn new moves." I grimaced, my mood at that moment not conducive to the intricacies of the fight.

Trent recovered, springing to his feet unsteadily, his shirt ripped from the shoulders. Gabriel continued his assault with renewed enthusiasm, swinging his legs with precision through the air, attempting to avoid the lunges of the knife.

One severe kick by Gabriel to Trent's hand and the knife flew into the air. With a frantic scramble they both dropped to the ground but Hock had already extracted it deftly from the dirt with one swift lunge. His queue still swung with the speed of his movement.

My sharp look made him shrug his shoulders in return. Naturally, the two men fighting were under his care, Gabriel an adopted nephew, Trent the son of his benefactor. Clearly, creating a balanced fight for both men was a family obligation, if not for his own honour.

Who would Hock back in the end? Master Trent or Master Gab? I knew Gabriel regarded him as an uncle, but Hock's allegiance lay with the Willoughby family.

Gabriel took a severe kick to the skull and then a good pummel to the stomach as he ricocheted off the fence, shaking his head in befuddlement. "That was a dirty move, Trent, but you have always played dirty!" he smirked, blood trickling from his mouth.

"You surprise me Gab, those years on the ships have made you flabby!" Trent leapt forward skilfully kicking Gabriel's chest; the intensity knocked the wind from the Captains lungs. He collapsed in the dirt.

God, please don't let Trent win, the situation would change inexorably! Maybe I should think about what I could do? I gazed around – the horses were grazing near the front fence, a short distance from the front gate. It would take me seconds to leap onto the back of the smaller beast. My chemise would create little resistance to riding! Luckily, I still had my boots on. The thought of riding into Sandhurst half-naked was shocking. Maybe I could ride to a house closer to town and throw myself on the mercy of the owner.

As I contemplated my alternatives, Gabriel charged like a Jerez bull, grabbing Trent around the waist and pushing him backwards. With surprising dexterity he flipped Trent over and applied a death lock. Perspiration dripped from Gabriel's face and soaked his shirt. It was clearly taking all his strength to subdue Trent.

"Do you relent?" Gabriel said, puffing while holding Trent firm.

"Go to hell, Gabriel."

"Gladly, but after you!" An exasperated Gabriel raised his fist and connected with his companion's jaw. Trent Willoughby's face sagged and with a thud his head fell to the ground.

Hock nodded. "It is done."

Gabriel stood and bowed before collapsing to his knees.

Running into the house, I returned with a silk dressing gown, ripping it into shreds. "Stay still" I complained as he swayed and his breath still rasped with the exertion. Locks of his thick auburn hair were plastered to his forehead with a mixture of dirt, blood and perspiration.

"God damn it, Charlotte! You will be the death of me," he croaked, his troubled eyes level with mine as I knelt, fumbling to stem the blood flow from the deep cut. As if in agreement, a passing rose-breasted galah squawked, its grey wings luminous in the fading light. A quick smile of satisfaction played on my lips as I continued my ministrations.

30

CIVILISATION

Criterion Hotel, 17 November 1853

I lay cocooned within the plush bedcovers of the Criterion suite, staring thoughtfully at the intricate gold leaf peacock stucco. My mind still reeled with the toxic events that had transported me from Port Phillip to the goldfields and to the heart of Celestial activity. It had been nearly a week since Captain Sterling had battled Mr Trent Willoughby. A week since Hock had transported me safely back to Melbourne via Castlemaine. My brother was a little peaked but had recovered sufficiently to tear strips off me for absconding. Our reunion was a jumble of tears, remonstrations and promises.

It had been a week since I had quarrelled, challenged or needled Captain Sterling. He was the most obstinate, determined and honourable man I had ever encountered – my father and brother excepted, of course! I had gleaned a little information from Hock when he'd arrived with a letter of apologies from old man Willoughby. Hock, uncharacteristically subdued, advised that Master Trent had set forth on a passage to Dutch East India to manage his father's spice assets. I shivered at the mention of his name and prayed for his soul.

Apparently, Gabriel was immersed in the affairs of the *John Robinson* (naturally) and accommodating its cargo of Celestials bound for their homes in and around Canton. I wondered whether Long Song was bound for home. Soft brown eyes with a sensual mouth came to mind.

Well, it had certainly been a disturbing month, one which still haunted my dreams. I vowed not to dwell on the matter but immerse myself into Melbourne society. Captain Sterling was in his place of residence clearly enjoying whatever he did, and here I was totally at a loose end, contemplating a life in the colony as a single lady. Sighing, I rolled over to confront an ostentatious lamp crafted from Venetian glass. Its garish colours were in keeping with the gauche surroundings.

A scratch on my door alerted me to company. It was late in the morning, but the day was chilly for December and I had forgone any idea of greeting it early, swathed in my newly acquired luxury. Well, luxury for Melbourne! Sun filtered through the heavy festooned curtains as I rose on my elbows.

A head poked around the door. "I thought you would be awake by now, sweetness. Do you wish to join me for a late breakfast or have it sent up?" Alexander asked, his elegant figure sporting a suitably well-tailored sling.

"A tray would be delightful. I am determined to lie in, all day!" I yawned. My face had healed beautifully, thanks to Ju and now only by looking closely could you see a slight yellow tinge around my jaw. I could have easily ventured downstairs but I felt lazy and slightly despondent.

"As you wish. I will call on you later." With a bow he left the room.

Relieved, I sank into garishly coloured feather pillows. Alexander had exerted an exorbitant degree of leverage to obtain the suite. Its outlandish colours and furnishing suggested it was regarded as the height of fashion by wealthy miners. Alexander had entertained me with amusing stories of the vagaries of the diggers in Melbourne in the past week, no doubt to raise my spirits. He told me tales of weddings, sometimes mock and sometimes real, that were a constant source of excitement in the Melbourne streets. A special bridal carriage with hearts painted on the door would be hired for the excessively high price of twenty pounds to drive the merry wedding party around the town. Some diggers were married each time they came to Melbourne with 'wives' provided from bars or brothels. It seemed ludicrous, but after seeing the hardships of the fields I was not surprised. The diggers spent ridiculous amounts of gold on lifestyles they were totally unaccustomed to or to 'cut a flash' in the town. I chuckled at their eccentricities and their desire to make an impression. And it hit me like lightning. *Charlotte Lavender, you are a genius!* I threw the covers aside and leapt to my feet. Ringing the bell for assistance, I clambered madly for my clothes. It was trade, and yes, I was a woman, but what better way to make a living? Alexander was scouting new ventures for Father to invest in – surely the idea was plausible?

In a flurry of silk, undergarments and hairpins, I raced downstairs in a most unladylike manner to confront my brother. The idea was brilliant, and if I were to be an independent lady of means, this was truly an amazing opportunity. Mother would be horrified but recent events had desensitised me to the demands of society. Life and its opportunities was here to embrace and yes, if that meant I did it on my terms how freeing was that?

Alexander sat stiffly in the dining room reading *The Times* and sipping hot chocolate. His injury gave him grief but he was resilient. "Charlotte," he said, attempting to rise to his feet. I wavered him down and slid in beside him.

"Alexander, I have the most brilliant idea. A business proposition for you – please let me finish before you make any derogatory comments. This is important to me." I placed my gloved hands on the table to give me the strength to speak coherently. Taking a deep breath, I proposed my idea.

Alexander listened intently strumming his fingers upon the table intermittently. His brow furrowed at times and he looked thoughtful.

"Well?" I asked breathlessly.

"It is an interesting proposal, one I will shall investigate on your behalf, Charlotte." Seeing my face collapse, he continued quickly, "I do not wish to dampen your enthusiasm, my dear, but it is in your best interest that I consult our bankers. So remove that glum expression from your lovely face. I promise you I will even make a head start today."

"Thank you, Alexander. You have made my week – my year!" I declared, grasping his good arm in affection.

"On that note, I should also inform you that Captain Sterling has requested an interview with you this evening." He passed me a stained vellum paper note. The script inside was bold and assertive.

"It's a wonder he has the time!" I said defiantly. "Hock mentioned that he sails shortly for China. I cannot imagine what he wishes to discuss."

"Charlotte, you cannot be so naive. We have discussed this matter already in Castlemaine. Captain Sterling – as a gentleman – has a commitment to you." His forehead frowned as he brought his flaxen eyebrows together in concern, a copy of my father's own expression when he was displeased. It was his cornflower blue eyes, however, that gave him away.

"Tosh, Alexander! It's so... it's so barbaric. Forcing two people to marry because they've travelled together."

"I seriously do not think the travelling together was the issue, my dear sister," he said compassionately, his hand reaching over to touch mine.

"Well, it is all behind me now. I have moved on! I am truly excited by this idea and look forward to discussing it with you this evening."

"And Captain Sterling?"

"Captain Sterling has not bothered to see me or communicate with me in over a week. I am sure he can bear the deprivation," I stated churlishly.

"Charlotte!"

"Goodness, Alexander, you sound like Father. Very well, after dinner, but I am positive I will be plagued by shocking indigestion." I rose and, kissing his forehead, begged him to stay seated.

I had things to attend to, people to talk to, and certainly an establishment to find. With a light step I headed for reception. I required a chaperone, a manservant and directions.

By late afternoon I had collapsed onto the chaise longue – it had been decorously piped with a cringing pink satin against a lavender brocade backdrop, hideous! It made my head spin. The day had been most successful. Alexander had eventually joined me in Collins Street to peruse various establishments. I was in excellent spirits and dinner was a bubbling affair with endless chatter, mainly from my side of the table. Alexander became caught up in my enthusiasm, toasting the new venture with copious amounts of claret. It was so refreshing and exhilarating I had almost forgotten my appointment with Captain Sterling. Almost! My stomach felt like a swarm of butterflies. I refused to be intimidated by the man, although he obviously felt it was important to do the right thing. I respected his point of view but that did not mean I was obliged to surrender.

Mr Hamilton, the maître d', politely informed me that Captain Sterling was waiting in the Wellington room, at my convenience. Raising my eyebrows at Alexander, I left him to his cigar and port.

I had dressed carefully for the evening. Subtle elegance with a touch of devil-may-care. The waist-hugging duck blue-coloured silk dropped in gentle folds to the ground. The sheer organza sleeves were gathered at the elbows with matching ties. A wide belt of wrapped white satin accentuated my waistline, tied simply to one side with a soft bow. My décolletage was unadorned, except for a simple cameo that rested on my cleavage. Understated and elegant; most becoming to a lady about to enter a new enterprise.

❧❀❧

He had not taken a seat but leant casually against the mantelpiece, looking thoughtfully at the smouldering fire. Surprisingly, he was dressed in high fashion. His only concession to utility was a morning jacket rather than an evening one. I paused in the doorway, watching his expressive face. It was still weathered by the sun and his hair was decidedly too long for fashion. However, you could never say Gabriel was a man who would be overlooked. His firm jaw, his piercing eyes and commanding stance spoke of power and determination. Gabriel Sterling was a striking individual.

"Captain Sterling, how kind of you to call after all this time." I said offhandedly, gliding in with my head held high, my cheeks becoming unfortunately heated as his gaze travelled up the length of my body.

"Miss Lavender, Charlotte, you look captivating." He acknowledged my cutting comment with a mocking grin. With a swiftness that astonished me, he had my hand clasped in his. A soft kiss ensued, before my hand was returned, tingling with goose bumps. *Damn the man! This was business.*

"I thank you for this opportunity to discuss a business venture that has captured my heart and imagination," I continued, noticing the stunned look within his penetrating green eyes.

"A business arrangement?" he enquired, watching me carefully. His mouth was curved in an enigmatic manner.

"Yes, I have been consumed by an enterprise and seek your assistance."

"You wish my assistance?"

"Captain Sterling, I would appreciate if you would be serious and stop repeating everything I say as a question!" Clasping my hands in front I refused to sit. This man could be intimidating at the best of times and if I sat he would literally dominate the space!

"Pray, continue. I am bemused by this revelation."

"Oh, please behave. I have persuaded my brother to finance a venture to supply fashionable goods to wealthy miners and colonists."

"This is because –?" One eyebrow rose in surprise.

"This is so I may be an independent lady of means. One who does not require their virtue defended." I met this eyes challengingly, daring him to comment. Moving to the fire he turned, folding his hands firmly across his chest.

"And may I ask what credentials you have for this type of occupation?" The sombre tone of his voice was certainly not conciliatory but I had expected as much. For my sanity and heart, I desperately needed to be in control of this conversation.

"Well, someone with taste and a certain amount of flair is needed to guide them in spending their gold! Why not me? I have style, good taste, an eye for detail, and, I believe, the necessary appearance."

"You would be charming. condescending at times, but I hope always the lady!" he declared.

Unsettled by his answer, I continued, "I do hope to duly control those unladylike qualities."

Gabriel cocked his head to one side and raised his other eyebrow in the infuriating manner I had grown to love. Love? My goodness! "Yes, yes, Well it will be a learning process! Fortunately, I have a partner who will supply the necessary quality goods on time." Instinctively I moved forward placing my hands on his crossed arms. I had surprised him, wonderful! His body tensed as I raised my chin, serenely meeting his eyes. He hadn't expected that move.

"May I venture to ask, who is the lucky partner?" He croaked overwhelmed by my closeness and probably unnerved by my hands gently caressing his forearms.

"Well, you of course! You have the *John Robinson*. I am not naïve enough to imagine that you would feel comfortable settling down in a quaint four bedroom townhouse in East Melbourne. You would suffocate within a month; your passion is the sea!" The silence wove tentacles around the unyielding space. Relaxing, he clasped my hands affectionately and brought them to his lips.

"Did I tell you I love you? No, I adore you!" he whispered between kisses to each finger.

"No!" I stammered as his feline eyes scrutinised my face. I stepped back, his hands tenderly caressing my palms. "There is but one obstacle, and please do not distract me!"

"Pray share it. I am fascinated by this line of conversation." A broad grin transformed his serious face. His eyes sparkled with mischief as he relaxed against a mahogany carved desk.

I barrelled along, avoiding his gaze. "Alexander believes – and this vexes me no end – that a lady's name on the shop front may preclude certain customers from entering the establishment or alternatively the name may cause misunderstanding by certain elements in our society, so...."

"So. You believe a respectable gentleman's name should grace the building?"

"Yes, exactly!" My eyes widened with excitement.

"Would you object to the name Sterling and Sons?" Gabriel whispered pulling me into his arms. Soft lips brushed my ear as he murmured. "Proprietor in charge, Mrs Charlotte Sterling?"

Stiffening I stepped back from the warm circle of his arms, placing my hands firmly on his chest. "Gabriel, be serious! As we will be partners in this enterprise and for providence I believe that yes, Sterling and Sons, maybe, would be, acceptable. I certainly do not wish to convey... that is to say, I do not wish to appear presumptuous." Lost for words I threw my hands in the air. "I am prepared to use my own name, Charlotte Lavender, but trade under yours!"

"But where would the fun be in that?" He smiled.

"Gabriel!" I was slipping and I could feel the ground dissolving beneath me.

"Miss Charlotte Lavender, would you do me the honour of becoming my partner." He smiled conspiratorially, his body so close and enticing that I felt electrified, humming with excitement. His strong long fingered hands clasped mine and gently raised one after the other to his warm lips, divesting a kiss upon each palm. "It will not be an easy task. At times we will be apart for many months, but I can guarantee you will be my only port! And when we are together, it will be exquisite!"

I watched him tenderly. His unyielding green gaze possessed my soul. It was nigh impossible to retain my resolution next to this man. "Captain Sterling, Gabriel," I stammered. "I accept your proposal but be guaranteed that if I discover your ports have changed, I will track you down!" I threw back my head in defiance.

"Spoken like a true Sterling." Gabriel declared running his moist lips down the exposed arch of my neck. "Now, tell me what you will do when you catch me." His rumbling voice created sensual tingles down the length of my body.

END

AUTHOR'S NOTE

The actual *John Robinson* sailed from Jamaica in 1853 for the goldfields of Port Phillip. On board were several merchant families including Charlotte, the eldest daughter of a wealthy Jamaican plantation owner and magistrate. Her journey to the colonies was a wonderful catalyst for this historical novel, for this was the time of the famous gold discoveries in the colony of Victoria. A time when Melbourne became one of the fastest growing cities in the world. A time of great growth and great despair. When a community of people from all corners of the world and from all walks of life came together, their one dream to find gold and become wealthy beyond words!

Added to this bizarre pot of humanity came the Chinese, a determined and well-oiled machine of men. Here was an opportunity for them to obtain great riches from the 'golden mountain' for their family and their villages. At times this diverse ethnic mix was understandably volatile. Their leveller was the harshness of the land and comradeship against loneliness.